Rise of the Sparrows

Also by Sarina Langer

Relics of Ar'Zac

Wardens of Archos (#2)
Blood of the Dragon (#3)
Shadow in Ar'Sanciond (#0.5)
The Relics of Ar'Zac Box Set (#0.5 - #3)

Darkened Light

Darkened Light (#1)
Brightened Shadows (#2)

Rise of the Sparrows

Relics of Ar'Zac Book One

Sarina Langer

Content Warning

Please be advised that *Rise of the Sparrows* contains content some readers may find upsetting such as, but not limited to, suicide. Please proceed with caution if this might cause distress.

ISBN-13 978-1530016969
ISBN-10 1530016967

Cover Design © Design for Writers
Map Design © MonkeyBlood Design

To my Sellybean

You tried so hard, but I finished it despite your best efforts.

Acknowledgments

When I started writing this book in early 2015 I had no idea what I was in for. I knew it'd be stressful, I knew there'd be a lot of work, and I knew that, by the time the release date came around, I most likely wouldn't want to look at it anymore. Two of those are true.

I *didn't* know how incredibly welcoming and supportive the writing community would be—on Twitter, on WordPress, and in several other corners of the internet, too.

THANK YOU to my thorough beta readers Kay, Faith Rivens, Paul Broome, Vanessa Moore, Mollie Wallace, Kayleigh Osborne, Gerry Klabis and Sarah. Without them this book wouldn't have been the same.

THANK YOU to my editor Briana Mae Morgan. You've been a pleasure to work with, and I owe you a tea.

THANK YOU to Glynn from MonkeyBlood Design, who designed my awesome map and who taught me a few things about cartography in the process.

THANK YOU to Rebecca and Andrew for my beautiful book cover. You were such a joy to work with, and I'll be back for the sequel.

THANK YOU to Claire Huston, Nicolette Elzie,

Alan Morgan and Rhianne Williams.

A special THANK YOU to Sarah, who always had time to discuss ideas with me when I was stuck, and who contributed more to this book than she knows.

THANK YOU to the incredible writing community on twitter and Cookie Break. You're all amazing, and I owe all of you teas and cookies.

And, finally, THANK YOU to you, dear reader. There are so many amazing books out there, and I'm humbled that you've chosen to read mine. I hope you enjoy it, and if you don't—no hard feelings. Thank you for giving me a chance.

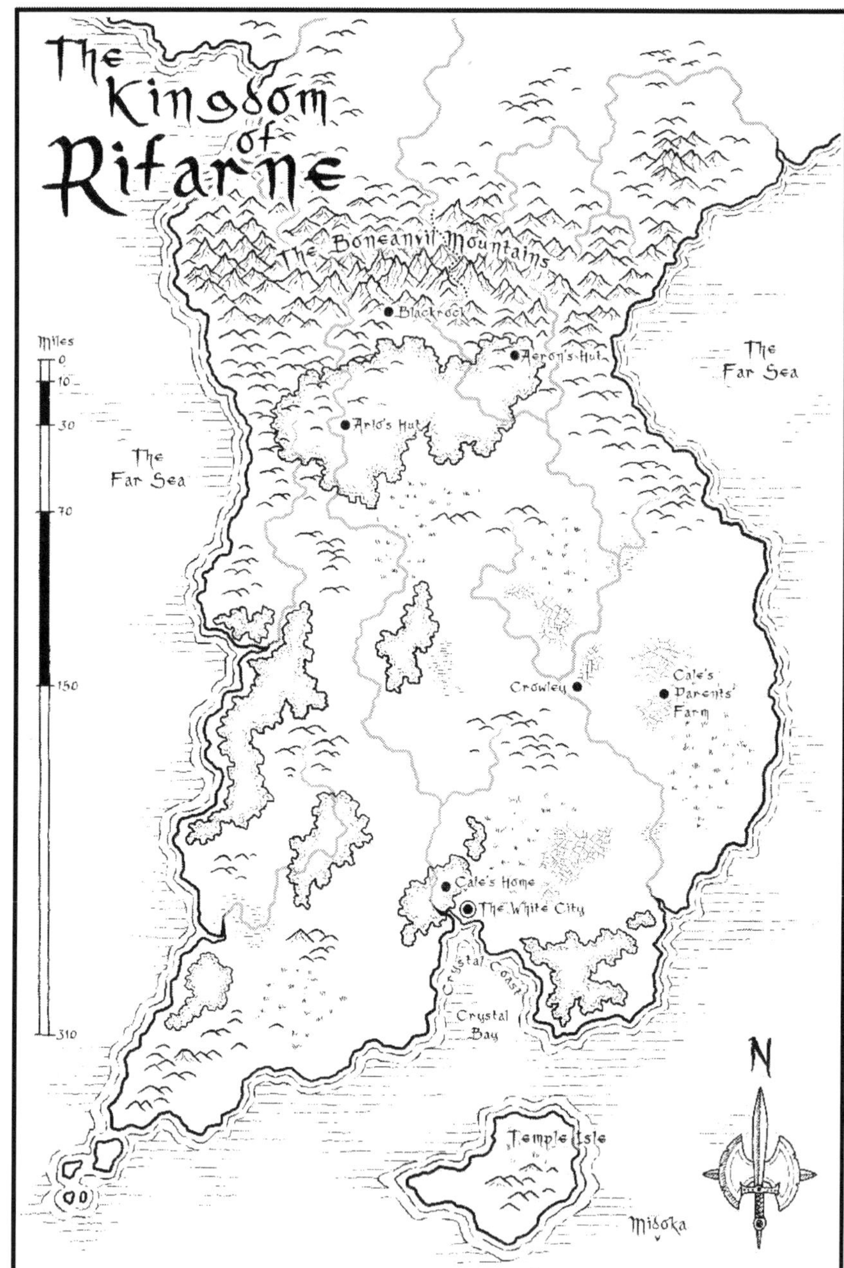

The Kingdom of Rifarne
The Boneanvil Mountains
Blackrock
Aeron's Hut
Arlo's Hut
The Far Sea
The Far Sea
Miles
0
10
30
70
150
310
Crowley
Cale's Parents' Farm
Cale's Home
The White City
Crystal Coast
Crystal Bay
Temple Isle
Midoka
N

Prologue

The island of Kaethe didn't get many visitors. Aeron and the dead baby she held loosely in one hand were a rarity. She took her time walking up the three hundred steps to the Mothers despite the Dark One's infernal servants' impatient glares. There'd be no doubt that she, not they, were in charge today. Their master's temple was their charge, but Aeron outranked them in power and ability. The Mist's crones wouldn't get in her way.

The sacrifices at the temple's base watched her every step; she felt their concerned eyes on her. They'd likely never seen another living soul and they were too inconsequential to attend any events of import—unless the Dark One demanded they die to strengthen Him, of course. After all, that was their only purpose. The farmer didn't inform his sheep when a butcher had come to talk business. It simply happened to them.

Aeron smiled. She'd finally bring death to the world—something the Mothers had failed to achieve after centuries of exile. It was beyond her what they were waiting for, but it didn't matter now. She'd come to take things into her own hands.

The two Mothers guarding the temple's entrance greeted her with indifference. They were creatures of the Mists, the dark realm the Dark One inhabited, and didn't look human. The Mists that gave them shape were ever-shifting, ever-flowing around them in evervescent wisps. They were made of darkness and shadows. Aeron had never seen one in person before. They were formidable, but Aeron wasn't impressed.

She saw more than they. Their time was coming to an end. The Dark One wouldn't need them now she was here—she'd come all this way from Rifarne to ensure just that.

The Mothers didn't speak. They were the perfect servants—obedient without doubt or question, deadly, and impossible to harm with normal weapons. They saw both worlds at once—Aeron's world and their world, the Mists—to better do their Master's bidding. It worked both ways—He saw through them when he needed to. Their cries came from the Mists too. They were low, animalistic hisses, the breaths of demons laced with a moral's terror and the promise of pain.

Aeron put more effort into her false smile. The Mothers were powerful and perhaps deserved more respect than she'd given them, but she still held more power than all Mothers combined. She could wipe them all out with a flick of her hand if she wished.

But she hadn't come for that.

"The offering." She dropped the bloody lump in her hand on the cold stone floor, not taking her eyes off her hosts.

The space where a face would have been on humans

twisted into vicious grins.

"I have work to do. Take me to the sacrifices."

One of the two Mothers turned around and opened the heavy stone doors with its dark gift. The intricate spellwork wouldn't react to anything else—the Mothers were her only way inside, and her only way out.

Aeron had wasted enough time. It was a privilege to walk inside these halls, an honour without equal to spill blood inside their sacred chambers. She'd bleed the sacrifices until not one drop of blood was left in their bodies.

Aeron placed a small light of raw magical energy over the Mother's shoulder, following it wherever it went as it escorted Aeron.

They stopped by an unassuming stone door. While it didn't look special, Aeron could feel the leftover magic of old sacrifices' anguish pulse behind it. She walked past the Mother and placed one hand on the cold stone. She fed her gift into its own spells and forced it open—she could have been more delicate, but it would have taken more time and she was eager to get started.

"I won't need you for the rest," she said to the Mother. "Return to your duties."

The Mother hissed, but Aeron dismissed it. They'd die soon enough, like the rest of the livestock awaiting its day below in the village.

For now, they'd done as she had asked. Aeron closed the door behind her, feeling more excited than she'd done in years. Terrified whimpers from the seven people cowering in the middle of the room filled the darkness. They clung to each other like defiance alone could save them. They'd been raised for this—had lived their whole lives knowing what would be expected of them one day—but now the time had come they were afraid nonetheless.

Good. Their terror would please the Dark One.

Aeron called a flame into her palm with her gift and centred it above the sacrifices. She smiled. They were already stripped bare, and their faces spoke volumes of the horrors inside their minds. Whatever they imagined was coming, she'd do worse. They were shaking. All seven had left children behind—a rule the Mothers reinforced without mercy to ensure the sacrifices' continued survival Sadly, she'd end the world before their children could to maturity, but perhaps they'd find another way for them to serve the Dark One.

Aeron took off her clothes and joined the sacrifices in the centre. Her knife, a gift the Mist Women had given her on the day she graduated, was restless in her hand. To think it had once been her pride and joy… It was intended for so much *more.*

Despite their visible fear, none of the sacrifices spoke or begged for mercy. They weren't foolish enough to defy the Dark One—not when His darkness was about to embrace them.

With practised precision, Aeron drew a long cut across her arm and walked around them, her blood forming the circle she needed for the spell to work. Aeron had rehearsed the intricate magic many times. The incisions had always healed quickly, but today they'd leave scars. The Dark One would drink from her and feed on the sacrifices. He'd finally make her weak world His. Aeron was more than happy to pay in cuts of any size to ensure it. They'd be a reminder, a promise of what she could do for this world and its pitiful ants.

She send out her gift into the sacrifices and pulled out theirs. Finally, they screamed, like sweet confirmation that her spell was working. It was a painful affair to have your gift removed by force, but they'd be grateful once it was over. Their pain ensured something better. Their gifts were weak, but Aeron's was strong enough to make up the difference. She commanded her gift to the centre of her circle, and it obediently pulled the sacrifices' thin threads behind.

She swallowed. She had waited her entire life for this moment.

The air around her vibrated with power when she shoved their gifts together and opened a door into the Mists. It was forbidden, yet so easy once you knew how to do it and willing to pay the price.

She cut the sacrifices deeply. They screamed when her blade pierced their skin, but not one asked for an end. Her own body ached from the many cuts covering every inch of her naked skin. She lifted her head, spread her arms, and welcomed the Dark One's touch on her soul.

Aeron was surprised she could feel His presence already. She had expected Him to need more convincing, but He seemed just as eager as she.

"Come to me! I, your loyal servant Aeron, set you free!"

Dark tendrils blacker than the night sky burst into the chamber from every direction. They rushed to the sacrifices and encased them until Aeron couldn't see them anymore. They gasped as He drained their lives. . Aeron herself couldn't stifle all sound as death filled her, licking at her wounds and considering her body as a potential host. A chill colder than ice filled her as a darkness of which she'd only dreamed poured into every aspect of her being. It was violent, the pain too great for screams, but it was done.

Her vision had changed. She now shared her consciousness with His vision. Within herself, she felt His appreciation at her power.

Now the real joy began. She'd kill the Sparrow once she had toyed with it and handed its blood over to her infernal master, and then she'd see herself on the throne of a world doomed to burn screaming under her reign.

Chapter One

Rachael kept her eyes on the shadows in the alley ahead of her while she picked small chunks off the bread she'd secured for herself the day before. Someone was following her. Whoever it was had been on her trail for a while, tailing her through Blackrock while she clung to her shadows. She had a bad feeling about it made worse by her headache, but right now, her pursuer stayed hidden in the dark alley while she sat on her hole-ridden blanket, the prize of yesterday's hunt in her hands.

It wasn't much. The woman who'd thrown the loaf at her feet only gave her half—the rest she kept for Blackrock's other strays. She had been generous in giving Rachael such a big portion, which was far bigger than what she usually found for herself. Not enough by any means, but more. No one cared about a stray dog or another homeless child. Now winter had reached the small town the villagers were less willing to share their food, and she knew they disliked her even more than the other strays. The half loaf was a gift she'd make last as long as she could. It'd be a rough winter, but she'd survive this one too.

From the corner of her eye, the alley's shadows moved. Blackrock's people were clumsy and went as quietly through their lives as any rabbit in the wolf's clearing; most of them had no use for silence, whereas Rachael depended on it. She didn't need to watch the shadows in the alley closely to know they were there. If they shifted, she knew.

Her stomach was still begging for more, but she was used to the feeling and wrapped the rest of the bread in her blanket for later. Holes punctured the fabric all over and it was wearing thin, but it had kept her warm all her life. Old and ineffective as it was, she wasn't willing to steal a new one. It was her only memory of her parents save for the rare hazy dream of a woman humming a soothing melody. Rachael couldn't even remember her last name. This blanket was something real, something physical she could cling on to. It was in bad shape, but so was she. They were perfect for each other.

She sank into the thin fabric and held one hand to her pounding head. Her last nightmare had been bad and left her bruised in some places. Her head had smashed into a small rock on the frozen ground when she had thrashed around in her sleep, and her right ankle had rammed into a wall. The pain from her foot had woken her. The dream left her aching, her nose bleeding, and her head thrumming so hard she saw stars, but then again, hers weren't normal dreams.

She'd dreamed about a merchant from Blackrock's wealthier quarter, who was about to leave town with his wife and two children. They were heading to Tramura across the Boneanvil Mountains. In her dream she saw them get attacked, robbed, and murdered before they reached the safe end of the narrow mountain pass.

A long time ago, Rachael had warned the villagers. They had ignored her, believing she was just another homeless child craving attention. When the first woman whose death Rachael had foreseen died, they blamed her.

The gift, called *magic* by some and *a curse bestowed by the Dark One Himself* by others, was a terrifying thing for most people, including Rachael. They didn't understand how it worked and neither did she, but they did understand that Rachael had seen a death before it happened. It was easiest to blame her.

She'd tried to help once more after that. In response, the villagers had tried to burn her alive. Rachael had spent months in hiding before she dared step out into the daylight again. The people had moved on to some new gossip and a new tragedy and had paid her no mind. From overheard whispers she knew they'd decided it'd be in their best interest to leave her alone, and so life had continued. Rachael was a bad omen, but as long as she found enough food to survive she didn't care. There were enough people left who took pity on her, like the baker's wife who had given her a whole half loaf. If she lost their charity, she'd have to get more daring, but for now it would do. She was more scared of what lay beyond Blackrock's walls than she was of their hatred. Their loathing, at least, was familiar.

Nothing good had ever come of helping others. Rachael knew better than to get involved. The merchant and his family would have to die in the

Boneanvil Mountains. She didn't like it, but there was nothing she could say that they wanted to hear.

The shadows darted out of the alley, but she was faster. Two men, taller and much stronger than her, reached her spot on the frozen cobblestones within seconds, but Rachael was already on her feet and prepared.

"What d'ye think? Ye wanna go first?"

Men like them had frightened her once. But then she'd grown up, and now they were just another nuisance, like fresh snow or several days without food. They were annoying, but she could cope.

The man's friend grinned, exposing several gaps in his teeth and a smell bad enough to make a finer lady faint. Lucky for her, life on the streets had sharpened her edges so much that it didn't bother her.

"Aye, I think I will." He grabbed for her with two beefy hands, but Rachael had seen it coming. As scared as the villagers were of her, there'd always been other strays like these two who wanted her bread or her. They were taller than her and stronger, but clumsy. Rachael was fast and flexible, and the harsh terms of her survival had been a good teacher.

She moved aside, stepped behind him, and laid her hands on his arm and shoulder. She pulled with everything she had, causing him to stumble and fall face-first onto the cobblestones. There was a crunch as his nose broke. It would never have worked had he been prepared, but people had a habit of underestimating starving strays.

His friend stood stunned for only a second before letting out a drunk laugh and grabbing for her. His arms lunged forwards, but he never stood a chance. Rachael flew around him and kicked his back towards the ground, shoving him down next to his friend.

The first man was unconscious. A small pool of blood stained the snow underneath him. Rachael kicked him onto his side so he wouldn't drown in it; no matter what the villagers wanted to believe, she was no murderer. The second man was still moving. She kicked him in the head. It would buy her enough time to get away. They wouldn't try to rape or otherwise hurt her again. Most men were embarrassed to be defeated by a girl—a homeless orphan no less, whose feet were blistered from the cold and whose body was dangerously thin. Plus, no one knew Blackrock like Rachael did; she could easily disappear for a while if their pride hurt worse after all. Usually, their first attempt was always their last. None of them were willing to admit they'd been bested so easily—by Blackrock's bad luck charm, of all people.

Rachael wrapped her blanket around herself, imagined it was her mother's hug, and cradled the rest of her bread in her arms. It was time to find a new hiding place, until the next shadows watched her.

Chapter Two

Only two days after Rachael had abandoned her previous hiding place, new uncertain steps followed her. At first Rachael thought the men had come back for revenge after all, but the more she listened to the tiny footsteps in the shadows the more she realised this follower wasn't as clumsy as the men had been. No drunk waddling. No alcohol on the breeze. Just careful silence in the fresh snow which had barely fallen enough to cover the cobblestones, and the hasty brush of fabric against air whenever Rachael turned around. This follower was smaller, lighter, and seemingly scared of her.

In itself, that wasn't unusual. All kinds of people followed her for all kinds of reasons. Most were like the two men, but sometimes other orphans followed her. Sometimes, people who wanted to kill her followed her home and waited until she slept. Rachael always watched them, and never relaxed until their anxious breathing had left her alleys. Once they were gone, so was she. It wasn't safe to stay in places others had tracked her to with knives and prejudice.

But this one was different, their footsteps more cautious. Rachael was curious, but she wouldn't approach them while they hid; she had learned not to bother people who bothered her only indirectly.

Her frost-blistered feet carried her past the market and into the dark back alleys. Blackrock could be a treasure cove of free food scraps—one just needed to know where to look. Today, the pavement was empty. Her stomach complained, but Rachael paid no attention to it. It always hurt more when she did.

Tired and hungry, she returned to the small spot she called home for now. It was a good spot, because most people avoided this part of the town. Not because it was dangerous or unsavoury. There was simply nothing here. If she was lucky, she'd be able to stay for a while.

But she wasn't alone today. Her silent follower was still there. They were more persistent than most, but then most would have attacked by now. This shadow was watching her from a distance, and it put Rachael on edge. She preferred honesty, even when sharpened blades were involved—or perhaps especially then. It was better to know where she stood.

"You might as well come out," Rachael said to the shadows. "I know you've been following me all day."

A small girl tripped into sight, clutching a stuffed bear that had seen better days. It looked like her dress—like it had cost a lot of money once but had since been dragged through mud, snow, and fear. The baker's daughter. As far as Rachael knew, her father kept a tight leash on her and her siblings. Both parents were alive—the one baker in town that had never given Rachael or the other strays anything. Their bakery was always busy, but the girl didn't look like the child of a rich man.

She nearly fell when she tripped but caught herself just in time and clung to her bear all the tighter. Younger than Rachael by at least five years, her tiny frame was more fragile but better fed—if she was homeless for whatever reason, she hadn't been on the streets for long Her eyes looked a watery red even from this distance, and her shaking arms were bruised.

She was the most vulnerable thing Rachael had ever seen.

Her face and feet were covered in dirt, her hands holding a loaf of bread. Rachael's mouth watered.

"What do you want?" The girl didn't look dangerous, but looks could be deceiving. Suspicion was healthy and could be the difference between dying and surviving another day.

"I…" The girl shot nervous glances back the way she'd come. Instinctively, Rachael knew why the girl was here. It had happened before, more times than Rachael cared to count.

"If someone has sent you on a dare, you can go. You've seen me, there's nothing more for you here." Children with families and warm homes had made a game out of sending shy or unpopular children to her on a dare. They considered seeing Blackrock's bad omen up close brave. Talking to her earned them respect. Of course the baker's daughter was with them, all the rich kids were.

"I..."

"Go away." Being harsh was often the only way to get rid of people. Rachael refused to be nice to someone who'd only come here to prove her courage, dangling a tasty loaf of bread before her just to taunt her.

The girl took slow, uncertain steps towards Rachael. She ripped the bread in two and laid one half at Rachael's feet when Rachael didn't take it from her outstretched hand.

"I'm not scared of you, and—" Her shaking body and thin arms wrapped around herself told a different story. The girl swallowed, like the lie had cost all her nerves. "And I want you to have this." She spun around and ran off before Rachael had the chance to reply.

This was the strangest dare Rachael had ever seen. Her eyes were glued to the bread by her feet. The snow gently melted around it and washed its fleeting warmth to Rachael's feet; it was fresh as could be. She couldn't remember the last time she'd had such a big piece. Why would the rich kids bring her food? They didn't usually care.

The smell reached her nose and made her mouth water. Her stomach tightened, urging her to take a bite. What if it was poisoned? Maybe the two men had been so humiliated they put something in the dough and paid the girl to bring it to her, knowing fully well Rachael would be too hungry to resist. Was it possible the villagers had given up trying to kill her with knives and had thought up this new plan? Perhaps that night they'd tried to burn her hadn't been forgotten after all.

But her hunger was too strong. She finished most of it within a few short minutes and wrapped the rest in her blanket for later, if it didn't kill her in the meantime. Any food was valuable, she couldn't afford to waste any. This loaf might have been the only food she'd get all week. If it killed her, she'd at least die with a full belly.

Rachael sought the dark alley ahead of her for the girl, but she had disappeared. She heard a boy teasing and laughing, but for all she knew it was unrelated. The loaf had been nothing to the girl—her rich parents could easily bake more. They were human, she was a stray and an unwelcome reminder that magic was dangerous. If someone wanted to poke her with a sharp stick they'd prod until she bled, and no one would step in to save her. If the bread was poisoned, it was too late to worry about it. If it wasn't, it had been a taunt, a reminder of what she couldn't have whenever she needed it.

Rachael had learned a long time ago that the only one who could save her was herself. The bread hadn't been a kindness, her survival was up to her alone. Hoping for anything else was foolish and an unwanted child's tear-stained dream.For the first time in a long while, Rachael fell asleep with a full stomach. Her thoughts wandered to the girl as she drifted off. She couldn't shake the thought that the girl hadn't looked like a baker's daughter. Not well groomed like the many times Rachael had seen the family around town. She had looked poor and dirty, like Rachael. And she'd been bruised. Maybe there hadn't been a dare after all. Maybe she was just another unwanted child, cast out by her father when he couldn't afford to feed them all. The youngest were often the first to go. Rachael had seen it before.

Rachael couldn't care. There were too many strays for her to take pity on one, and no one had ever taken pity on her. Survival on the streets, especially during winter, was only learned the hard way.

And yet her dreams that night were haunted by a thin girl with black-and-blue limbs, clutching her stuffed bear like Rachael clutched her hole-ridden blanket.

Chapter Three

A hot, searing pain burnt through Rachael beyond anything she'd ever felt before. She was used to blistered feet, frozen ankles, and an empty stomach; this was worse, cut deeper. Frantically, she looked around, spread out her hands hoping to find something she could hold on to, but if anything was there she didn't reach it. The darkness was too perfect.

A shadow stepped into view above her. It wore the baker's daughter's face, her eyes dead and empty and not her own. They saw into her soul and terrified her more than anything she'd ever experienced. There was no getting away this time. The darkest shadow finally had her where He'd wanted her. His promise of unimaginable suffering, of her begging him to stop, echoed in her numb mind.

Rachael's heart pounded with fear. At the same time, she felt so empty she wanted to vanish. She was hollow, a disappointing shell of the girl she'd been supposed to be. She should have faded away a long time ago, but He'd kept her alive for this moment, for this glint of the impossible sword above her heart.

She had run so very far. None of it mattered.

Someone screamed. She wanted to help, but she couldn't move. Rachael had thought she knew despair in Blackrock, but it had been nothing compared to the end of days. Her body wouldn't obey and her mind was slipping away from her into His control, even as the screams were dragged farther away from her. Or perhaps they died along with her friend? She hoped they died.

She screamed, begging Him to end it with words that wouldn't come, but the darkest Shadow had disappeared.

Desperate to get away, her legs eventually responded. A sharp pain in her head responded. Her head felt ready to burst and her nose was bleeding for reasons she couldn't remember, only that the two were linked.

*A door—*her *door—scraped over cold stone floor, and she braced herself. A demon entered.*

This was it—the end she had prayed for. Everything she'd fought for was over.

Black mists closed around her hair and dragged her across the floor. Rachael cried; it didn't matter now, no one could see her.

Rachael woke with a silent scream that died in her throat. Her body was drenched in cold sweat, and she shivered.

That hadn't been a nightmare. It had been one of those dreams, only this time it had been about her.

None of it made sense, least of all the shadow wearing the baker's girl's face—whatever that meant—but she knew it had been her. These dreams always left her a little shaken, but she felt better when she woke. This time, her core was rattled, and she couldn't escape the feeling that it had cost her something she'd never get back.

The only thing she understood was that she couldn't trust the girl. She was the only part Rachael had recognised, and Rachael had been terrified. The rest didn't matter. If she avoided the girl, she'd avoid the dream.

The place had felt like a prison or a dungeon, but there were none like it in Blackrock. Unless... Blackrock used to be a mining town. Rachael knew where the old entrance to the mines was, but she'd never been inside and as far as she knew, neither had anyone else in at least ten years. The place in her dream had been dark and filled with shadows. A space below Blackrock? But no, that wasn't right. She relied on the shadows, she didn't fear them. But, to be on the safe side, she'd avoid the mines and she'd avoid the girl. Nothing would happen if she stuck to herself.

Something moved between the buildings before her. Rachael jumped to her feet and wiped her cold tears away with one hand while reaching for a loose brick with the other. After the dream, she wasn't willing to take chances.

The shadows stilled. Maybe she had overreacted after last night. She still felt the dream in her bones, so perhaps she'd panicked when it was just a gust of wind. But the harder she stared into the dark alley ahead of her, the more she made out a tiny frame. Someone was there, and they were watching her.

"Come out." She didn't trust her voice enough to shout. Even so, the small silhouette jumped but didn't come closer. She wasn't in the mood for playing games. "I know you're there. What do you want from me?"

Her eyes flicked to the frozen brick in her hands. She didn't want to use it, but she'd defend herself if she had to. She'd never seriously injured anyone, but she had hurt people enough to be left alone.

The small frame walked out of the darkness with scared steps. The little girl from before. The one she'd feared in her dream. The other children had never sent anyone to her on a dare more than once. It had to be related to her dream.

"Please don't hurt me," the girl said. "I've got a weapon too. I'll use it if I have to."

Rachael had never heard a bigger lie. She'd also never felt this conflicted. The girl's whole body was shaking and she was stammering, but Rachael didn't know if that was from the cold, out of fear, or a condition she had.

"What do you want?" For now, the brick stayed in her hand. Hunger could drive even the youngest children to desperate crimes. Maybe the girl had returned for the bread, having realised she needed it herself. How would she react when she learned that Rachael had eaten it all? Angry enough to make her nightmare come true?

"I want to talk. Please, don't hurt me."

No one had ever approached her like this before. Was it possible that the girl really meant her no harm? Her gut told Rachael not to let her come any closer, but how dangerous could she possibly be? Rachael's instincts had never let her down before. Despite her warning, the girl didn't have a weapon. She was just a young girl in rags, arms closed around her stuffed bear.

"Fine," Rachael said. "But if you try anything, I'll defend myself."

The baker's daughter crept closer to Rachael but stopped when Rachael raised her brick in warning. The girl from her nightmare flinched. Rachael sighed, and, as a sign of goodwill, put down her brick. She hoped she wouldn't regret it.

Chapter Four

Rachael motioned for the girl to come closer. "Come here."

Being an orphan in Blackrock had taught her how to react when someone was making fun of her, when someone was avoiding her, or when someone tried to rob her or worse, but not once had something like this happened. People being scared of her had become an inevitable part of Rachael's life, and it hadn't bothered her in a long time. That it bothered her now made her feel like a child again, newly abandoned and unused to being shunned. Too vulnerable.

The girl inched closer without taking her eyes off the brick. When it stayed on the ground, she cast an uneasy glance at Rachael and sped up until they stood next to each other. Rachael wanted to step away—a habit born of survival—but showing weakness or her own fear was a mistake the streets never let go unpunished.

"Have a seat," Rachael said. There was only really her old blanket, but Rachael feared the girl might collapse if she stood much longer.

The girl did as she was told, but remained silent,

chewing on her bottom lip.

"Are you here on another dare?"

The girl shook her head and stared at her shuffling feet.

"Then what are you doing here?" Rachael scolded herself for letting a stranger come this close to her. Caution was best, but she'd learned that not everyone was the same. This girl was a first in many ways. Rachael's gut told her that aggression wasn't the way to go if she wanted answers or to be left alone, uncomfortable as the closeness made her. If the girl had a shiv inside her stuffed bear, Rachael would struggle to dodge.

Then again, the only people who'd tried to come this close were those who came to rape her, and she couldn't imagine this girl had followed her for that.

"I…" Her shaking voice was as tiny as her thin body.

"What's your name?"

"Cephy."

Progress. "How old are you, Cephy?" "Ten." Cephy kept her eyes fixated on the frozen ground. She looked more out of her comfort zone than Rachael had realised. Neither of them was used to this.

"How long have you been homeless?"

Cephy was seven years younger than her and didn't carry herself with that special confidence only orphans who had survived long enough could muster.

Intriguing as it was, it didn't explain why Cephy had come to her. Twice. Even if the other orphans hadn't sent her on a dare, she must have overheard them talking about Rachael—Blackrock's omen was never far from anyone's lips.

"Three weeks, I think."

Rachael watched Cephy with curiosity. It was hard when you first became homeless. Not knowing where to sleep or where to find your next meal was difficult in any season, but to become homeless at the beginning of winter must have been worse. Rachael remembered her first season well. It had been warm, and finding water had been more important than finding food. She'd got lucky—it had rained often that summer. But she hadn't seen it as lucky, not having known any better. She'd only known that she was scared and cried herself to sleep every night, praying for help. When the few trees in Blackrock had shed their first brittle leaves, Rachael accepted no one listened to her prayers and her parents weren't coming back. She'd been five years younger than Cephy, but she had coped. She had made it work. If she went easy on Cephy, the girl would never learn how to take care of herself.

"What do you want from me?"

"I…" Silent tears ran down Cephy's flushed cheeks.

Rachael didn't know what to say. She'd never had to offer her sympathy before. What if her understanding got Cephy killed? Kindness wasn't the rule on Blackrock's street—she'd spent many nights as a child praying for that to be different.

"Go live with the other homeless kids. They're your age, they'll take you in." There were groups of strays all over Blackrock. They stuck together for safety and always took in new kids. Unlike her, they knew how to deal with something like this.

"I don't want to die."

Something inside Rachael ached worse than anything she'd ever felt. This was the monster she'd feared in her dream?

"You know where to find food," Cephy said. "You sure know how to defend yourself. I thought, maybe, if I watched you….

"I brought you this." Cephy took a small loaf of bread from under her dress, which she'd hidden behind her stuffed bear. It didn't seem to be warm any more, but it still looked good. "You sure were twitching in your sleep a lot, and you were crying. I… was scared. I thought about getting help, but then you woke up and you looked scared too."

Rachael stared at Cephy, lost for words. Cephy wouldn't actually have found anyone willing to help Rachael, but that wasn't the point. No one had ever wanted to help her before.

"I was having a bad dream," Rachael said.

Although, in the cold light of winter's morning, the nightmare no longer seemed scary. Cephy nodded like she understood. Rachael was glad that she didn't.

Rachael nodded at the bread. "You brought this for me?" She hoped to lighten the mood a little. The faint blush on Cephy's cheeks told her it had worked.

"Hmh. And I want to tell you something."

"Oh? And what could that be?" Rachael was getting more and more comfortable talking to the girl. The queasy feeling in her gut was still there, but the more they talked the more natural it felt. Her gut feeling had never been so conflicted, and Rachael saw it as a good sign. If Cephy was all bad, Rachael's instincts wouldn't be torn. "I'm not scared of you." Cephy's voice was as delicate as frost's first soft touches.

"That's not very convincing when you're shaking. You can't even look at me." Although, Cephy wasn't shaking as much as she had been. Still, Cephy was lying. The villagers had made it clear to her that there was no kind word for her here, and she reminded herself that she couldn't blame them—it was in their nature to fear what they believed to be evil. Cephy had only been homeless for three weeks, her parents would have taught her.

"I'm cold, is all," Cephy said. "I know how the mean kids make you feel. The grown-ups, too."

Rachael scowled. "I doubt you—"

"They are mean to me, too."

She knew Cephy meant well, but she didn't understand. How could she? They hadn't tried to burn Cephy alive for trying to help.

"It's not the same."

Cephy's eyes glazed over with the shadow of a painful memory. "They said I'm a monster. They said I should go to you so we can go to the Mists together."

Rachael shivered and hugged her legs a little tighter. "Why would they say that?"

"My father kicked me out when I set fire to my bed." Cephy was staring at the ground again, her hands balled into fists.

"Accidents happen. He shouldn't have left matches lying around." Rachael wasn't sure if Cephy was the youngest in her family, but either way it was a stupid thing to do with young children in the house. Even worse to punish her for his mistake.

Cephy shook harder and her bottom lip quivered. "I didn't mean to. Father was shouting at me, at my mummy, and it scared me. Suddenly everyone was screaming and father threw me over his shoulder. He shoved me into the street. Mummy told him to stop, but he pushed me so hard I fell.

"It wasn't his fault. See?" Cephy held out her hand to the pile of wet branches Rachael had been struggling to light since it had started snowing, opened it—

and fire flared to life. Rachael jumped to her feet and stepped back, eyes wide and heart pounding. How could the villagers be scared of her *dreams*?

Cephy hugged herself and cried. "I hoped you'd understand."

Her dream made more sense now, but Cephy hadn't set fire to her then. She hadn't even sounded like herself. Rachael had never seen such a pitiful creature. Wasn't it possible that her dream had only shown her Cephy because they'd met that day and Rachael had been thinking about her? Yes, she had lit wet branches on fire with a thought, but more than anything she seemed terrified. In her dream, she hadn't thought of Cephy as herself but as some shadow wearing her face. That had to be all it was..

Rachael sat back next to Cephy and pulled her into her arms. Rachael held her so tight Cephy couldn't have got away if she'd wanted to.

"I do understand," Rachael said. "I think. But how did you do that?" She knew many people had the gift—merchants returning from farther south talked about it—but she'd never met anyone else who had it. It had only ever been her and her dreams of death.

"I don't know, I just do."

Rachael didn't know what to do with a crying child, so she held Cephy until her tears stopped flowing and her shaking calmed.

"I want to stay with you," Cephy said. "Can I? Please?"

Rachael was about to agree when her stomach twisted into a painful knot. Her bad gut feeling spiked, its message clear. Cephy was a danger to her. If she stayed, Rachael would face the dark despair from her nightmare one day.

Rachael couldn't help. She hated the idea of Cephy feeling as lonely and unwanted as she had all her life, but she feared that place from her dream more.

Gently, Rachael pushed her away. "No." Saying it out loud didn't make her feel any better. If anything, the pain grew worse when she saw the desperate look in Cephy's eyes.

"I thought you understood."

"I do, but you can't stay with me. I'm sorry." Rachael sighed and hoped her excuse would be convincing enough. "I barely find enough food for myself. I have no shelter, just this blanket. It'll be easier without me." Their eyes met just in time for Rachael to see Cephy's eyes glaze over with the same acceptance she'd felt herself so often. There was no love for her in Blackrock. No place to call home. Cephy's last hope shattered inside her, and Rachael was the one who'd swung the hammer.

Cephy stood and walked away. "Keep the bread. I'll get a new one tomorrow."

Rachael wanted to stop her, to say that she'd changed her mind, but every time she opened her mouth, fear punched her in the gut. The pain only stopped once Cephy was out of sight.

Rachael hated herself for it. She'd had the chance to spare Cephy the same loneliness she had suffered for so long, and she had refused. It wasn't right, but what else could she have done? She'd never experienced a reaction like that; she'd be a fool to ignore it.

Rachael sat on her blanket and stared at the alley Cephy had disappeared into. She wished Cephy came back, that things were different. Cephy's fire was still burning strong despite the snow which was falling thicker every minute. It wasn't enough to keep the chill out of her bones, so she wrapped herself in her blanket and ignored the torn feeling that she'd made a terrible mistake and saved her life in the same frost-kissed breath.

Chapter Five

A week went by without any sign of Cephy. If it wasn't for the small presents of still-warm bread Rachael received every day, she'd have wondered if Cephy was dead. They were waiting on her blanket when Rachael returned after searching for food, or a few feet away from her on a bed of bricks when Rachael woke up. She'd been wrong about Cephy; the girl could look after herself just fine. Her excuse that she was struggling enough to find food for herself rang hollow in her ears.

Rachael wasn't used to feeling so conflicted. Life on the streets had simple rules: don't trust anyone, stick to yourself, and survive by any means necessary. They had served her well. So, even though she often caught herself wishing she could talk to Cephy again, she was grateful the girl was staying away.

And yet she'd felt guilty ever since Cephy had walked away from her, that delicious loaf of bread by her feet. The gift that should have swayed her but hadn't. All her life, Rachael had hated Blackrock's people for being cold to her. She'd had a chance to be better, and she hadn't taken it. She didn't even want to stay away from Cephy. Talking to her had made Rachael long for a friend again, and while she knew it was safer on her own she couldn't convince herself that wanting a friend was wrong.

Another loaf of bread was waiting for Rachael when she returned to her hideout. Two days after she'd told Cephy to leave, she had moved again, hoping that would be the end of it, but the girl had found her. The abandoned firewood store behind the empty house was a tight squeeze, but it protected her better from fresh snow and the breeze than the open air did. She felt guilty for eating the bread, but her hunger convinced her otherwise every day. She was in no position to waste food, and Cephy brought her more than Rachael had ever found on her own.

It was just getting dark when Rachael settled on her blanket and tore a chunk off the bread. The sun dipped the town in an orange-pink too pretty for Blackrock. Rachael felt watched but chose to ignore it. If someone had followed her hoping to hurt her, she'd do better once her stomach was full.

But then she heard a faint whimpering, and her heart grew heavy as stone. Usually, she left crying children alone since there was nothing she could do for them, but this time her gut urged her to investigate. The sound was soft, so the child must have been close or Rachael wouldn't have heard it. Her heart told her it was Cephy, but her mind insisted on caution. She'd take a look, but only help if it was Cephy. She owed her that much. .

It wasn't difficult to follow the crying. At this time of day, the silence of families having dinner inside their homes settled over the town; the crying stood out. Rachael followed it into the dark alley off to the left from her hideout, and into a narrow alley between houses on the right halfway down the first. Cephy was curled up on the ground, quietly sobbing into her stuffed bear.

When Rachael took a step towards her this time, her body didn't respond. She felt nothing but pity. Rachael had no idea what she'd say when she reached Cephy, but she wouldn't turn her away again.

"Cephy?" Rachael wanted to hold her and comfort her, but it was one thing to take her in and quite another to grow attached. Most new strays didn't survive their first winter, with or without help—the emotional strain often proved too much, and Cephy looked at the end of what she could take Cephy didn't seem to even hear her.

Rachael moved closer and put a gentle hand on the girl's shoulder. "Cephy? Can you hear me?"

Cephy rolled onto her other side, away from Rachael. She hugged the bear to her chest like it was the only thing that could comfort her. She was shaking from the cold and suppressed sobs. A weak ray of dying sunlight lit up Cephy's face, and Rachael's heart froze.

Cephy was bleeding.

Chapter Six

Rachael knew she should have turned around. This was none of her business—children died on the streets all the time, especially in winter. Someone had likely tried to rob Cephy and beaten her or worse when they saw she had nothing worth taking. Rachael knew better than to get involved, but this time it was different. This time she knew the girl.

Slowly, so as not to startle her even more, Rachael sat next to Cephy, carefully took her face into her hands and turned it towards her. Cephy tried to resist, but Rachael was stronger.

"Cephy, it's me. See? It's all right. What happened?"

Cephy focussed on Rachael, and through slow, ragged breaths her body relaxed. Her eyes were wide and wild. Gentle tremors still shuddered through her, but relief outshone the fear in her eyes.

"Who did this?"

"My father." Her voice shook harder again, as if she feared he'd hear and punish her for admitting it.

Rachael pulled Cephy into her arms and held her.

Somewhere in the back of her mind she remembered someone holding her like this once, stroking her hair to comfort her, so Rachael did the same. She understood. Her father hadn't wanted her either.

"Your father did this to you?"

Cephy nodded into Rachael's arms. "To me and my mother." Her voice had calmed down and was muffled from speaking against Rachael.

Stroking Cephy's hair seemed to help her, so Rachael continued. "Why did he do that?" She tried not to let her anger show in her voice. While she understood and had accepted a long time ago that she couldn't trust anyone, this was still wrong. Her old fury at the people who had abandoned her rose to the surface again, but Rachael tried to suppress it. Cephy needed calm comfort, not a shared enemy.

"He found out that mummy left me bread every day while he was at work."

That explained how Cephy had been able to spare so much. Now that her father knew what had been going on behind his back, he had asserted his authority.

Rachael felt ill at the picture Cephy was painting of her father. What kind of man raised a child with love, only to abandon her in a storm of violence?

But Rachael had learned never to make assumptions, and her gut told her there was more.

"I'm sorry," Rachael said.

It was cruel that Cephy had been treated like this, but it would make her new life easier for her in the long run. Maybe now she'd learn to look after herself rather than have someone else do it for her. Maybe now she'd understand that you only survived if you stood alone.

"Nobody loves me," Cephy said. Her voice sounded

far away, resigned. "Father doesn't. Mummy doesn't, or she'd help me. You don't want me, either."

Rachael was lost for words. How could she argue with that after she'd sent Cephy away? She could only think of one thing to do, and Rachael wasn't convinced it wouldn't make things worse. The light dimmed behind Cephy's eyes, and it made the decision for her. "Your mother loves you," Rachael said. "She gave you bread every day, right? Fresh bread, still warm. Every day. Because of her, you—"

"They are replacing me." Rachael found it odd that a voice as tiny as this could interrupt her so easily. "They are having a new baby. When father beat me and mummy, I heard my brothers say it's to replace me, because I'm not good enough."

There were no words that would make Cephy's pain go away. Was this why she was alone? Had her parents abandoned her when her first dream promised death? Had her mother left her the blanket like Cephy's mother had left her the bread? She remembered the soft melody humming her to sleep, the gentle hands caressing her hair. There'd been love in her life once. Rachael chided herself. Maybe her dreams had something to do with it, but more likely her parents had struggled for food like everyone else. Leaving a young child behind had probably been the easiest option. She doubted things were much better wherever they'd gone, but two mouths to feed were better than three.

There was one thing she could say that would make it better. "Cephy." Rachael steeled herself for the wave of pain, but nothing happened. The only hurt she felt was the one that already existed. If her nightmare had warned her then, it'd warn her again now; what she'd felt last time must have been empathy for Cephy, for the situation they were in. For how similar they were.

The cursed omen who dreamed of death, and the girl who called fire with a wish. They only had each other. Was it really so wrong to hold on to that?

Cephy had become numb in her arms. The girl stared at the snow in front of them with wide bloodshot eyes, her stuffed bear hanging into the snow from her limp hand slowly soaking up ice.

"If you want to stay with me, you can."

Cephy's eyes grew even wider than before and darted up at Rachael. She threw her arms around Rachael and held on so tightly Rachael was worried she'd bruise herself more..

"Thank you, thank you, *thank you*." Rachael had made her choice. There was no point in dwelling on the discomfort that flashed inside her core like a final warning.

Chapter Seven

The explosion filled every corner of her consciousness. Everyone was screaming. Not her; she was crying and angry and terrified.

"What have you d—" A falling wooden plank silenced his accusation. Its heat and fire shielded her from his glare.

She couldn't stay—he'd kill her if he got hold of her. The door was open, an inviting escape route, but could she really leave everyone she loved behind in this mess she'd started? This was her fault Every accusation he'd ever thrown at her would be true if she left now. She'd be the monster he always told her she was. His reasons for throwing her into the street like unwanted leftovers... Everything would be justified.

She spun around to get her mother, but the cupboard where the lamp oil was stored exploded. The force of the blast threw her across the room and forced white-hot deafness on her. The screaming had stopped, but so had every other sound. The flames were consuming the house around her, but its silence was worse.

Her ears were ringing, but the explosion had

brought her closer to the door. She couldn't reach the rest of the house, and her hearing was slowly returning. She didn't want to hear their screams again. Her mother's. Her brothers'. Even her father's, although his hatred had pushed her to this.

She ignored the pain in her back and ankle and leapt for the door. A frosty wind and cold snow welcomed her. A crowd had gathered to observe the flames and watched her stumble out, alone. They knew the rumours. They knew it was her doing.

Her hearing wasn't good enough yet to pick up on their insults and accusations, but she didn't need to hear them. Her father had been an unmoving heap on the floor last she'd seen him. Her mother had been trapped, trying to save her brothers. The crowd knew she had killed her family, and so did she.

The strength left her legs and she sank to the ground. Her arms went up around her ears to block whatever she did hear. She sobbed without offers of kindness or help, and rocked herself into madness.

Rachael woke drenched in cold sweat. She'd now had two vivid dreams since she met Cephy, and both left her panicked. Her reaction wasn't unusual, but normally, months passed between dreams.

But it was too late for doubts. Cephy was staying with her, and Rachael didn't have the heart to send her away again. Now she'd seen what Cephy would do, she could stop it from happening.

Rachael filled her fists with snow and rubbed them into her face to chase away her lingering doubt. As much as she tried, she couldn't shake the feeling that something was going on, and that something was shifting every time she made a decision yet felt out of her control. Rachael hated not knowing; that she couldn't figure out the details was as frustrating as her situation in the nightmare had been.

Still tired despite the snow, Rachael looked around. She squinted in the flickering light from Cephy's dying fire as her eyes adjusted. It was still dark. Her blanket, which she'd wrapped around herself in a hopeless attempt to stay warm, was dusted in a thin layer of fresh snow.

Cephy's spot was empty.

Rachael got up. Cephy never strayed far from Rachael and had seemed too grateful not to sleep alone tonight to wander off. In the short amount of time they'd spent together, Rachael had figured out that Cephy didn't like the dark. Odd sounds didn't scare her as much as the shadows between buildings, which always seemed to come alive in the faint moonlight. The sound of Rachael's bare feet in the snow was unnaturally loud. Something was wrong, her last dream too fresh in her mind for her to relax.

A week had passed since Rachael had taken in Cephy. She'd insisted that Cephy recover from her shock and her injuries while Rachael went out to find food. Cephy was young and not used to her new life, but she was clever—she hated being on her own, but she had agreed to Rachael leaving her alone to find food after she'd thought about it.

Maybe this had nothing to do with her dream, but Rachael's gut told her to find Cephy and fast. Blackrock wasn't safe at night, especially for trusting children like Cephy. Rachael called her name. No one answered. She walked away from their firewood store, stepped into an alley—

And the smell hit her. Burning wood. Ash. Fire.

Rachael's eyes shot up between the buildings. Thick black smoke smothered the night sky, the bright orange glow of nearby flames dancing across its surface.

She froze. Her dream hadn't been a warning, it had happened at the same time.

Rachael ran. She knew where Cephy's old home was, but the flames showed her the way regardless. The closer she got, the bigger the mocking play of light and dark against the night around her. She cut a corner, and there it was. The whole house was engulfed in flames. An oppressive smell filled the air, and a crowd had gathered to watch their neighbours burn. Cephy was sitting on the ground between them and the smouldering ruin, her face buried in her hands.

Rachael forced her way through the onlookers as fast as she could and fell to her knees beside Cephy.

"Cephy. It's me, Rachael." Cephy didn't look up. Her body had gone rigid. "Can you hear me?"

Three people with buckets full of water rushed past her. Rachael thought she heard screaming but wasn't sure whether it was coming from inside the house or from the crowd.

"I only wanted to hug my mother."

Rachael had to strain her ears to hear the tiny voice, but wouldn't ask Cephy to repeat anything. This was none of the villagers' business, and Cephy shouldn't have to relive it.

Rachael helped Cephy to her feet. "Come on, I'll get you home." Rachael regretted her words immediately. Home to Cephy was the burning ruin behind her, not the frozen spot under the too-small firewood store, and there was no going back there.

"I just wanted to see her one more time. He saw me, and hit me harder than ever before and I—"

Rachael silenced her with a hug. She could imagine what had happened after that. Carefully, Rachael picked her up. It took all her strength to carry Cephy in her arms, but the girl wasn't making any effort to walk on her own and Rachael wanted to get her away from this place.

No one tried to stop them. Rachael hoped Cephy had her eyes shut; the looks the crowd threw her said more than words could have done; Chances were, if Cephy hadn't burned down a whole house by herself—if the damage had been any less—things would have been a lot worse. For the first time, Rachael wondered if their curses could be small gifts. Everyone knew what they could do. They wouldn't arrest someone who could tell them about their death or easily reduce a building to ashes.

Cephy had committed a terrible crime. Thanks to her, they were safe.

Chapter Eight

That night, Rachael fell asleep cradling Cephy in her arms. She'd lain awake for several hours before the gentle cloak of sleep had finally embraced her. wondering just how her life had taken a turn such as this.

How had her life taken such an odd turn? She'd been content on her own—not happy, perhaps, but accepting. How had she come to look after a child? Not any child, either—a child with a talent far more dangerous than hers.

Rachael held Cephy and stroked her hair when the girl whimpered in her sleep. She was lying to herself, and had been for years. She had been lonely. She had wanted her mother to come back and embrace her, just like Cephy had craved one last hug. The lie had been a necessity, but that necessity was obsolete now. She had Cephy, and they'd chosen each other. In a way, that was better than family.

A week later, Rachael missed being on her own. There was comfort in having someone else, but after what

Cephy had done, the villagers didn't just avoid them, they went out of their way to stay clear of Rachael and Cephy. No one left food out for them now. The few people that had sometimes granted them a pitiful smile no longer did so. Even the fearful whispers behind their backs had quieted. It was like Blackrock was trying to pretend they didn't exist.

It made Rachael uneasy. Her gut told her to be on her guard and listen to every hushed whisper. The villagers had thought Rachael dangerous, but now Cephy was with her and there wasn't one soul alive in Blackrock that didn't know about the fire. Rumours spread fast and could do far more damage than truth—and in that case, they were likely all true. She worried the fire had been the last straw.

The snow was falling heavier every day. They'd starve or freeze to death if they couldn't find food soon, but there was no more sympathy amongst the people, no more mercy from those who had children themselves. In her twelve years on the street, Rachael had considered leaving Blackrock most days, but the uncertainty of the world behind the familiar walls stopped her. Cursed people like her were hated everywhere; they wouldn't fare any better in another town. Neither her nor Cephy had ever left the small village and didn't know what lay beyond the gates. Rachael had heard of dangerous animals in the woods just outside, but she'd also heard of edible berries growing in the shrubs. Death was almost guaranteed either way unless they got lucky. For the first time in twelve years, however, food was only a given outside Blackrock. Leaving would be worth the risk. Maybe they could find a cave or a clearing. They could catch river fish, learn to hunt small animals like rabbits, and eat all the berries they could find. They'd have each other. Maybe they could have something close to freedom. But Rachael was getting ahead of herself. Cephy had already lost one home this month; Rachael would wait to see if things improved. If they didn't, they'd leave. Blackrock was cruel, but she knew its shadows. The forest was an unknown. For all she knew, things would be worse, and she didn't want to make things worse if she didn't have to.

Rachael made up her mind. They had a little bit of bread left, but she could only ration it for so long. If they found no food in the next week, they would leave and never look back.

Exhausted, Cale brought Barnaby to a gradual stop. They'd ridden hard for the past few days, hoping to reach Arlo in time. Reeve's intel said she'd come this way soon, and Cale wanted to be here when she did. She'd have questions and would need a friend.

Arlo's hut wasn't much farther now. Cale petted Barnaby's head, her coat wet with sweat and her ears flicking in appreciation. She'd earned a break after their sprint all the way from the White City; he could lead her the rest of the way.

"Come on. He'll have a treat for you."

Barnaby whinnied and sped up.

Cale hated to put his old friend in danger, but too much was at stake and not many people knew Arlo lived out here. It would be the safest place for her—Rachael, Reeve had said her name was. Of course, compared to the trouble he had back home with the king and his White Guard, this trip felt like a holiday. A holiday with consequences for the country, true, but it was still a nice change from sneaking in and out of the prison and hiding in their safe houses. Not that he disliked any of it, but it was nice to leave Kiana in charge for a few days.

The trees grew close this deep into the forest. Arlo had chosen this spot because it could be hard to get to and Cale loved the hut for its seclusion, but leading Barnaby through the frosted trees and untouched snow was a challenge—but then, neither Cale nor his horse had ever shied away from one of those. Maker knew they wouldn't be here today if they had.

The scent of grilled fish teased his nose before he saw the smoke rise.

"Do you smell that? We're nearly there. Just a little more."

Barnaby needed no encouragement. She nuzzled Cale to let him know she understood and hurried along his lead as they made their way over to the hut.

Cale entered the clearing only to find it deserted. "Arlo?"

The fire pit was empty, the smell all that remained of what seemed like a feast now. It wasn't snowing right now, and there was only one set of boot prints in the snow. No one knew Cale was coming—he hadn't even told Arlo to minimise the risk. Cale relaxed a little; wherever Arlo was, he wasn't in danger.

He knocked on the door. "Arlo? Are you in there?"

Snow crunched behind him. Cale spun around, one hand on his sword.

"Quiet, my boy, or you'll scare away the game." Arlo's deep voice thundered through the clearing louder than anything Cale could manage. That and Arlo's imposing stature were more likely to scare away any animals had the wildlife not been used to him by now. If anything, they got along just fine. Arlo made sure they had enough food and shelter during the winter and only took what he needed, and in return the animals seemed to like him.

Cale sighed in relief. Worrying was a habit, and not one he was willing to abandon no matter how often Arlo or Ailis asked him to. It had saved his life too many times.

Cale nodded to the empty fire pit. “Looks to me like you’ve already eaten.”

Arlo patted his belly with a proud grin. “A man who works hard needs to eat hard, lad. Especially during winter.”

“I doubt you’re about to starve.”

Arlo wasn’t overweight by any means, but he was a good hunter and skilled with most weapons. If he wanted to eat, he’d eat.

His deep, hearty laugh resonated in the trees and seemed to make the ground vibrate with soft tremors. “Come, sit. I’ll see to it that you won’t suffer that fate either, my boy.” Grateful, Cale sat by the extinguished fire. Arlo always kept out an extra log to sit on in case Cale visited without warning. It had been too long, but the White Guard had kept him on his toes. His back ached from the long ride and his muscles were sore; he’d have sat on the ground if he’d needed to.

Arlo threw some dry branches on the fire pit and lit them with two rocks. “Does your visit mean it’s time?” His voice hadn’t lost all cheer, but there was no mistaking that he knew this situation for what it was. They’d all been waiting for this day to come, but now it was here they couldn’t celebrate just yet. Too much work to do, too much that could go wrong. Still, things were about to get exciting. Cale grinned. "Yes. I don't know when exactly, but it won't be long now. I left before the White Guard did and rode harder. They'll reach Blackrock by tomorrow evening if we are correct." Arlo sat next to him and Cale sighed. Rachael hadn't even left Blackrock yet but he already didn't have enough fingers to count the things that could go wrong. "Maker, Arlo, I hope we've done enough. Reeve is good, I know he'll help if necessary, but I wish I could be there with them."

"You know she'll have more chance of leaving unnoticed if fewer people are there to help her," Arlo said. "Besides, that old grump Reeve is there. But something else is worrying you. Spit it out, my boy."

Living by himself had kept Arlo's senses sharp. He didn't go amongst people often, but he was better at reading people than most. More importantly, he knew Cale better than most. There was no point trying to talk around the issue.

"Commander Videl left with them."

Arlo stared into the embers which were slowly growing into a nice fire. "Does he know who she is to us?"

Maker, he hoped not. "I don't think so, but we can't be sure. Reeve said there've been no spies in Blackrock besides him, and he's been keeping a close eye on her. He'd know. They are going for Rachael and someone else, but I don't think it's related to the prophecy. Kiana and I spied on them just before they left; they've been called to Blackrock to deal with a girl who kills people with dreams and another who killed her family in a fire. I don't think Videl knows, but he's no idiot.

If he connects the dots before Rachael makes it out… I should be there, Arlo."

He knew they'd done everything they could to allow things to proceed naturally without their interference, but it didn't help. The stakes were too high for peace of mind, the person too valuable.

"Hmph. Do you doubt me or Reeve, lad?"

Cale smiled. "Never."

"You worry too much, my boy. I'll be ready. There'll be a hot stew and a made bed waiting for her when she gets here."

"We can't let any harm come to her."

"Aye, lad, you don't need to remind me." Arlo put his large hand on Cale's shoulder. "The girl'll be safe with me. Do we know her name?"

Cale nodded. "It's Rachael. Another girl has been with her lately, they might flee together. Her name is Cephy, she's a good few years younger than Rachael."

Arlo skewered two fish on an arrow and placed them over the fire. "The prophecy mentioned only one other person, lad. Any chance this is her?"

The thought had occurred to him, but he wouldn't let fear control him. "She's a child, Arlo. If it's really her, don't forget prophecies are warnings, they're not set in stone. I won't turn her away."

"Don't fret, my boy. I'm not suggesting we abandon a child to this forest. I'll be ready for them."

Cale smiled. "Just like the good old days."

It seemed like another lifetime that Arlo had unofficially adopted Cale and his sister Ailis. Since they'd moved out and revived the Sparrows, Arlo had often looked after the gifted for him and nursed them back to health. Some of those gifted had become

Sparrows, others had been desperate to get on the first ship to Midoka or Krymistis and start a new life. Cale owed him his life as well as that of many others.

Arlo chuckled. "You youngsters are quick to speak of the good old days when all you've seen is chaos. Aren't you too young to speak of things that happened a long time ago? What are you, five?"

Cale couldn't help laughing. "I'll have you know, I'm almost twenty-six. I've seen enough."

"Don't be too keen to grow old, my boy. If you think you're hurting now…" Arlo handed him the fish. "Don't worry yourself mad, lad, or Ailis will never let me hear the last of it. They'll be safe here. You have my word."

Cale bit into his fish. "You wouldn't have a carrot for Barnaby, would you? I promised her a treat."

"I always have something for the old girl. Sit tight, I'll be right back."

There was no safer place in the world than under Arlo's watchful protection, but Cale couldn't shake the feeling that something was about to go terribly wrong.

Chapter Nine

Rachael woke to muffled but urgent shouting coming from the town square. Cephy shifted slightly in her arms, unfazed by the noises, but Rachael couldn't shake the feeling that something was very wrong.

She blinked. It was a clear night; the moon and her stars made the fresh snow sparkle. Blackrock was usually quiet at this time save for the occasional drunk men's laughter. But what she was hearing now was too energetic. The people of Blackrock were cheering.

Dread settled in her gut. It told her to run and made the fine hairs on her arms stand on end. She sat up, careful not to wake Cephy, and looked around. There was no immediate threat and she couldn't be sure the cheering had anything to do with her, but her gut feeling was never wrong. Rachael pulled her thin blanket over herself and Cephy and grasped it with both hands. If it was nothing and her sleepy mind had overreacted, she didn't want to disturb Cephy. But if it was more than that…

Again, the joined voices of the villagers reached her hideout. She couldn't make out words, but the way time passed between short shouts… were they responding to someone? Was someone rallying them?

It was just starting to snow again. The flakes were thick already—a new blanket would cover Blackrock by morning. If they left now, it would hide their steps before long.

Her heart was racing, her instincts on edge. She trusted her gut, and it told her to run. This wasn't how she'd been planning it, but it couldn't be helped.

A dog shot out of the dark, chasing something only it could see. Rachael jumped and gasped, suddenly very awake. They had to go *now*.

"Cephy." She gently shook the little girl cuddling to her. Part of her wanted to sneak closer to the danger and see what was going on. Knowledge was a worthy weapon, and if she knew what they were shouting… Maybe it would give them an advantage. "Cephy, wake up."

Cephy squinted, barely awake and unable to focus on Rachael. "What—"

"We need to go. Get up."

"What do you—"

"Up. Now."

Cephy sat up, worry in her eyes. "What's wrong?" Rachael's intuition had saved her life many times. Her gut didn't make mistakes. It told her to run, so she'd run as fast as her snow-burned feet would carry her. She knew Blackrock's hidden corners, knew of places most other people didn't know existed. She knew all its shadows, all the tight alleys only children on the brink of starvation could fit through.

"I don't know." Rachael didn't want Cephy to panic—it made people unreliable—but there was no time to find out how Cephy coped under pressure. The last time she'd been backed into a corner, she had burned a house down. Rachael couldn't afford the same thing tonight or it would lead the people right to them. "Come on, we need to go. We're not safe here anymore."

She pulled Cephy to her feet and rushed to the other end of the alley, into a small gap between buildings. Rachael hadn't used the passage for years, but that's what made it perfect. She couldn't use any of her usual routes tonight in case someone had been watching. Cats and dogs dragged their prey here to either devour it or leave it once they got bored with their new toy. The ground would be littered with the corpses of mice and other small critters, but it was the best route away from their spot. The villagers would never think to look for them here, and they could sneak closer unseen.

"Be careful where you step," Rachael said. "Don't look down." It was unlikely that anyone would hear a young girl's shriek or the cracking of squirrel bones in this weather, but the rush of adrenaline told Rachael to take no chances.

The snow was growing heavier. Luck was on their side.

Cephy clung to her bear and Rachael's hand. "The ground feels weird."

"It's nothing, don't worry about it. Hold on."

They had reached the end of the narrow alley. Rachael stuck her head out just enough to make sure the road was clear. It was empty.

She turned around to Cephy. "Let's run across to the other side, okay? Look, there's another alley over there."

"Hmh."

They dashed across the broad street, disappearing inside the next tight alley as fast as their feet could carry them through the thick layer of frozen snow.

They were close to the square now, and Rachael made out single words here and there. Words like *witches*, *death*, and *fire*. Words like *Dark One*, *servants*, and Mists. The villagers were coming for them, no doubt about it. If they stayed in Blackrock or were followed tonight, they would die—and it didn't sound like Blackrock would show them the mercy of a quick death.

"Stay right behind me."

Cephy whimpered in response. The alley was too slim for them both to fit next to each other, but they could make it work if they walked sideways.

They just needed to stay unseen and leave Blackrock before anyone noticed they were gone. Nothing else mattered.

Rachael hurried to the other end of the alley, terrified of making any sound at all. The square was on the other side. If anyone heard her or glanced their way at the wrong moment…

Rachael held her breath and pressed herself against the wall. Cephy was copying her every movement. She didn't dare get any closer, but she heard enough.

"Have faith, good people. After tonight, your struggle will be over. Justice will be served."

The crowd cheered and raised their fists into the air. Their shouts were no longer joyful. They were angry. Blackrock demanded blood—*her* blood, and Cephy's.

"Don't forget this day, because today the White Guard freed you of the evil influence of the Dark One's spawn."

Rachael peeked around the corner enough to see the speaker. White armour and white banners, cold as frost. The king's White Guard. She pressed herself back against the wall, praying it would swallow her and hide her. If even the king wanted them dead, where could they possibly run?

"Long live King Aeric!" the man in white shouted.

"Long live King Aeric!" The crowd spoke in perfect sync. Rachael had never seen them so united.

"Onwards, good people, to the witches' lair!"

Her heart was racing, but Rachael inched forwards to see what was happening. Four guards in white armour on white horses led the angry group away from the square. The people were carrying torches, as were two of the guards. Some carried axes and pitchforks. The man who had rallied them walked out front, leading their charge.

They wouldn't get another opening like this again.

"Rachael?" Cephy looked up at her with wide, terrified eyes. "Are those people after us?"

With a grim frown, she nodded.

"What will they do if they find us?"

Better to spare her the details. "They won't."

Cephy nodded, her eyes focussed on the ground. "What do we do?"

Rachael was out of ideas. The White Guard meant the king had issued the order to kill her and Cephy. Where could they go that the king's influence wouldn't reach them? They had to leave, but then what? A vast forest lay outside Blackrock—at least she'd always imagined it to be vast—and she'd seen the slaughtered animals hunters brought from the woods. Big, dangerous animals with sharp teeth. Even if they somehow evaded those, the White Guard would track them.

But what else was there? Blackrock bordered Tramura, but she didn't know enough about it to go there—she'd only heard rumours that Tramura had almost hunted their gifted to extinction So much was uncertain about the forest, but it was their best option. Were dangerous animals really that different to an entire town hunting them?

She knew of a gap in the wall big enough for them both to squeeze through. If they hurried, they'd be gone and their steps hidden under fresh snow before the villagers reached their empty hiding place.

"There are cracks and small holes in the wall in several places. I know one we can fit through." She'd never attempted it herself for fear of what might be lurking beyond, but she'd children better fed than her sneak out that way. If well-fed, spoiled brats could fit through, then so could they. The White Guards' heavy armour wouldn't fit, and that was all that mattered.

Getting there was another issue. They'd have to sneak through at least one richer neighbourhood, and there were no narrow passages there. It was on the other side of town and there'd be nowhere to hide. For the first time in her life, Rachael was grateful for the heavy snow. It was odd that something she'd hated for so long would now save her life. It would hide their tracks and she knew the town better than the White Guard. They had the advantage while they were still in Blackrock.

"Follow me," Rachael said. "Don't hesitate. We can't afford to be slow tonight."

Cephy nodded, a determined gleam in her eyes. Perhaps she'd do all right under pressure after all.

Rachael squeezed out of the narrow gap onto the open road. Cephy was right behind her. She ran across the road, praying to whatever deity wanted to listen that no one was looking out their windows in that moment. The commotion had passed, there was nothing to see. Their luck had to hold just a little while longer.

The faint uproar of an angry, disappointed mob reached their ears.

"We need to run."

The fear on Cephy's face was reassuring. It would keep her moving and alive, if they were quick. They were nowhere near where they needed to be, and now the townspeople knew they were hiding somewhere.

"Don't take your eyes off me, Cephy. No matter what happens, don't look back."

Rachael took off into the nearest alley.

Rachael dashed through one narrow alley, disappeared inside another, and jumped across a side road into yet another passage. The numb thuds in the snow behind her told her Cephy was keeping up.

Rachael paused, eyes glued on the scene ahead of her.

Cephy pressed herself against her. "Why are we stopping?" she whispered. "We're close." Rachael said. Her lungs were burning. The angry shouts had grown quieter as they'd flown through Blackrock, but anything could happen between now and coming out on the other side of the wall.

"So, let's keep going."

Only one large square separated them from the final

two alleys that stood between them and freedom. Just one square filled with fifteen residents, two armed guards, and three dogs.

"We can't go this way," Rachael said. "We need to turn around."

"Why, what's there?"

"People. Guards. I bet they've been told to watch out for us. They wouldn't be here at this time otherwise."

There was no other alley they could take that would bring them closer to the other side. The wall was right behind them, but it was too smooth to climb and it was in good shape since it was in a better part of Blackrock.

"Which way do we go?" Cephy asked.

Rachael didn't take her eyes off the people for one moment, scared she might miss something if she did. If one of those dogs caught their scent… But they wouldn't know what they smelled like. They'd have to wait for Rachael to step out to know anything was amiss.

"We can go around, but it'll take longer." Rachael didn't want to go back the way they'd come even if it was only for a short time, but there was no other choice.

"Can't we distract them?"

"Distract them how? We don't have anything we could throw. Even then it wouldn't distract them for long enough for us to slip through."

"I could set a fire." Rachael paused. She hadn't considered that. Cephy sounded confident, maybe it could work. "Can you do that from here?"

Cephy shook her head. "No, but I can set fire to that cart over there if I get closer."

Rachael saw the one. It was full of goods from the

local shops. They'd burn easily. It was on the other side of the square, but if Cephy could pull it off it would create the distraction they needed.

Rachael shook her head. "It's too far away. You'd never make it back in time."

Cephy shrugged. "They won't fit in here, they're not small enough. It'll burn for a while, and they won't search all the way back here." She nodded to her left. "I bet this alley leads right to it."

Rachael didn't like it, but it was all they had. "Be quick. I'll be right behind you."

The distant shouting grew louder—the angry crowd was catching up.

Cephy nodded. Together, they hurried down the left alley towards the cart and closer to the shouting. It wasn't far, but they'd still need to hurry back and run across the square once the cart was on fire. With the whole town out for their blood, time stretched differently. Roads were longer than they'd been before, Rachael was slower than she normally was, every sound was louder and high-pitched. She couldn't tell if the mob was only a few more streets away or if her fear made it sound that way.

They reached the cart, and Racheal took a deep breath. The villagers were on edge and pacing. It wouldn't take much to draw them away. This either worked or she'd die tonight.

"When you're ready and there's no one in the way, you can—"

The cart burst into flames. The sudden heat tore through the snow and seemed to singe her face.

Rachael grabbed Cephy's wrist and pulled her back the way they'd come. She didn't turn around until they were back in their previous spot.

Cephy's trick had worked a miracle. Everyone was running towards the fire and screaming in terror. The guards had drawn their swords and held their shields in front of them, but they were focussing on the fire. No one was looking this way.

If they ran along the walls, the snow and bright light from the fire would hide them. Hopefully, it'd be enough.

"*Now.*"

They didn't take their eyes off the crowd when they stepped into the road.

Rachael's heart felt ready to explode. She didn't remember the last time it'd beaten so hard.

They sneaked along the houses as fast as they dared. The heavy snowfall helped conceal them, and the alley leading to freedom was only a few short moments away. Once they were there, it'd be difficult for anyone to follow. "*Mum.*"

Their heads shot up. A little boy was sticking his head out of a window right above them. He was pointing down at them. "*Mum, the witches are getting away.*"

There was no time to see if anyone was looking— their angered cry told her all she needed to know. She sprinted towards the gap dragging Cephy behind her, praying it would be enough. They couldn't fail now, freedom was too close. From the corner of her eye, Rachael saw the group get closer fast— but she was closer to the alley. A muscly man grabbed for Cephy's arm, but Rachael pulled her away from him. They jumped between the buildings, running faster than she'd ever done before, the sounds of mad screaming and cursing of their souls too close behind them.

They'd never catch up with her now they'd reached the alley, but it didn't reassure her. The dogs were barking, and they'd fit through the alley.

The hole was smaller than Rachael remembered, but it would have to do. She shoved Cephy through first, and squeezed herself through right after. A dog bit at her ankle—she felt its breath and spit on her—but it wasn't quick enough. The girls shared a brief look, then took off into a world they knew nothing about.

Chapter Ten

"Where did they go?" Commander Videl's calm voice didn't betray the disgust he felt on the inside. The witches must have had an accomplice or he and his men would have caught them without problems.

Behind him, the burnt-out ruins of a house forced a grim reminder of what the witches were capable of on Blackrock's people. The baker's home. His own daughter, one of the witches Commander Videl had come to kill, had burnt him and his family to ashes. Many locals had witnessed the foul magic first-hand, yet they all stood rigid before him now, too terrified to speak.

Commander Videl's grip on his sword tightened and the creases on his forehead deepened. "I said, where the fuck did the witches go?" The crowd looked sheepish and terrified. He hated both, cowardice and fear. Normally, he was a calm and collected man, but the people of Blackrock were testing his patience.

Finally, a man raised his hand without looking up from his black leather shoes.

"Speak up."

"We don't know, good sir."

"You don't know?" Commander Videl hit the man's face, his heavy gauntlet drawing thick streaks of blood. "Men!" Behind him, his three subordinates straightened and saluted. "Find them. They are two young girls, damn it. I won't be outwitted by two children, understood?"

The guards nodded, saluted once more, and spread out.

"Now, you lot need to be taught a lesson," he said to the shivering crowd before him. Normally, he lived for ridding the world of the Dark One's plague, but they'd ridden for several days just to come here. His skin crawled at the thought of all the witches he could have prosecuted in the White City in that time. "You call us to your town, asking us to rid you of the Dark One's spawn, and then you have the nerve to lose them?" He spat every word.

"We're awfully sorry, good sir," a young man said. "We don't know where they might have—"

Commander Videl punched him in the face, leaving another deep red smear on his gauntlet.

"Show me every crack in the wall around this damned town. I want to know every last rabbit hole, understood?"

"But, good sir, our walls are old. They have held for centuries, they have. Not a crack large enough in any of them, we assure you."

His patience was running low. How stupid did they think he was? How incapable did they think him and his men? He was a commander of the White Guard, damn it, not some badly trained youth from some backwater like this one.

"Are you saying, then, that the witches are still in Blackrock? That they have simply outwitted my men and me?"

"Aye, good sir, they must—" The raspy gurgling of blood filled his lungs and cut him off.

The crowd gasped. A woman screamed and ran to the man's side.

"Adam!" She broke down in front of him and held his blood-soaked hands, pleading with the Maker to save him.

Commander Videl had pledged his life to the execution of the Dark One's spawn. How did these people not see the danger the witches posed after they'd burned down a house and the family trapped inside? Why didn't the people of Blackrock care? Just what, Maker forbid, needed to happen before they saw reason?

Commander Videl kicked her with his steel boot. "Excuses. You people have allowed two dangerous criminals to flee your city and you blame us. This man, *Adam*, has conspired with evil to fool us and buy the witches time. He died for his sins, may the Maker forgive him. Would you allow one such as him to live among you? Are you no better, that you won't speak up and allow us to do the Maker's work?"

Mumbled apologies shuddered through the shaking crowd.

"Let me ask again." Commander Videl tried hard to control his breathing and be professional, but these people were driving him mad. It wasn't this hard in the White City. Some fools sympathised with witches, but he always delivered them to the Maker and most knew the danger. "Show me every crack, hole, and gap in these walls. Now."

The people looked down, too scared to meet his demanding gaze. Mothers turned their children away from him and held them close. No one was brave enough to do the right thing.

Commander Videl shook his head; such weakness in the face of justice. He drew his sword, grabbed the wife of the dead man, and pressed the blade into her neck. She whimpered when it drew the thinnest sliver of blood.

"If you do not cooperate, I will have to assume that all of you think as Adam did. If your town is as rotten as I fear, I and my men will have to purge it to spare the world your corruption."

The people looked mortified, but no one spoke a word. Their fear seemed to have disintegrated all rational thought.

He sighed. It was a pity, but it was better to lose one town and save the country than spare a few on good faith and doom their neighbours because he'd been careless. He wouldn't take risks with the Dark One's taint.

"Very well. My men will be back soon, but I can start the purging of this corrupted shithole without them." The cold promise of his sword cutting through the winter air sang through the square.

"Stop! Wait!" A panicked voice parted the shaking crowd. A heavy-set woman dragged a small child through the snow. Her face was flushed from running, but there was a spark in her eyes he'd seen before. This would be good.

"Explain yourself."

"My boy here, my Peter, he saw 'em. He saw 'em

escape. They squeezed through a gap in the wall, he saw it himself. Isn't that right, Peter?"

The boy looked as scared as the rest of them, but he peered up at Commander Videl without flinching. "Yes, sir.."

"Where?" Excitement replaced his anger. Maker willing this trip wasn't a waste after all.

"That way, good sir. The other end of town."

"How long ago?"

"I dunno, maybe—"

Commander Videl pressed his blade into the child's neck. The crowd gasped, a few screamed, but he ignored them. This was more important than any one life. "I asked you, how long ago?"

The boy nodded as quickly as the situation allowed him. "It wasn't a half hour ago, sir."

"Did they have horses waiting for them?"

"No, sir. I saw them run into the forest, I swear."

Commander Videl smiled. No horses? The witches stood no chance now.

"You've done well, Peter. You'd make a fine soldier of the White Guard one day."

The boy beamed with pride and looked at his mother for confirmation. She nodded, the same proud grin on her face.

Commander Videl cleared his throat to recapture the people's attention. "Today, this young lad's honesty saved you. May you learn from his virtue and remember the White City's mercy, for we have rid you of evil and given you a second chance."

Their cheering followed him as he rode out of town, where he promised himself he'd never set foot in this hole again.

Chapter Eleven

Rachael stopped to catch her breath once she couldn't hear the eager barking of the guards' hounds any more. She leant against a tree, exhausted from their narrow escape, but struggled to calm down. Those guards had arrived on horses. How could she possibly hope to outrun them? Maybe, if she'd been on her own…

Cephy wasn't far behind and was watching her. Every surface was covered in undisturbed snow, every small branch and leaf. Rachael had never thought of snow as peaceful or beautiful, but the serene silence of this forest was starting to change her mind. How far had they run? She no longer heard the dogs or the angry mob, so perhaps it didn't matter. They had escaped Blackrock and the White Guard for now; they'd be fine. She wasn't familiar with her new surroundings, but she doubted guards all the way from the White City knew this forest any better. It was still snowing slightly, and their tracks were slowly filling in. They had the advantage.

Rachael looked around, trying to find something they could eat, but their panicked escape had scared off any wild animals and she didn't know if she could trust the few red berries. Survival had been hard before, but now… She didn't know how to hunt deer or even a boar and was too inexperienced to make a bow or take any critter by surprise. Their best chance was to reach a town, but how far away was that? Which direction? What if the White Guard rode through there? Even if they did reach a town, it wouldn't do them much good. She knew from gossip she'd overheard that people like her and Cephy weren't wanted anywhere. These woods were a complete mystery to her, but at least they weren't outright hostile.

Whatever they ended up doing, she had to figure it out fast. Cephy was still out of breath, and neither of them had had a good meal in too long. If she didn't come up with a plan, the snow would hide more than their tracks.

"Are you all right?" Rachael asked.

Cephy nodded, looking lost, and it made Rachael's decision for her. They wouldn't be running from anyone again for a while. They'd reach a town far away from Blackrock and start over where no one knew they were cursed. They'd live normal lives. Maybe a nice couple would take them in.

Rachael huffed at herself. She hadn't allowed herself to think like that in years. Wishful thinking had never got her anywhere, and the only dreams she still had were out of her control and had got her into this position to begin with. If she wanted to achieve anything, wishing hard enough wouldn't get her there. She just needed to start somewhere, and for that, any action was better than standing around hoping the world would change.

They needed to find a cave. Then, Cephy could light a fire and they'd be warm for the first time in years. Rachael wasn't as strong as the hunters she'd seen but she knew how to move without drawing attention to herself. She could hunt smaller animals. They would take one small step at a time, and they would survive.

But for now, she needed to calm Cephy down. The girl still looked like she was on the run. Her eyes were bloodshot, her breathing hadn't slowed, and she was looking over her shoulder every other second.

"Are you sure you're all right? We can rest longer if you need it."

"I'm fine." Cephy's small whisper was loud in the silence.

"What is it?"

Cephy shuffled her feet. "Thank you for taking me with you."

Rachael didn't remember the last time anyone had thanked her. She shrugged and pretended the mild heat in her cheeks was a delayed reaction from their sprint. "I couldn't leave you behind, could I?"

Cephy nodded. "You could. They almost got you. That man would have killed you if they had."

Rachael shivered. Was that what her dream had shown her? Her last days in a prison, waiting for her execution. She'd felt like she'd let someone down—it must have been Cephy. Had Cephy spoken with the commander's voice? She had been more worried about Cephy at the time, so perhaps her dream had merged the two. Either way, she had somehow evaded that fate. That had to count for something.

She had a chance to start over, and she wouldn't leave Cephy behind. Cephy was relying on her, and

Rachael refused to be just someone else who abandoned her. Neither of them needed another. They had each other, and she wouldn't throw that away.

"Do you think you can go on?" Rachael herself didn't want to take another step, but they needed to put more distance between themselves and Blackrock. Their filthy rags stood out among the forest's white. If anyone followed them out here, they'd be easy to spot.

Cephy clung on to Rachael's hand like it was the only lifeline she needed and nodded.

"We should find a cave," Rachael said. "Maybe a hollow tree. We should get out of the open for a while."

Cephy looked up at her. "You mean like a hiding place?"

"Yes, just like that. Tell me if you see anything."

The snow got deeper the farther they went. It had never been this high in Blackrock; the daily traffic of people, animals, and carts hadn't allowed it to settle higher than her toes. Rachael doubted they were making any progress towards the next town, but at least they were moving farther away from the road, too. If only the snow weren't covering her ankles. She was worried she'd stop feeling her toes. Cephy was shaking, but there was nothing Rachael could do about that. They'd be in trouble if they didn't find shelter soon, but as far as she could see there was nowhere to hide. There were no caves, and the trees stood too far apart to stop the snow from reaching the ground.

"Look, over there." Cephy pointed at a tree to their right. Its trunk was hollow. "Could we hide there?"

Blackrock's streets had taught her that, if something seemed too good to be true, it usually was. But the ground inside the tree was a pale green, the tree wide enough that it would hide them from most directions. It was just big enough for both of them to sit inside, maybe even a small fire. They'd have to keep an eye on it, but it would be better than this.

"That's perfect. Well done, Cephy."

Cephy's beaming smile was the first she'd seen in… a while. They hurried over, and sighed when the inside of the tree was a little warmer than the outside. It wasn't a big difference, but it was good enough until they could get a fire going.

"Can you make a fire?"

Cephy nodded, her hands already glowing with the promise of warmth. Lighting it inside the tree's dry base was a risk, but Cephy had controlled her fire perfectly before. They wouldn't burn unless Cephy wished it.

Rachael leaned into the tree's embrace and felt her lips twitch into a content smile. This was the best shelter she'd had in years. For now, it was better than good enough.

Commander Videl pointed towards the small, slowly vanishing trail of footprints in the snow. "This way." It was starting to snow heavier again. If they didn't hurry, the witches' trail would disappear completely and they'd miss their chance.

His men followed behind him, weapons drawn and ready to attack anyone standing in their way. The real hunt had begun. This—doing the Maker's work, chasing the corrupted—was what they'd trained for.

Commander Videl held up one hand to signal his men to stop. His most trusted soldier rode up beside him.

" Off your horses. We'll go the rest on foot." His men dismounted and gathered around him. "You two—get over there and drag them here. We've waited long enough." The men saluted and made their way over to the tree, their hands on their weapons. The witches had lit a beacon leading him straight to their lair. Even from a distance he saw the soft glow of a fire lighting up the immediate area around the tree. That they'd outrun him this long was offensive, but they'd pay soon enough.

He basked in the righteous feeling of victory while his men marched over to the witches' hole. He'd bring them to the White City, where they'd rot in their cells until King Aeric gave the order to have them skinned and executed in Market Square. King Aeric would give the order on Videl's recommendation. They made a good team—the fair king who wanted the best for his people, and the commander who was prepared to do what the king couldn't. He grinned thinking about it. At the very least, the younger girl would hang—he'd take no chances with a public burning. The older witch was no danger to anyone now, so she'd get the usual punishment. Either way, they'd both die, and that's why he did his job—to make his country a safer place.

Rachael turned around so she could warm her side. Cephy had started the fire almost an hour ago, but it was still burning as hot as it had done when Cephy had first lit the small pile of snow-covered branches. Not one spark had jumped out of place, kept in place and alive by Cephy's will alone. Cephy was relying on Rachael, but Rachael wasn't fooling herself--without Cephy, she wouldn't have stood a chance. Her toes were tingling and for the first time this winter, she wasn't cold. She owed Cephy.

Although, she couldn't help envying the girl just a little. Cephy was so much younger than her, but her power was more useful, had saved their lives today, and Cephy had perfect control over it. Rachael had nothing like that with her dreams. What would it be like to control them? She doubted she'd ever know.

"Tomorrow, I'll show you how to defend yourself in case we get separated."

Cephy's face fell. "But I want to stick with you."

"I know, but we might not have a choice. If we have to split up, I want you to be able to look after yourself until we find each other again."

They needed each other. To her surprise, Rachael didn't mind. She was the stealth, Cephy the fire. They knew what it was like to be on their own. She could trust Cephy, and in return she'd look after her.

Cephy was quiet for a moment, then nodded. "Can you show me how to hunt?"

Rachael frowned—if only. "I'll show you what I know, but it probably won't be enough to feed you. You'll need to find a town if we get separated. Find a couple, or maybe an old lady. They'll have no reason to be suspicious if you don't set anything on fire."

"And if they are mean to me?"

Rachael hesitated. When people had been mean to her, she'd run away or kicked them where it hurt if they'd tried anything, but setting fire to someone wasn't the same. She wanted Cephy to be brave enough to defend herself without killing anyone. A trail of dead bodies and missing people would only add to their problems no matter how mean they were.

"You can't burn someone just because they are mean

to you. Defend yourself if someone tries to hurt you, but don't use your fire unless there's no other way."

Cephy nodded but looked unsure. "Can I use it to hunt rabbits?"

"Only if no one is watching."

Starting a new life would be difficult enough as it was. Being careless wasn't an option.

A shadow over their faces caused the fire to flicker.

"Look at that, cornered like foxes."

Rachael's heart stopped. Two men wearing white armour stood in front of them, blocking their only exit. She didn't dare move. She'd forgotten how, and she wasn't convinced it mattered. There was nowhere to run. She doubted the guards had come alone. The hairs on the back of her neck stood on end as she remembered the merciless voice of their commander. One guard was stronger than Rachael and Cephy together; fighting them would be pointless. If the commander was nearby, it was over.

The man who'd spoken had the nastiest grin Rachael had ever seen, like he knew exactly what his commander would do to her and was looking forward to it.

"Like pretty little foxes. Let's take them back to the commander. He'll be happy to see them unharmed—more fun for him."

The bigger of the two reached out and grabbed Rachael's arms. His grip was so tight it hurt. He pulled her outside, jerked her up onto her feet, and her bones twisted under his rough hands.

Cephy screamed. She tried to duck out of the other man's reach but wasn't fast enough. His arms closed around her. He carried her away slung over his shoulder like she was nothing but a half-filled sack of flour. The other dragged Rachael after him by her arm. She tried to pull free, but it was no use. He was much taller than her, stronger than her. Had she punched him right between his ribs he wouldn't have felt a thing under that armour. She tried to kick herself free, but her feet hit snow.

Her nightmare echoed in her mind. The prison, the darkness filled with horrors, that terrible voice. The veiled demons. She refused to let him drag her to that place.

"Cephy! Do it!" Cephy stopped screaming, but nothing happened.

"Now!"

A nearby tree caught fire. The man carrying Cephy laughed and pulled her closer to his face by her hair.

"Was that supposed to hurt me, you little bitch? You're not as dangerous as the commander told us."

His head caught fire and he dropped Cephy with a desperate scream. The smell of burning flesh filled the air. Rachael's captor tightened his grip on her arm and twisted her around as he turned to Cephy, who was cowering wide-eyed in the snow.

"Why you filthy little sh—" His arm went up in flames and he let go of Rachael.. They screamed as they tried to put out the flames, but Rachael knew they'd only stop if Cephy willed it—and Cephy looked too terrified for any rational thought.

Rachael tried not to gag as boiling blood thawed the frost and the first man collapsed into the snow. His head was a charred, bloody mess. Too close to them, more soldiers and the commander's terrible voice cried out as they took up their pursuit. The clanging of steel filled the air, followed by the fast trampling of horse hooves.

Rachael grabbed Cephy's hand. "*Run.*"

They ran deeper into the forest, praying to whichever god might listen that they'd somehow make it out of this alive.

Chapter Twelve

Aeron poured herself a steaming cup of tea and inhaled the rich fragrance before taking the first sip. To think the Fox was finally within reach, after all these years of patience and waiting—and better yet, it was bringing her the Sparrow. She'd lived a long life waiting for prophecy to find her, to come alive, but she'd never dared dream it would happen right outside her front door. Her mother had prepared her well almost two-hundred years ago. Now that she was so close…, It'd have been hard to sit still if it hadn't been for the patience training all Mist Women went through...

Careful not to waste any of the tea's aroma, Aeron inhaled the scent of five different herbs and leaves. It was her favourite tea, fatal if not made properly but so very useful when prepared by the right hands. *Her* hands. Her mother had taught her how many years ago. It was the only thing Aeron still had left of the woman besides the dagger and her name. *Aeron*. The bringer of destruction. 'Maiden of Death', her mother had once called her. Aeron had revelled in it, had loved the power her mother had bestowed upon her. She'd been given an important fate and now, finally, she'd fulfil it.

She'd already taken the first steps and vital precautions, but she couldn't be too careful. She had to succeed, no matter the cost. Her sacrifices on Kaethe had been small, but worth it. The Dark One shared her mind and soul—all she had to do was wait for the right moment and do His bidding. Nothing was more important. Aeron reminded herself of the prophecy her mother had force-fed her until the day Aeron had killed her. The ancient words were beautiful, stunning perfection.

A smile played on her full lips. Her wait was nearly over. Soon, her Fox would lead the Sparrow right to her door, and then the world would die in a flawless explosion of burning horror.

Rachael was struggling to catch her breath. She stopped running and dropped into the snow to steady her shaking legs. Cephy was hiding her tears in Rachael's moth-eaten sleeves as they both inhaled the crisp winter air, but Rachael felt the girl tremble worse than she was.

The screaming had stopped a while ago. The breeze no longer carried the stench of burning flesh. Rachael hadn't seen them all die, but from what she'd heard Cephy had panicked and unleashed merciless fire on the soldiers. The last time she'd dared to turn around, even the commander had been too preoccupied with his burning armour to come after them. How long ago had that been? Her legs felt like she'd been running for years. Her feet were too heavy to move another inch. It was tempting to stay in the powdery snow until she was sure the madness had ended.

"Are the bad men gone?"

Shaking from fear and fatigue, Rachael looked back the way they'd come. The snow was undisturbed apart from the small indents their feet had made. In this wintery perfection, it would have been easy to spot anyone who wasn't supposed to be there, even a soldier dressed in white.

Rachael nodded. "Yes, they're gone. I think they're all dead."

She didn't know what to make of Cephy. The girl had burnt down seasoned soldiers without another thought, yet was now holding onto Rachael and crying into her rags. She'd never met anyone as fragile or as dangerous as Cephy. The guards' screams were still ringing in her ears. They'd been terrible people, but they hadn't deserved that. Rachael just wanted to live in peace. No one needed to die for that—or was that what it would take? Was she prepared to pay such a high price?

If Cephy hadn't done anything, they'd be on their way to her nightmare right now, tied up and helpless in the back of a cart. Rachael had heard stories of men like them. The smile that guard had given her was forever burned into her memory. She couldn't deny that she owed Cephy her life. They'd had no other choice.

Fight or be hunted down and suffer—it was how things were. Rachael had learned that lesson early, but it had never been more true than today.

"Come on," Rachael said. "We need to find shelter, light another fire."

"Are we far from the next town?"

Rachael wished she had the answer. They were too exposed here, and if the White Guard returned with reinforcements… They'd be long gone by then. But the woods housed other dangers too—wolves and probably darker things Rachael didn't know about. The sooner they found shelter, the better.

"I don't know," she said. "We've been out here for a while. There's got to be something."

Cephy followed her through the snow without letting go of her rags. The snow wasn't as thick here as it had been when they found the hollow tree. Maybe it was a sign there were people nearby.

The forest grew denser the farther they walked. The slowly falling sun dipped the forest into a dark shade of red until the snow looked stained with blood. She hadn't realised they'd been running all day, but it had been dark when they fled Blackrock. The time of day hadn't mattered, but now they got this far she'd use it to their advantage more.

"Keep an eye out for another tree like the one you saw earlier. We could rest inside and continue tomorrow."

It didn't fix that they had no food, but they were used to that. Travelling would be easier once they'd slept by a fire, and it was better than being hunted across the forest or being despised within Blackrock. This was the closest to freedom Rachael had ever had. Nightfall brought unsettling sounds. A creaking branch here, an owl there, and Rachael was no longer sure spending the night outside was a good idea. She was exhausted, but the waking forest kept her awake.

"Rachael, look." Cephy pointed at small bright spots burning through the darkness like a beacon. "I think it's a house."

Relief washed through her. "I think you're right. Come on, maybe they'll let us stay the night." It was beyond her why anyone would want to live out here, but she wouldn't argue with luck. Maybe they were closer to a town than she'd thought?

They ran, energised by the warm lights amidst the trees. They stumbled over small branches hidden beneath the snow and large rocks in their way several times, but slowly the house became more than a faint silhouette. The light from inside the small hut illuminated the glistening snow around it. The orange glow from behind the windows was the most beautiful sight Rachael had ever seen. "Stay behind me," Rachael said. "I'll knock."

Cephy nodded, peeking out from behind Rachael..

Faint, homely sounds came from the other side of the door. Cooking pots clanged against a worktop surface, a chair scratched across the floor, and the sweet smell of tea hung in the air. It was a perfect home with all the perfect sounds and scents.

Cephy grabbed hold of her hand. Rachael had often been thrown off someone's doorstep for begging, but whoever lived here didn't know her or Cephy. They had no reason to be afraid of two young girls who'd got lost in the forest at night.

It wasn't enough to stop her heart from racing.

The door opened. "Yes? Can I help you?"

In Blackrock, people had grown contemptuous and lazy since the mine had closed and it showed in their figures. This lady was nothing like them. Her silky hair matched the darkness outside, her kind smile put the stars into her midnight eyes. Rachael had never seen anyone so beautiful. She looked like a good spirit come to save them, and for a second, Rachael didn't know what to say.

She gulped. "We're lost. We were playing in the forest but lost track of time, and now we can't find our way back." She'd never wanted anyone to believe her quite so badly.

The woman touched her heart, eyes heavy with sympathy. "You poor things. Come inside, I'll brew you some tea so you girls can warm up. I don't have much room, but I have some blankets stored away. They'll warm you right up."

Relieved, Rachael nodded and followed the lady inside. This was so much more than Rachael had hoped for.

She held a steaming mug of tea that warmed her frozen insides while the lady rummaged through cupboards and cabinets until she pulled out two comfortable-looking blankets twice hers and Cephy's size combined.

"Wrap up warm," the lady said. "I'll make you some more tea. Are you hungry? I have a bit of rabbit stew left. It's not much, but you're welcome to it."

"Yes!" The word had left Rachael's mouth before she could think better of herself. "I mean, please. If it's no trouble."

No one had ever offered her food like this. The stew smelled divine and made her stomach contort into painful knots. Somewhere in the back of her mind, her gut whispered something about things that were too good to be true, but she didn't care. Not tonight. If this turned out to be a mistake, they could sneak out and run once they were full.

The lady smiled. “Not at all. What are your names?”

“I’m Rachael. This is Cephy. We’re... sisters. From Blackrock.”

Cephy beamed up at Rachael from under the small gap she’d left in her blanket.

“I’m glad you found me in this weather, Rachael and Cephy. My name is Aeron.”

Chapter Thirteen

Rachael had never been so comfortable. Aeron had handed her and Cephy a nightgown each, and had offered to repair their clothes. They'd both worn rags, but Rachael's clothes especially were in bad shape. She'd worn the same rags for years, and weather as well as her growing limbs had stretched them out of shape. Lady Aeron had even seemed certain she could fix Rachael's blanket, which she'd accepted to be beyond hope.

Her gut was still whispering that this was too good to be true, but it was getting quieter after a good night's sleep. Lady Aeron had been nothing but nice to them. Of course Rachael had expected the worst—it was what she was used to. Was it so strange to think that some people were genuinely kind? With every smile, Rachael grew more convinced that her gut was overreacting out of habit. She wouldn't let her paranoia ruin something good. They'd been lucky when they stumbled across Aeron's hut, and that was all there was to it.

Lady Aeron's nightgowns were soft and fluffy, and

had caressed Rachael's skin when she snuggled into it. They had their own beds and their own large blankets. Last night had been the most luxurious Rachael had ever experienced. She'd never slept so deeply. No dreams had ruined her night, and sleep had come easily knowing she didn't need to worry about thieves, rapists, or the White Guard.

Rachael had woken to the wonderful smells of tea and fresh bread, and the happy chirping of birds. Cephy was still asleep, but Rachael couldn't stay put any longer. She'd never dreamed that a place like this could exist, or people that looked after her so kindly.

Lady Aeron couldn't find out they were cursed or she'd throw them out. Maybe she'd even alert the guards. Rachael didn't want to overstay her welcome, but maybe Lady Aeron would allow them to stay a little while longer. She'd need a good reason if Lady Aeron asked why—after all, Lady Aeron thought they had parents to go home to and wouldn't want to worry them.

Rachael wrapped the blanket around herself and got up. She opened the door a tiny bit. Soft sunlight poured into the main room, and Aeron was sitting in one of its beams. She was humming to herself as she sipped a cup of tea. She looked like Rachael had always imagined a caring mother would look, waiting for her family to wake up. "Good morning, Rachael. Have you slept well?"

Rachael blushed. Embarrassed she'd been caught, she stepped out of the small room and closed the door behind her so they wouldn't wake Cephy.

"I'm sorry," Rachael said. "I didn't mean to spy on you."

Aeron offered her the kindest smile Rachael had ever seen. "Nonsense. Come here, I have something for you."

Rachael sat down next to Aeron, and Aeron spread out her rags on the table. Only, they weren't rags any more. They were beautiful clothes dyed vibrant reds and blues.

"How did you—" She touched the fabric. The clothes were as soft as they looked; if it wasn't for the tailoring itself, Rachael wouldn't have believed them to be the same shirt and trousers.

Aeron winked. "I'll let you in on a secret, if you promise not to tell anyone."

Rachael nodded. She owed Lady Aeron too much to even consider it and knew what it was like to keep a big secret. Lady Aeron spread her old, hole-ridden blanket over the beautiful clothes. "Do you like the colour red?"

"I do, but—" She couldn't dye it. As much as she resented her parents for abandoning her, it was all she had left. "It has sentimental value," Lady Aeron said. "I understand. I'll restore it to the way it was when you received it."

Rachael blinked. She would have loved for her blanket to be whole again, but it couldn't be done. She had accepted it years ago and was fine with it as it was. It was imperfect and flawed, but so was she. Rachael didn't even remember how it used to look.

Lady Aeron placed her hands on the tattered fabric and spoke words in a language Rachael didn't understand. She'd never heard words of such beauty before. They didn't sound like they belonged in this world.

Before her eyes, the blanket began to patch itself up. The holes stitched back together until they were gone. Even the fine seams disappeared, leaving nothing but the fabric itself. Stains disappeared, rough patches softened.

Her blanket, which had been beyond repair, was whole again.

"You promised not to tell anyone, remember?" Rachael didn't trust her voice, so she nodded. "I'm a Mist Woman. I can use magic to do things for me, like fix your clothes or make you tea."

Rachael was lost for words. Out of all the places they could have stumbled upon, they'd found someone like them. Lady Aeron wouldn't betray them. They were the same, she'd understand Rachael's need for secrecy.

"Cephy and I have magic too." It felt strange to say it out loud, but more than anything, it was exciting and right. She didn't need to hide anymore. "But we can't do anything as beautiful as you."

Aeron gave her a sympathetic smile. "And your parents don't mind? I didn't believe there was anyone in this world willing to tolerate us."

It didn't look like excuses would be necessary.

"We don't have parents. We're from Blackrock, but they asked the White Guard to take us away. I'm so sorry, we didn't mean to lie to you, but—"

Aeron laid a gentle finger on Rachael's broken lips. "It's all right. You don't have to explain. You and your sister are welcome to stay for as long as you like."

Sometimes, things that seemed too good to be true were simply luck. "Thank you. We won't be a burden, I promise."

Lady Aeron smiled. "Don't worry. I've waited all

my life for girls like you to find me."

Cale paced the small living room in Arlo's cabin. "I don't understand, they should be here by now. They can't have disappeared, they must be around here somewhere."

"It's possible they took the wrong turn when they left Blackrock and didn't follow the main road, lad. It's not like we left them detailed instructions. Maybe they—"

"No." Things couldn't have gone that wrong. If they'd gone left, if *she* had them... His palms were sweating, his heart racing. Something had gone wrong, but it couldn't be that bad. Maker, or could it? He needed to fix this.

"But if they have, lad?"

Cale shook his head. There had to be another reason. He'd come too far for it to end like this.

"Have you searched the forest?"

"Of course I have, my boy. This isn't the first time I've done this."

"And there were no traces at all?" Cale stopped and looked around the room like the curtains might have answers. He steadied himself on the heavy oak table. Maybe Arlo was right. Maybe they had to consider the worst.

Maker, he'd never felt so tired.

"No, my boy. I'm sorry."

"Then we need to find them. They are two girls without any tracking experience, they must have left a trail. The Sparrows need them. I won't sit here and hope for the best."

"And what do you suggest we do?"

It wasn't ideal, but there was only really one option. "I need to go see her. At best she's seen the girls pass through. At worst... I don't know what I can do if she has them, Arlo. I don't know why she'd co-operate."

Mist Women didn't argue, they issued orders and were obeyed. Aeron was the only one in Rifarne, but she was bad enough. If she wanted to keep the girls, it'd be near impossible to convince her otherwise. She was young by Mist Women standards, and he'd heard she was more impulsive than others. Arlo had met her fifty years ago, when his greying hair had still been a warm brown. The scar across his chest was all the proof Cale needed. He couldn't let the Sparrow anywhere near the Mist Woman.

"You know I can't let you go, my boy. She'll do worse to you than she ever did to me, and I'm—"

"Lucky to be alive, I know. That's why I have to go. We need them."

"You need only one."

Cale didn't like arguing with Arlo, but he couldn't leave the Sparrow with Aeron.

"And you think the Sparrow will leave the other girl alone? They've escaped Blackrock together, Arlo."

"I think it's a deal Aeron might just agree to. She's more likely to be interested in the younger one, don't you think? Children these days are so impressionable. What did you say her name was again? Cedar, Cider…"

"It's Cephy. For the love of the Maker, how did you expect to recognise them if you don't even know their names?"

Arlo chuckled. "I'm kidding, lad. Sit down, you're working yourself into a right frenzy."

The earthy, warming smell of Arlo's boar stew filled the room. Cale didn't know anyone who could cook a stew with boar as well as Arlo, but his old friend had a gift.

Cale breathed deeply, allowing the familiar smell to calm him, and sank into a chair. He sighed. "I just can't leave them in the clutches of that woman. Who knows what she'll do to them? What if she knows the prophecy, Arlo? Maker forbid, Rachael might already be dead. What then?"

Cale watched Arlo's heart sink behind his eyes. If Aeron killed Rachael, it would be the end of their resistance. Rifarne would burn. The whole world would die. He saw it as a good sign that the dead weren't marching across his country right now—Rachael had to still be alive. He'd put a lot of effort into finding Rachael and arranging for her to reach the White City safely. If there was anything he could do, he'd do it. They'd lost too much for him to be defeated now.

Arlo scratched his head. "Well, my boy, there's one thing you can do. But I can't guarantee your safety if you try it."

Cale had promised his Sparrows he'd get her to safety. Her life was more important than his. "I understand the risks. Let's begin."

Chapter Fourteen

For the first time in her life, Rachael settled into a comfortable routine without worrying about where her next meal would come from or whether the shadows were watching her.

Cephy had been overjoyed to learn that Lady Aeron was like them. They both helped out around the house, and in return, Lady Aeron helped them with their gifts. Lady Aeron herself seemed skilled in several kinds, and taught Cephy to control her fire even better. In return, Cephy helped with their lunches.

Rachael had told Lady Aeron about her nightmares, and Lady Aeron offered to brew her a tea which would stop them. It wasn't as sweet as the tea she'd served their first night, but Rachael went to bed without fear of what her dreams might show her—it was worth the slightly bitter taste. In exchange, Rachael helped with dinner. She knew nothing about cooking, but Lady Aeron was a good teacher and Rachael realised she loved learning. It wasn't much, but she was glad to be useful. Lady Aeron gave them the peace Rachael had craved. Cephy was enjoying herself and was excited to learn more about her gift. Rachael tried to think differently about her dreams, too—they'd warned her about the White Guard and led her to Cephy the night she'd burnt down her parents' house, after all. If it wasn't for her dreams, the White Guard would have delivered them to the demons and her nightmare would be real.

Still, she was glad to be rid of them. At least for now. It hurt, but they couldn't stay. Aeron was a wonderful host, but this was her home and it seemed too small even for her alone. With all three of them, it felt too crowded. Rachael was grateful, but she didn't want to intrude. It'd be better if they moved on, made something for themselves. Lady Aeron managed to live in peace, and so would Rachael.

Cale hurried through the forest towards Aeron's hut as fast as he could. The thought that she might kill Rachael at any moment was enough to let him ignore the burning pain in his legs and ankles. He'd left Barnaby a little way off to make sure his loyal friend would be safe and not end up as stew should this meeting not go well.

He still wasn't sure what to do about the other girl. He and Arlo hadn't talked more about it but Arlo had been right, as much as it pained him to consider the option. The Sparrows—Rifarne—needed Rachael. Rachael and Cephy had been together since before they escaped Blackrock and had likely grown attached to each other, but if he needed a bargaining chip…

He gritted his teeth. What was happening to him? Cephy was a human being, not currency. He refused to treat her like a means to an end. He refused to let this war make a monster out of him. The Sparrows didn't need Cephy to succeed, but she was innocent and he couldn't turn away another gifted, no matter what happened. He'd sworn to protect the gifted and he wouldn't make an exception now. There was a way to rescue both of them, he just needed to find it.

Of course, if this plan worked, he'd save Rachael, take Cephy along, and Aeron would never know he'd been there.

Aeron smiled in the dark as she waited. A man was coming to her home. A Sparrow. One of those her mother and the prophecy had warned her about. He wanted the girls, and she'd spent a long time wondering whether she should just let it happen. Let him believe she didn't know.

But where was the fun in that?

She had consulted the tome of Ar'Zac D'Ar, a relic from an ancient fallen empire. Her favourite prophecy—the Rise of the Sparrows—was right at the end, but she wasn't interested in that this time. She had leafed through the whole book, reminded herself of every word, until one prophecy had caught her eye: *The child will return to its mistress willingly and freely.*

She was sure Cephy was the Fox. Why this prophecy didn't name her as such made no sense, but it didn't matter. It couldn't mean anyone else. Rachael was the real danger to her plan, but she wasn't ready to let her die just yet. The Dark One protested in her mind, but she was stronger than He'd anticipated. He'd have to wait until she was ready. Rachael had no talent for her gift and was no threat right now. Besides, Aeron was nothing if not curious. It seemed unlikely Rachael would ever rise to become this threat to her plans, but she wasn't one to ignore prophecy. She'd watch and interfere if things got out of hand.

It'd be more fun if she let them go for now. Prophecy said Cephy would return when the time was right, and she could sacrifice Rachael to the Dark One whenever she pleased.

There was no rush.

Rachael was reading a book on the history of seers when Cephy sat down next to her with an exhausted sigh. The girl fell back into the pillows and sighed into the soft fabric.

Aeron had been working Cephy hard, teaching her everything she knew. The lessons were rough on Cephy and tired her out, but Rachael was sure it was only because Aeron saw so much potential in her. Cephy's ability was useful. Rachael had no control over her dreams, and Aeron had no skill as a seer either. So, she'd given Rachael a book, and Rachael was glad to have this much. It wasn't as good as learning something practical, but she felt less alone knowing there were others with the same gift.

Rachael looked up from her book. "How did your lesson go?"

"I'm *tired.*" Cephy slowly turned around until she was lying on her back, showing Rachael her charred fingertips and bleary eyes. "My hands hurt, but Lady Aeron won't heal them."

The feeling that things were too good to be true tugged at her again; Lady Aeron hadn't seemed like someone who wouldn't heal an injured child.

"She's trying to teach you to be more careful next

time." Lady Aeron had done them a huge favour. Now she was doing them another by teaching them. Lady Aeron knew her magic better than they did and knew what was best. Rachael wanted to trust her decision and support her, but to let Cephy suffer didn't seem like her.

"I *am* careful."

Cephy was pouting now, but Rachael knew the moment Lady Aeron entered the room her frown would be gone. They both wanted to please her—there was no other way to repay her for her kindness.

Rachael held out her hands. "Show me."

Cephy scooted closer and gently placed her hands into Rachael's. She hissed when they touched and winced but left her hands with Rachael. Her fingertips were burned. Small blisters had burst and left bloody streaks behind. Rachael tried to hide her frown. Why wasn't Lady Aeron healing them?

"Does it hurt?" Rachael asked. Cephy nodded, her eyes brimmed red. "Want me to get you some snow from outside? It would cool the wounds, and maybe—"

Cephy shook her head. "Don't. Lady Aeron would know. She'd punish both of us."

Rachael doubted it but nodded. Lady Aeron's methods were harsh and didn't quite fit the image Rachael had of her, but she wouldn't punish them for a bit of pain relief. She was kind and teaching Cephy a lesson, but she wasn't unnecessarily cruel.

"Go to sleep," Rachael said. "They'll feel better in the morning." She set the book aside and stretched. They were both tired; sleep could only help.

Most nights they fell asleep quickly, but Rachael

struggled having seen Cephy's fingers. An uncomfortable feeling was growing in her stomach. The voice at the back of her mind telling her that something was wrong had grown louder again. Just this once, Rachael wished she knew what would happen. Seeing someone's death was horrible, but this sense of foreboding was worse. At least her visions had been detailed.

Rachael was still lying awake when the pale glow of the moon filled their room and everything was silent save for the sound of owls hooting outside their window.

She held her breath when she heard something else. Faint creaking—someone was opening the front door, but… Lady Aeron would already be asleep. Someone was breaking in.

Her heart was racing. She wasn't sure whether to get up and spy on whoever had entered, or pull the blanket further over herself and pretend she hadn't noticed.

Aeron's muffled voice filled the dark. She spoke in hushed tones, so it was difficult to hear; Rachael strained her ears to hear anything at all. She got up and sneaked to the door to hear better.

"… you've come," Aeron said. "But stealing into my house? My, my, Sparrow, you should know better than this." A shiver ran down Rachael's spine; the softness in Aeron's voice was gone. Something else had replaced it. Something cold and amused.

Something that played with its prey before it ended its misery.

It was so unlike the Lady Aeron Rachael had come to know that she pressed herself against the door, eager and scared to hear more.

"Then you know why I'm here, too." The second voice belonged to a man, but Rachael didn't recognise it. He sounded older than her, strong and defiant. She could picture him glaring at Aeron even though their door was shut tight and it was too dark to see much of anything.

Aeron chuckled. "I do indeed. You can have them."

Rachael's heart felt ready to jump out of her chest. She wasn't supposed to hear this. If Aeron found out she'd been listening… But her curiosity won.

For a moment, neither said anything. Aeron's soft laughter broke the silence, but it didn't sound like her. It wasn't warm or wonderful. It made her regret leaving the comforting safety of her duvet.

"Surprised, Sparrow? I knew you were coming and I knew what you want even before you arrived. Take them. I have no use for them at the moment."

Pain shot through her heart. They were talking about her and Cephy. Aeron didn't need them—no, had no use for them. Like they were some goods to be bought at the market. What did that make the man?

Rachael had believed Aeron to be different, better than the others, but she was just as selfish. She didn't care for her or Cephy.

"What do you want?" His voice had a hard edge to it—he didn't trust her, and now neither did Rachael. But did that mean she could trust him? What did he want with them?

That terrible laugh that made her want to run back to Blackrock cut through the night. "Why, Sparrow, I don't want anything. They are yours."

"Fine. Have it your way. I will come back tomorrow with some horses. Don't you dare go back on your word, witch."

Aeron huffed. "I didn't know my word meant anything to you, but I promise if it makes you feel better. They'll be ready for you in the morning. You don't need to come here again. I'll bring them to you when they are ready to leave."

"And you had better make sure they are unharmed."

Rachael glanced at Cephy. Did her burnt, blistered fingers count as *unharmed*?

"Or you'll do what, Sparrow? Punish me? I'd love to see you try." Aeron's voice was a silky purr, but the threat was unmistakable.

Rachael wanted to warn the stranger, tell him Aeron could burn him to a crisp if she wanted to, but her gut told her that he already knew. He acted strong but she recognised fear in a man's voice when she heard it, and his was thick with it.

The door slammed shut and Rachael hid under her blanket. She was scared of the Aeron she'd heard tonight. Had Aeron ever cared about them or had it been an act this whole time? Why would she take them in, feed them and teach them, if they were so worthless? She had no idea what this man wanted with them and wouldn't trust him, but if he was here to take them away they could go with him until it was save to run.

They were better off on their own after all. Rachael wouldn't forget it again.

Chapter Fifteen

Rachael woke to the delicious smells of sweet tea and honey and the even sound of Cephy's breathing. The rising sun was dipping their room in a warm orange glow, and the first birds had begun to sing.

Rachael gently shook Cephy's arm until the girl was awake, and hurried to dress herself. She felt like she'd had the worst night's rest, like she'd suffered a nightmare she couldn't remember. *Something* wasn't right, and it made her uneasy.

She sighed. Had her body got used to the medicine Aeron prepared for her every morning? Maybe she needed something stronger to keep the bad dreams at bay.

Aeron was sitting at the table pouring tea when Rachael and Cephy entered together.

"Good morning, girls," Lady Aeron said "Have you slept well?"

Cephy nodded and sat down close to Aeron, but Rachael couldn't shake the feeling that Lady Aeron's smile didn't seem as genuine. Now she was so close to her, the feeling in her gut grew worse, twisting her insides and putting her mind on edge. Something she'd dreamed? Aeron sounded less sincere, her smile looked cooler. Even the warm comfort of this room seemed strange, like paint that had started to peel.

"Sit, Rachael," Lady Aeron said. The words—soft on the outside but sharp underneath—made the hairs on Rachael's arms stand on end. "Here, have some honey on white bread while you still can. My little Fox here won't leave you any otherwise."

Had Aeron always called Cephy that? Rachael felt like she'd heard it before, but not—

She remembered. Aeron had called Cephy her Fox last night, when a man came to the hut and they talked about her and Cephy. When Aeron had said she didn't care about them, had no use for them.

They weren't wanted in Blackrock and they weren't wanted here either. Their home with Aeron had been a lie and had proven what she'd always known deep down—they weren't wanted anywhere.

She felt so stupid. In Blackrock, she'd never have trusted anyone like she had trusted Aeron. People always betrayed one another—Rachael had lived by this rule all her life and it had served her well. Were a few days away from the mining town and a false smile really enough to let her guard down? Had she really thought Aeron was different, just because she was cursed too?

Rachael had never felt so childish. A bit of kindness had never fooled her, and now Cephy's hands had suffered because she'd been ignorant. Never again.

"Rachael?" Aeron's voice called her back into the hut. "Aren't you hungry?"

She hadn't touched her honeyed bread, whereas

Cephy only had crumbs left. Aeron herself wasn't eating anything but was slowly sipping her tea. Rachael felt sick just watching her.

"Not very." She wasn't convinced she'd keep it down if she tried. How had she been so blind? Her gut had tried to warn her when they'd arrived, but she ignored it because Aeron had given them comfort. Of course this was too good to be true, how couldn't it be? Aeron had given them everything she'd wanted, and she had fallen for it like a hungry rabbit that spotted a carrot in a barely disguised trap.

Rachael's instincts told her to run, but she doubted Aeron would let them get far. This was some kind of twisted game for which Rachael didn't know the rules but that Aeron had mastered. All she could do was go along for now and run as soon as she got the chance.

"Try to eat a little bit," Aeron said. "You have a busy day ahead of you."

"A busy day?" Cephy looked hopeful. "Are you going to teach me how to cast the special flames you told me about?"

Aeron shook her head and took one of their hands into each of hers. "I'm afraid not, my little Fox. Today is an important day for you both. I've arranged for someone to take you into their custody." *Lies*. Rachael remembered his every word—this had been his idea, not Aeron's. "He'll be back for you soon. You need to be ready when he arrives."

The disappointment on Cephy's face nearly broke Rachael's heart. If only she'd woken Cephy up last night; Cephy would have heard the venom from Aeron's lips herself, and this would have been easier on her.

Rachael didn't say a word. They'd be safer away from Aeron. She'd tell Cephy what she'd overheard once they were out of Aeron's reach.

"You're sending us away?" Cephy asked. "Why?"

Aeron squeezed Cephy's hand. "I will explain when you're older."

Cephy didn't look happy with that answer, but didn't argue. "So, we *will* come back?"

Rachael doubted Cephy noticed the terrifying smile that flashed on Aeron's lips. "Of course you will, my little Fox. You can return any time you like. I promise you'll always have a home here."

Rachael wanted to interrupt, tell Cephy that it was a trap, but this wasn't the moment to do it.

"Come, now," Aeron said. "He'll be here soon. He's bringing horses, so you won't have to walk."

"Where is he taking us?" Cephy's voice was trembling, her hands tight fists in her lap. Rachael wasn't sure she should comfort her, but last night she'd felt excited right before the man had arrived. Maybe it was a sign he was better for them, at least until they could get away.

"It doesn't matter," Aeron said. "You only need to know that he'll look after you from now on. You might say he's adopting you."

"When do we leave?" Rachael asked. She should have thanked Aeron for everything she'd done, pretended she didn't know what had been said, but she couldn't bring herself to lie. Aeron hadn't bothered last night—if anything, she'd been very open about her opinion of Rachael and Cephy. If they weren't worth the lie, neither was Aeron.

"As soon as you've eaten," Aeron said. "Finish your

bread, Rachael, and I'll see you off. He's not far from here."

Rachael nodded and started eating. She'd need her strength to escape.

Chapter Sixteen

The faint glow of a fire shining through the trees stood out among the white of winter. They'd only been trudging through the snow for a short while, but Rachael was beginning to feel the familiar chill in her bones. The clothes Aeron had made for them kept the worst of it out, but she was still relieved to see the flickering orange ahead.

Cephy clutched her hand and Rachael squeezed it. It was good they were getting away from Aeron, but Rachael didn't like returning to the unknown either. She'd grab Cephy and escape as soon as they could, and then they'd build something for themselves. Something permanent and peaceful.

At least she doubted this man was worse than Aeron. Rachael had heard a coldness in the woman's voice the night before, a promise of a cruelty she hadn't known people were capable of. Aeron's friendly act reminded Rachael of an incident many years ago, when a boy had visited his aunt in Blackrock with his family. He had changed his personality like that too. Around his family he'd been nice, but as soon as he was alone for a moment he'd kicked dogs and other children. She'd heard his parents say he was sick, that he couldn't control his own personality, but no doctor could help him. They'd left again within a week and Rachael never saw the boy again. Maybe Aeron was sick like that too.

Whoever this man was, he couldn't be worse. They'd stick it out for now, maybe get some food they could store for later, and wait until he was asleep.

"Sparrow." Aeron's voice was quiet but carried across the frost-kissed snow regardless. The birds in the trees startled and flew off as if sudden rain had surprised them. They weren't far away now but still far enough that the man shouldn't have heard her, yet he looked up and frowned at Aeron all the same.

She'd called him that last night, too. It didn't sound like a name somehow, but for now, it was all Rachael had. It would have to do.

Sparrow got up from a log by the fire and walked towards them. He glanced at her and Cephy, but his eyes were focussed on Aeron. Rachael had never seen eyes like his. She'd seen determination before, loads of times, but it had always been determination to hurt her. Sparrow looked genuine and it made her more cautious; Aeron had seemed genuine, too.

But she couldn't deny that something about him was different. He wasn't like the others—Rachael knew that the moment his grey eyes fell on her. His voice had betrayed his fear last night, but now she wondered if he could snap Aeron in two, after all. He wasn't packed with muscles, but he wasn't gangly either. He was a head taller than her, and the scar across his face told her he was used to fighting. But did he fight to defend himself or because he liked hurting people? It had begun to scab over but was still a little raw and belied the boyish face underneath.

"I'm impressed you kept your promise, witch." He sounded more confident than last night, but a hint of fear remained.

"I always keep my promises, Sparrow. Treat them well. They are very dear to me."

Pure hatred flickered in Sparrow's eyes. "You care as much about these girls as you care for the ground under your feet."

"If the ground under my feet weren't there, Sparrow, I'd fall into the abyss. I care greatly." Her silky voice was dripping enough venom to kill the entire White Guard. Even Cephy caught on and held Rachael's hand tighter.

Cephy's hands were still raw from practising her spells. The wounds hadn't scabbed over yet, and Rachael felt every blister against her own rough skin.

"We need to be leaving," Sparrow said. "There's a long road between you and where I'd rather be."

An amused smile played on Aeron's lips. "Of course. Treat them well, Sparrow, or I'll be back before it's time."

Just like that, Aeron was gone. Cephy gasped. The spot where Aeron had been standing was empty even of footprints in the snow.

A warm smile replaced Sparrow's frown. "I'm glad you're all right. Has she hurt either of you?" He sounded honest and a part of her wanted to trust him, but she wouldn't fall for it again. If he wanted her trust, he'd have to earn it, and she wouldn't make it easy ever again.

Rachael didn't take her eyes off him, waiting for the first sign of danger. "I'm okay. Cephy, show him your hands." Rachael smiled at Cephy to let her know it was all right and glanced at the horses. "She won't be able to ride."

Shaking, Cephy held up her hands.

Sparrow's eyes went wide and he paled. "What did she do?" He inspected the burns, gently turned Cephy's hand to see the wounds from other angles, seemingly careful not to hurt Cephy more.

Cephy didn't wince. "She taught me magic. I burn things and she was teaching me how to—"

Rachael wasn't fast enough. By the time her hand reached Cephy's mouth, the secret was already out. Only moments ago, he'd called Aeron *witch* with enough spite to make a lesser woman die of shame. Rachael was surprised his smile was still there. Not mocking, amused, or pitiful, but genuinely warm.

"It's all right," Sparrow said. "Magic is nothing to be ashamed of where we're going. My sister Ailis lives with me, she heals with her gift. She'll be able to teach you better than Aeron did." He ruffled Cephy's hair. "No more pain."

"Do you…?" Rachael didn't know how to finish. All her life, her curse had been just that—terrible and unwanted. Now, within two weeks, she'd met two people who weren't afraid of it and even used it themselves. She'd never realised it was so common.

"Do I have magic?" Sparrow asked and they nodded. "The gene seems to have jumped over me. Our parents were talented and Ailis is a healer, but all I'm good at is swinging a sword and rescuing people like you."

"Like us?" Cephy was still hiding by Rachael's side,

but she hadn't taken Rachael's hand again after Sparrow let go.

"Are there many?" Rachael asked.

She had believed herself to be the only one until she' met Cephy, and then they'd met Aeron, who hadn't hidden her magic. Now Sparrow was telling them his whole family was like them. Rachael and Cephy had hidden their gifts for so long, afraid of what others would think. How many more like them were there, too afraid to use their magic?

Sparrow's smile widened. "There are. You're not the first ones we've saved, but—well, it can wait."

His eyes briefly examined her like she was some valuable cargo finally delivered.

She narrowed her eyes at him. "Why?"

"I'll explain later but for now, we should bandage your hands, Cephy. A friend of mine lives nearby, we'll rest there for the day and then get an early start tomorrow. He'll be relieved to know you're unharmed."

Rachael scoffed—Cephy was anything but with her fingers charred like this—but she was glad to get Cephy's hands treated. Cephy was relaxing, so Rachael would need to be twice as cautious. Once Cephy's hands were healed, they'd escape.

But why had Sparrow gone to all this trouble? What made them so special he'd faced Aeron to see them safe? Why did his friend care? Sparrow talked like he'd known them all his life, but she was positive she'd never met him before.

He threw some snow on the fire and kicked dirt over it. "Follow me," he said. "I've got three horses tied up over there. Rachael is right, Cephy, you won't be able to ride so well with those hands. Could you share a horse with Rachael until your hands are better?”

Cephy nodded and stepped closer to Rachael. They were half-way to the horses when he turned around with the most sincere smile Rachael had ever seen. “Before I forget again—it’s nice to meet you. My name is Cale, and I swear to the Maker, I won’t let any more harm come to you.”

Chapter Seventeen

Cale was a strange man. They'd left his camp fire around an hour ago, and in that time he'd asked several times if they needed a break or if Cephy's hands were okay holding on to Rachael. Their horses had fallen into a gentle walk, which she doubted was for his benefit. He'd even bandaged Cephy's hands and given her some lady fern he'd rubbed into a paste to ease her pain. His constant smile shone past the scar and made him look boyish after all. He was a mystery to her, committed and determined but also cautious and caring at the same time.

Her gut whispered she could trust him, but she wouldn't make the same mistake again; people couldn't be trusted no matter how much they smiled or how sincere they seemed.

Behind her, Cephy was clinging to Rachael's waist. Rachael couldn't see her but had a feeling Cephy's eyes were shut tight. Aeron's betrayal must have been a shock to her, and now they were riding into the unknown again with another stranger.

"How much longer?" Rachael asked, earning her

another one of Cale's smiles. There didn't seem to be an end to his patience, and it had her stomach in twists.

"We'll get there by dusk if we keep up this pace. Do you need a break?"

She shook her head, hoping that Cephy was fine too. It was freezing outside, but she was used to that. The open forest on horseback gave her better chances if she needed to take Cephy and run.

They arrived at the cabin just as dusk dipped the snow in a bright pink. The comforting smell of fresh stew warmed the chilled air, and birds sang in the fading glow of the evening sun. It was similar to when they'd found Aeron's home—the delicious smell of her tea had drawn them in then too. But that night, only the sinister cooing of owls hidden in the shadows had filled the woods whereas today, birds were chirping. While Aeron's tea had smelled too sweet, this stew smelled soothing.

Rachael's eyes fell on little bags full of seeds hanging from most of the trees.

She pointed to the nearest one. "What are these?"

"Feed for birds," Cale said. "Arlo stuffs little nets with seeds and the birds eat from them over the winter."

She'd never seen anything so thoughtful. Even the birds were treated well here. Despite the promises she'd made herself, she began to feel safe.

"We can leave the horses here," Cale said. "Arlo will bring them some hay once he knows you're all right."

Rachael nodded and waited for Cephy to climb off the horse. Her cold hands had started to leak pus. "It's okay," Rachael said. "You can get off the horse now."

Cephy was shivering against her and shook her head against Rachael's back.

"Hang on," Cale said and jumped off his horse. He gave the animal some reassuring pets and scratches behind its ears, then walked over to them with his arms stretched out to Cephy. "It's a long way down. Come here, I've got you."

Cephy was as solid as the frozen ground beneath them, but Cale got her down without fuss regardless.

He extended his hand to Rachael.

"I'm fine."

They were getting too comfortable around Cale. People as nice as him and this Arlo didn't exist. People who reached out to strangers and went to great effort to feed birds when they couldn't feed themselves. People who looked after their horses like they were friends, and who looked after strangers in the same caring way.

Cale nodded and picked up Cephy, closing his arms around her. "You must be tired. How are your hands?"

Cephy's eyes flashed to Rachael. She was every bit as unsure of their situation, but nodded.

"They hurt."

"We'll get them looked at in a minute, I promise. Arlo has lived alone out here for a very long time, he's good at dressing wounds and healing minor injuries."

"*Minor*?" The word was out before Rachael could stop herself, but she refused to take it back now. How could he call Cephy's wounds minor? The paste he'd made from lady fern helped the pain, but the burns had still blistered badly.

Again, Cale smiled. "Arlo is a hunter and a veteran. I've seen him pull through wounds far worse than this.

He nearly died three times, but he always pulls through. He knows what he's doing." He looked at Cephy. "Your hands will stop hurting soon, I promise. Two days from now and they'll be good as new, you'll see."

The front door of the small house flew open and a bear of a man entered the snowy forest.

"By the Maker, lad, I thought I heard your voice." His own matched his rugged appearance, and Rachael wondered if he didn't hunt by usual means but by shouting his prey into submission. His booming voice coupled with his size was enough to intimidate any predator. Rachael had never seen anyone taller or heard anyone louder, and he wasn't even shouting yet. Oddly enough, the birds didn't seem bothered by it.

Cale grinned. "I'd have sent a message, but getting here was more important."

The bear-man reached them in only a few quick steps and stopped breaths short of walking into Cale. "Don't be rude, my boy. Introduce me."

The spark in his eyes and the way none of the critters had run for safety at his entrance spoke volumes of his kindness. Rachael guessed he was every bit as dangerous as he looked, but he was also the reason birds had food during the winter. He was another mystery, just like Cale.

Cale nodded. "Rachael, Cephy, this is my friend I've told you about, Arlo Braddock. Arlo, meet Rachael and Cephy."

A shadow crossed Arlo's smile. "So, your plan worked, then. You were able to sneak them out."

Cale grimaced. "No, she was waiting for me. She knew I was coming and was waiting at her table, sipping some tea. This is a game to her."

"How did you do it?"

"I'll tell you later. For now, these two need warm blankets, some hot food, and Cephy here needs her hands treated."

Arlo turned to Cephy. "Show me, girl."

Cephy stretched out one arm, hiding her face in Cale's neck.

The spark in his eyes turned angry. "Maker's soiled breeches, girl, where did you get this?"

Cephy giggled and peeked out from Cale's embrace. It worried Rachael that she trusted him so much already. Or did she simply trust him more than Arlo, who looked like he could wrestle three grown bears and win?

When Cephy didn't answer, Rachael did. "Aeron did this. She taught her how to—" She caught herself. Cale had mentioned that they didn't hate magic, but was it safe to talk about it so openly? Just the idea alone put her on edge, like the White Guard was waiting just around the corner for her to betray herself. It had been so much easier when the whole world was her sworn enemy and she hadn't talked to anyone.

"Cephy is very skilled with her gift already," Cale said. "Aeron taught her how to use it better, in her own way."

Arlo frowned. "Say no more, my boy. Come on inside. There's enough stew for all of us, and I've got just the thing for your hands, lass."

"Did you know we were coming?" Rachael asked.

"Aye, lass, I knew Cale was bringing you eventually. But me Ma always said to cook enough to end world hunger in case you have unexpected visitors or in case you need to end world hunger."

She had no idea what to make of Arlo, so she didn't say anything.

"I'll be right in," Cale said. "I'll just tie up Barnaby and get her some hay." Seeing Rachael's confused look, he added, "Barnaby is my horse. The two mares I brought for you are Kaori and Shelbie. You've been riding Kaori today. Shelbie is Cephy's as soon as her hands are better."

Rachael smiled; it wouldn't hurt to trust her gut and be careful at the same time.

Chapter Eighteen

The inside of Arlo's little hut was *cosy*. A warming fire crackled in a large hearth, two rabbits cooked on a stick over the open flames, and the stew Arlo had mentioned bubbled away in the corner. The meaty smell carrying a hint of potatoes and vegetables was almost overwhelming. Friendly shadows created by the flickering fire danced through the room and invited her inside.

It smelled of home, and Rachael raised her guard a little. She was too close to feeling comfortable while in a stranger's home.

"Come over here, lass."

Arlo was rummaging through a rather large cupboard with many drawers and small doors. It looked as though he'd crafted it by hand—not the most skilfully made piece of furniture, but it had a certain charm to it. It looked big enough to store every trinket in his house and more. In fact, now Rachael was looking around more, everything inside this hut looked self-made. Every piece was made of wood and looked a little rough around some edges, like Arlo had been more interested in practicality than style. They suited him, large and rough like the man who'd made them. She couldn't imagine dainty tea cups like the ones Aeron had used in this hut, or fancy glassware like what she'd sometimes seen in Blackrock. In Aeron's home, everything had looked polished and expensive, but here the furniture was larger than life without being intimidating. It felt like a home should feel, even though Rachael braced herself for splinters to pierce her fingertips at any moment.

Arlo waved Cephy over. He took out some bandages and a few small bottles, and sat down at the large oak table where Cale had already made himself at home.

"I'll clean the wound first," Arlo said. "It will sting a little, but it won't get infected that way. Once it's clean, I'll treat it with this tincture here." He held up one of the bottles so Cephy could see. "Then I'll bandage it nice and tight. You're all right with all that, lass?" Cephy nodded and took a few hesitant steps towards Arlo. "Good. Be a good lass and take a seat so I can get started."

She sat down next to him, the large chair much too big for her small body, and Arlo began his work. Judging by the twists Cephy's face distorted into, cleaning the wound was as painful as Arlo had warned.

"Here." Cale pulled out the chair closest to Cephy and nodded at Rachael.

She sat down and watched Cephy, uncomfortably aware that Cale was watching *her*.

Rachael turned around to frown at him when she couldn't take his stare any more. "Why are you staring at me?"

She decided she'd imagined his blush.

"I'm sorry," Cale said. "I don't want to upset you. I'm just relieved you're safe."

"Why? You don't even know me."

People were only this nice when they wanted something. Rachael was all too aware of the cramped space they were in and the two strong men who knew the area much better than she ever would. She doubted she'd outrun them. She and Cephy needed the rest and they definitely needed the food, but Rachael wanted to live more than she wanted their hospitality.

But why dress Cephy's wounds if they had ulterior motives? Wouldn't Cephy struggle less if her hands were hurting? Wouldn't they both be less of a problem if they were hungry and tired? She shouldn't have given them the benefit of the doubt. It could all be an act performed countless times on countless victims. But then why had Cale taken them away from Aeron? His fear had been real, Rachael was sure of that much. Why go to so much effort, why face his fears, when there had to be easier targets?

She promised herself not to fall asleep in this place. Not while these strangers were around.

Next to her, Cale smiled that irritating, reassuring smile of his. "I do know you, in a way. I don't know you personally, but I know *of* you. All of us do."

"All of you who?"

"The Sparrows, lass." Arlo's voice was a low grumble, his eyes focussed on Cephy's hands. The girl looked more relaxed now. Whatever their motives, Rachael was grateful Cephy was no longer in pain.

"Aeron mentioned them," Rachael said. "She called you *Sparrow*."

Cale scowled. "She calls all of us *Sparrow*. I doubt

she knows our names. We're in her way, that's all she cares about."

"What are they?" She wasn't sure she wanted to know, but any conversation was better than uncomfortable silence.

"We're a group of people who—"

"What do you know of Rifarne's politics, lass?" Arlo asked.

Every now and again, she'd caught a few whispers around Blackrock, but since none of it had helped her survive another day she hadn't been interested. She knew they had a king and she knew the White City was their capital, but what good had that knowledge ever done her?

She shook her head. "Nothing."

"Rifarne is ruled by a king," Arlo said. "The Ellerys have been the ruling family for centuries. They make fine rulers, but they have one flaw."

Frustrated, Rachael shook her head, feeling she was supposed to catch on but didn't. "What flaw?"

Arlo tied the ends of the bandage together and smiled at Cephy, who beamed at him. "There, lass, your hands'll be good as new." He got up and walked to his bubbling stew. "They distrust magic and everyone with it because it's easier than questioning tradition."

Rachael's heart sank. She'd known that for a very long time.

Arlo stirred his stew but took his eyes off it to look at her. "That's why the White Guard was after you and Cephy. Someone in your town reported you. The White Guard was there to take you to the White City for execution."

Rachael felt sick. She'd guessed as much, but hearing it confirmed made the truth worse somehow.

Tears welled up in her eyes, years of anger boiling to the surface. "Why?" She'd asked the Maker the same thing many times without an answer before she'd decided He either wasn't real or didn't care.

Cale and Arlo glanced at each other. Exhaustion clouded Cale's eyes when he said, "Who knows? It's because of power, we think."

"Power?" Cephy asked.

"Aye, lass. Many people feel threatened by the gift, so they slaughter it. Our good King Aeric Ellery is one of those people. They pretend they care, but they always turn to murder in the end."

Rachael remembered the terrible stench of burning soldiers. Cephy had taken down so many without any effort. Maybe the people of Rifarne were right to be afraid. How could they hope to defend themselves against something like that? The men Cephy had killed were seasoned soldiers, and they hadn't stood a chance against one frightened child.

"The gifted are tired of hiding," Cale said. "There've been attempts on his life, but no one got close enough. Not yet."

"I don't understand what this has to do with me," Rachael said. "Why does any of this mean that you know of me? And you didn't answer my question. Who are the Sparrows?"

"That's us," Cale said. "We're a group of people who are tired of the prejudice. Most of us have the gift, and we all want King Aeric's rule to end. We need a ruler who understands what the gifted go through every day just to stay alive."

Ice filled her veins. “You don’t mean—”

Cale nodded. “We’ve committed ourselves to killing the king, and we need you to lead us.”

Chapter Nineteen

Rachael sat back in stunned silence. Cale was giving her time to think, quietly waiting for her answer, while Arlo busied himself with the hot stew. Cephy's scared eyes flicked to Rachael.

Cale had to be joking. She didn't need political knowledge to know that regicide was the worst offense. If King Aeric wanted her dead now, she'd never stand a chance of a peaceful life if she as much as nodded in Cale's direction. What did she know of infiltration and assassination? They'd barely escaped the White Guard before, and that had been Cephy's doing. The king would have a lot more guards than that around him at all times. This idea was bound to fail whether she agreed or not, and she couldn't fathom why Cale thought they'd need her to begin with.

This had to be some kind of test, to make sure she wasn't gullible. Of course it was a joke.

But Cale didn't take it back. He was still watching her, waiting for an answer she couldn't give.

She leaned forwards in her chair and looked into his eyes so he knew she was serious. "I can't kill the king, that's madness. What makes you think I'd even consider that?"

Arlo came over and took her hands into his giant ones. "We know it's a lot to take in, lass. But the truth is we need you or we'll fail."

The walls were closing in around her. Arlo's oversized furniture pressed into her sides. The stew's steam seemed too thick suddenly and it was slowly suffocating her. She wanted out. Out of this wonderful hut and out of this dangerous forest. Anywhere as long as it was away from these people.

"Why?" She didn't know what else to say and the word came out in a croak.

"There's a prophecy that predicts it," Cale said. "We—the Sparrows—have named ourselves after it."

"Aye, lass. The *Rise of the Sparrows*. It's been around since the old empire."

This was ridiculous. A real-life prophecy? Her own magic was one thing, but it was another to predict things hundreds of years into the future. What could some long-dead prophet possibly know about what she was going to do hundreds of years before she was even born?

"Maybe if we told you the prophecy?" Cale said.

She sighed and nodded.

Cale cleared his throat. "'When the blue blood flows freely, the Sparrows will rise again. The Sparrow that sees ahead will lead you to victory. You will know them by their dreams. The Fox will lead you to ruin. You will know them by their malice.'"

Rachael was waiting for the rest when she realised this was all they had. "That's it?"

Cale nodded.

"I didn't hear my name, so I don't see what any of this has to do with me. It could mean anyone."

For the first time since they'd met, Cale's smile was gone. "It couldn't. We've looked for the Sparrow for years, Rachael, but you're the only seer we've found. You're the Sparrow that sees ahead, the one who dreams. There is no one else."

His growing enthusiasm didn't infect her. If only she were back on the streets of Blackrock. Life as a homeless orphan hadn't been great, but at least there'd been no prophecies or dreaming sparrows or evil foxes.

She sighed. "This is insane. I don't know what you think I'll do, but I won't do it."

"We don't need an answer tonight," Cale said. "Take time to think if you need it."

Arlo nodded. "You don't have to do anything right now, lass. Why don't you get some sleep? You must be exhausted after everything you've been through."

She doubted she'd reached the end of everything she'd been through, but Arlo was right. She was tired, and Cephy looked too exhausted to stay on her chair much longer. Sleep was the best option, but she refused to close her eyes with those two lunatics around.

Rachael got up. "Come on, Cephy." She turned towards the room Arlo had indicated but stopped herself by the door. "We'll be off tomorrow morning. Find someone else to fulfil your prophecy."

The room Arlo had readied for them was small but cosy. Cephy sat down on the duvet and sighed into the smooth fur. Rachael followed, happy to sit on something other than hard oak chairs.

She'd stay awake tonight while Cephy slept. If Cale

and Arlo were prepared to commit regicide, what stopped them from killing her and Cephy now she had refused? No one would miss them, and they knew of the plan. They were a danger to the Sparrows' mission.

If she saw the slightest hint of danger, they'd run, hopeless as it seemed. Or maybe they should run anyway once the two men were asleep. She wanted nothing to do with this plot, and she didn't want Cephy involved with it either. It was bad enough that Cephy looked conflicted, like she was considering what Cale and Arlo had suggested.

"How are your hands?" Rachael asked. She had to get Cephy's mind away from all this before the idea found roots.

Cuddled into the duvet and her eyes shut, Cephy nodded. "They don't hurt any more. It was real nice of Arlo to treat them."

"It was."

Rachael beat down the rising panic. What if Cephy wanted to stay? She hadn't been homeless long enough to smell a threat from a mile away with walls between her and the predator. The homely feel of Arlo's hut was a comforting trap that lured in its prey and spoke soft lies while it snapped shut and broke their necks.

Cephy sat up and stared at the floor, her feet shuffling back and forth.

"What is it?" Rachael hoped her gut feeling was wrong just this once.

"Would killing King Aeric be so bad?"

Maybe Cephy was too young to understand the moral issues around killing anyone, but the innocence with which she said it still made Rachael shiver.

She sat closer to Cephy. "Yes, it would be. It's the

worst criminal offence."

Cephy was silent for a long moment. "But he tried to kill us. Isn't that wrong too?"

Rachael didn't know how to argue with that, so she closed her arms around Cephy and held her close. How could she explain something like this—especially when, deep down, she agreed? Why should they have to die because King Aeric felt threatened by magic? Murder was wrong for any reason, no matter how grand the chair someone sat on. Didn't they have a right to live in peace, away from hateful glares and pointed fingers? Rachael had never hurt anyone unprovoked.

But that didn't change what they were discussing. King Aeric was wrong to want them dead, but if they killed him for it they'd be just as bad. Hate only ever birthed more of the same.

"You're right, that's also wrong," Rachael said. "But King Aeric is an important man. He rules Rifarne. Killing him would be treason." Her weak argument rang hollow in her own ears.

"Father once said it doesn't matter how important someone is to someone else if they do something bad. They have to be punished like everyone else."

Rachael figured he'd meant Cephy's magic but didn't say so aloud.

"That's true, but if that person rules a country then—"

"What does it matter?" Cephy's eyes flashed with anger. "He is human, isn't he? What gives him the right to kill us for being different?"

Rachael swallowed. "Do you think I should agree to Cale's plan?"

Cephy nodded. “If King Aeric were dead, there could be a new king. Maybe we wouldn’t have to hide then.”

Was that even possible? All her life, Rachael had done nothing but hide her magic. She was struggling to imagine a different reality, one where no one would hate her because of her dreams. It seemed too good to be true—and the last few days had reminded her of a few hard truths about that. She had wanted nothing more than to be accepted for who she was. What if Cale and Arlo had the answers to her unheard prayers?

She shook her head. Cale’s plan was foolish and too risky. If she wanted to survive, she’d have to find a secluded spot and make a home there, not walk right up to the king’s front door.

“Go to sleep,” she said. “We’ll leave tomorrow morning.”

“Do we have to?” Cephy sounded sad and as fed up with running away as Rachael.

Rachael nodded and tucked Cephy in. They’d find an abandoned cave or a clearing deep inside a different forest, maybe even a place like this one, and live their lives undisturbed away from hateful eyes. It wouldn’t be lonely because they’d have each other, and they’d be safe. She couldn’t ask for anything more.

Once she was sure that Cephy was comfortable, Rachael sat on the second bed and watched the door. This would be a long night.

Chapter Twenty

"Rachael."

She squinted at the light in her eyes and sat up. Cephy was sitting on her bed, but Rachael didn't remember her getting up. Why was it so bright in the room?

The sweet smells of honey and freshly baked bread entered her nose, and she jolted upright.

"How long was I asleep?" She couldn't believe she'd been so careless. "Come here."

Rachael pulled Cephy closer and examined her carefully. Her hands were still bandaged but no blood had stained the white sheets, and there were no new scratches on her. Cephy seemed fine. Nevertheless, Rachael jumped out of bed and searched the room for any signs Cale and Arlo had entered while they slept. It seemed undisturbed, but looks could be deceiving.

Cephy rubbed her eyes. "I don't know."

Cephy did look much better. A bit of colour had returned to her cheeks and she looked well-rested. Rachael relaxed; it didn't look like Cale or Arlo had entered the room.

Cephy took Rachael's hands into hers and pulled her towards the door. "Come on, Arlo made breakfast."

Rachael let Cephy pull her out of the small bed chamber and into the room they'd been in the night before. Soft sunlight embraced every corner. The front door stood wide open and a gentle breeze cleared the air. Chirping birds accompanied the thud of an axe hitting wood.

"Did you sleep well?"

Rachael jumped at Cale's voice. He was sitting on a chair in the corner, swirling whatever he was drinking around inside a large mug.

She frowned. "I did."

"Good! Have a seat. Arlo made some fresh bread earlier. It's still warm, I think."

Despite her reservations, Rachael felt saliva pooling around her tongue. Aeron's bread had been good, but Rachael doubted Aeron had made it herself. With magic spells, yes, but not with her own hands. Arlo had baked this himself, just like he'd made everything else in this hut.

Watching Cale from the corner of her eyes, Rachael sat beside Cephy, who was already spreading thick honey on a generous slice of bread.

Rachael copied her and took a bite. The bread was not only warm but also tasted amazing. It was soft, the crust firm and full of flavour, and bounced back when her knife dug into it. The honey was sweet and warmed by the bread. She'd have to thank Arlo when he came back in. Cale, too. They didn't have to take them in, treat their wounds, feed them, give them warm beds, and save them from Aeron. Thanking them was the right thing to do, no matter how suspicious she was of them.

Cale put down the mug and joined them at the table. "I'm sorry if our conversation last night was a little too much. I should have approached it better."

Her mood dropped; he'd ruined it. That conversation was the last thing she wanted to talk about, but Cephy's words echoed even louder.

Rachael dropped her bread on the wooden board Arlo used instead of plates. "I don't understand. Why me? I can't believe I'm the only one, there have to be others who do what I do." They were probably better at it too. No matter which way she turned it, she wasn't the right choice for this.

Cale shrugged and smiled sympathetically. "Killing King Aeric wasn't what you expected to hear, I take it?"

She scoffed and glared at him. "Is that the reason you saved us? Because you need something?"

Cale sighed. "Yes and no. It's true that the Sparrows have already lost without your help. We couldn't let Aeron kill you."

The lump in her throat tightened. "Why would she kill us? We only just met her."

"The prophecy names you as the one who kills the king. You would effectively end the world as we know it."

She didn't want to do either. "You say that like it's a good thing."

"Isn't it? Right now, a lot of people are hostile towards people like you. Didn't you wish just once when you were growing up that you could be like the other kids?"

Rachael almost nodded but stopped herself. Cephy

nodded, her eyes wide and on Cale.

"How will killing King Aeric achieve that?" Rachael asked. "There are others like him. Someone else will take his place and you'll have got nowhere."

Cale glanced away for a second, shuffling his feet under the table. "That's why we need you, Rachael. We need you to kill King Aeric and take his place."

Dumbfounded, Rachael stared at her breakfast. She wished she could ask the birds to stop singing for a moment while Cale's words sank in. He couldn't be serious.

"I wanted to tell you last night, but you already had so much to think about. I thought it could wait."

"You're mad."

"You have magic, Rachael, there's nothing you can't do. The ancient prophets wouldn't have named you if they didn't believe you could do it."

She doubted it worked like that—she didn't dream of people she thought should die but of whoever her dreams showed her—but right now she wanted to believe that someone had made one huge mistake. It was too much to think that something like fate actually existed and wanted this for her.

Her head was spinning. She'd wanted to run away before but now she was glad she was sitting down. "But why me? There must be others who can see bad things that are about to happen. I can't even control this."

"I told you, there aren't."

She hadn't forgotten, but it was as ridiculous as this whole idea of killing the king and taking his place. There were too many people in the world for her to be the only one. She *couldn't* be the only one.

“True prophets are rare, lass,” Arlo said. He leaned his axe against the doorframe and joined them at the table. “If there are others we haven’t found them, but Cale knows what he’s doing. His Sparrows have searched everywhere and only found you after years of trying. There really is no one else.”

She hadn’t thought like this in years because there was no point, but it wasn’t fair. Why was she the only one who saw terrible accidents before they happened? Why did she have to be some prophesied hero? She didn’t want it. She didn’t want any of this.

“We thought true prophets to be extinct for many years,” Cale said. “We almost gave up, to be honest. No seer, no revolution. But then we found you. I’m sorry, this is a lot. I wouldn’t ask this of you if there was another way.”

She scoffed. “What, now I’m not good enough?”

He smiled. “I don’t believe in forcing anyone to do something they don’t want. You don’t want this but here I am, asking for your help anyway. I only ask that you try, Rachael. Let me show you what we have. If you still want to walk away then, I won’t stop you.”

So, she could either be homeless in a town that hated her or she could commit regicide and become Rifarne’s ruler. Wasn’t there supposed to be a middle ground? She doubted Cale would just let her leave once he had her where he wanted her. And even if he did, she’d be trapped. She’d be in the White City crawling with White Guards, so just walking away wasn’t likely to work.

“Well, you’ve made a mistake,” she said. “I can’t control my magic, so I don’t see how I can help you.”

If she was their last hope, they were doomed to fail.

"We know," Cale said. "None of us have ever taught anyone how to be a prophet, but my sister has taught many who weren't healers like her. The only difference is in the magic they use, but the principles are the same. She will teach you as best as she can if you let her."

She couldn't bear how hopeful he sounded. His eyes were pleading with her to reconsider, even Arlo and Cephy were silently begging her. No matter where she turned, she saw hope. But how could they direct it at her? Couldn't they see she was their worst candidate? Even if she was the only seer in the world, she couldn't be a queen. No one in their right mind would allow her anywhere near the throne, let alone on it with a crown on her head. Only two weeks ago she had begged for just one slice of stale bread.

She got up, ignoring the pain when her knees bashed into the corner of the table. Cale moved to get up after her, but from the corner of her eye she saw Arlo shoot him a look. Arlo had left the door wide open, but the air inside was too oppressive nevertheless. She needed to get somewhere with an open sky and no walls where she could breathe and be alone.

"I can't do this," she said. Cale's face fell and her heart sank. "I'm sorry."

King Aeric Ellery paced his throne room, contemplating his options. Just when had life dealt him such a terrible hand? The gifted were a danger beyond belief, he couldn't argue that, but to slaughter them all... His people had spoken. Many years ago, at his coronation, he had vowed to listen. To be a caring king who looked after his people. If they were afraid and backed into a corner, he would stand between them and danger as their shield. But to seek help from the very people he'd promised to subdue… It wasn't right.

He stopped to look at his two guests. His most trusted commander and old friend Videl, and a Mist Woman he'd never heard of before. They were sitting at his table waiting for him to speak—or rather, his commander looked patient. The Mist Woman looked anything but, and as dangerous as his people had told him. She could have been beautiful if it weren't for the look in her eyes. Her long black curls flowed around her slender shoulders like silk and complimented her soft features. But that glare, cold as death itself, dug its way into his core.

"Commander Videl," King Aeric said. "A report of recent events, please. For our guest."

Videl nodded and rose from his chair. He was the king's embodiment of justice in the country, and in his shined armour, broad shoulders, and confident eyes he looked the part. Aeric had always admired that about him. In a way, his friend looked more like a king than he did, even wounded and covered in bandages. Or perhaps because of it—Aeric had vowed to be the people's shield, but Videl was the one fulfilling that promise. Aeric only made decisions. He couldn't risk his life like Videl did, but he still thought he could do more. He hoped the Mist Woman would be that chance.

"My Lord." Videl bowed. "I and my men rode to Blackrock, a small village to the north near the Boneanvil Mountains, on the urgent request of its people. Two witches were living there, one prophetess and one who controls fire."

A look darker and more terrifying than the Mist Woman's entered his expression. Aeric had seen his First Commander angry before, but Videl wasn't used to losing his entire unit. He wasn't used to being bested. Most prisoners came freely, knowing they had no options left. These two girls hadn't only run but they had burnt the flesh off his men. To be so young yet murder so many in cold blood… They had to be punished.

"And what happened when you got there?"

He had the usual sitting with his loyal subjects in an hour, but more than that he didn't want to be around the Mist Woman any longer than he had to. She made him uncomfortable. Of course, his people would report more crimes against their freedom, all of which caused by the gifted. It seemed magic was the reason behind every issue these days.

"We tracked them down and pulled them out of their hiding place," Videl said. "The younger one burnt my men down. I barely escaped myself and wouldn't have if she'd got one good look at me." Aeric recognised the hunger in Videl's eyes. His commander was always ready to bring another witch to justice and he'd have these two as well, especially now they'd made it personal. He simply needed a better unit.

The Mist Woman chuckled.

"What's so amusing to you, woman?" Aeric asked. "Don't you feel any grief for those who have died?" He knew she was far more dangerous than some little girl, but this was his city and his throne room and those had been good men. He wouldn't allow disrespect in his home.

"I'm merely laughing at your *men*. They were

children slaughtered by other children. You don't truly hope to murder the Fox with little boys' games, do you?"

Videl shot her a dangerous look. "Remember who you are talking to, witch. This is King Aeric, son of our beloved King Rorden, ruler of—"

She dismissed him with a wave of her hand. "I know and I don't care, commander. If you want to be a king, Aeric, you will have to grow up first."

"How *dare* you. We should hang you like all the others, you filthy b—"

"*Enough.*" Aeric's voiced thundered through his throne room. He appreciated Videl's restraint so far, but perhaps he had expected too much, asking him to stand beside a witch. Videl looked ready to strike her down with his bare hands. The Mist Woman, however, looked unmoved.

"Why don't you introduce me to our guest, commander?" Aeric asked.

Videl clenched his fists as much as his injuries allowed and scowled at the Mist Woman. He began to speak when she interrupted him.

"I can speak for myself, my *king*. I am Aeron, and I know how to defeat those girls."

He didn't like where this was going, but he stood at the beginning of a war he didn't want to wage. When the enemy had the upper hand, he had to employ the means to defeat them no matter how uncomfortable it made him. It was his duty as Rifarne's king to protect his people, no matter his personal preference.

"Speak."

"The one dangerous to you is the older girl. Her name is Rachael, the prophetess your commander mentioned. She is mostly harmless, her magic of no use whatsoever."

"How can she be of any danger to me, then?"

"Because prophecy names her so."

He was losing his patience. "We have no time for this nonsense. Get to the point."

Aeron sighed. "Then you will just have to lose this battle you want to call a war. Your people will die, but rest assured they will die quickly. I am sure they will find solace in that."

He bit his tongue. Sometimes, being king meant he had to suffer fools to protect his people. Disrespectful, insolent fools. "Explain yourself."

"Prophecies don't lie. You must find Rachael and kill her before she kills you."

He nodded, rummaging through his options. According to Aeron, Rachael wasn't dangerous and his own commander had reported that it was the younger girl who had destroyed his unit. Taking care of Rachael should be easy once they were separated.

"And the girl?"

"My Fox will come to me when the time is right. She will be an asset to your army."

"No, she won't." Videl was glaring at her, seemingly ready to tear her heart out where she stood. "My king, the girl needs to die for what she's done. I demand vengeance!"

"You demand nothing from me, Commander Videl. Stopping this war is our priority. Your personal grudge can wait."

Videl had been his loyal friend and advisor since childhood. Back then, they'd been so close people had thought them brothers. Aeric disliked having to remind him of their stations, but it had to be done. He was still the law in Rifarne, not Videl and certainly not Aeron.

Videl clutched his fist to his chest. “My king.”

“Now, Aeron, tell me what you have in mind and we will begin preparations.”

Her wicked smile made him regret his words. “With pleasure.”

Chapter Twenty-One

Two rabbits sat on the frozen grass not far from Rachael. Her legs were slowly growing damp from the snow under her, but she ignored it to watch the small animals, which were chewing on the grass only two shuffles away from her. They looked happy. Well fed, too. Little red berries grew everywhere despite the low temperatures, the grass was a verdant green under the frost, and nuts grew around Arlo's hut. She didn't know how deep into the forest they were, but things had to be in even better shape farther in away from Arlo, who needed some for himself. The rabbits had a good life here with all this free food. Arlo killed some for his suppers, but Rachael could tell by the larger hides drying on racks outside his hut that he shot bigger prey more often. The rabbits had nothing to fear with him around. They looked content eating the free reserves nature threw at their paws, and Arlo took care of their predators.

Rachael sighed. Even these tiny critters had a better life than she'd ever had.

Careful not to scare them, Rachael extended her

hand. The rabbits froze. She'd never seen one outside the butcher's window, but she had heard other children speak of petting them. They'd told each other stories about stroking a rabbit's coat and about how soft it felt to their hands. Just once, Rachael wanted the same normality in her life.

The moment her hand got too close, the rabbits bolted into the thicket. Rachael heard the soft rustle of leaves and branches for a moment, and then that was gone too. Only their small paw prints in the fresh snow remained.

Rachael let her hand sink and pulled her legs to her chest, seeking comfort in her own arms. She was sure the rabbits didn't have it easy at times too, but they were cautious enough not to get caught and they had each other. That was all she wanted too, but here they were with two madmen asking her to do the unthinkable.

She hid her head between her kneecaps and drew her arms tighter around herself. How could two men who'd never met her before expect her to just go and assassinate King Aeric? He was the best-protected man in the country. Even if she did agree, she'd never get close enough. And why did she have to be the one to do it anyway? Cale seemed keen enough. Why couldn't he do it? Because some ancient prophecy said so? She found it hard to believe in things like that. Her dreams were different, they had proved true many times. But prophecies had been written centuries ago by people who didn't know her. What made these strangers think she could walk up to the king, pierce his heart, and sit on the throne like it was her right? Rachael, queen of Rifarne.

Rachael hugged her legs closer to herself. A nervous smile touched her lips. Things were bad for people like her—no one knew that better than she did and she wouldn't disagreed—but killing the king was too much. Too extreme. There had to be another way. Surely the most powerful man in the country could be reasoned with? She wanted peace, but regicide was too high a price.

In the past, she had defended herself when necessary. She knew how to hurt a man if need be. But at most, she'd attacked two men at once in self-defence. She couldn't take on a whole army, it was physically impossible. She couldn't even swing a sword with confidence. The king himself had never lifted a finger against her, and Cephy had dealt with the men who had come after them. Rachael was no murderer, and she wouldn't allow Cale to turn her into one.

A choked sob escaped her throat. The king had done more than lift his finger. He had commanded his army to hunt her down and take her to the city for execution, because her dreams sometimes showed her the future. He hadn't made a mistake, neither had it just happened. Someone had presented him with the problem—her—and he had decided she should die for it. He had issued the command. He could have acted in any way he wanted, but he had decided her death was the best way. She couldn't even hurt anyone with her curse.

Cephy was the dangerous one, but they'd been together for a while now and she never tried to hurt Rachael. In fact, Rachael had never seen her hurt anyone. Cephy had defended herself, but she never attacked anyone for the sake of it. She was careful. Her gift had slipped out a few times in Blackrock, but there'd been no accidents since Rachael had left with her.

Cale had said his sister would teach them, that she could help Rachael understand her gift and grow it into something more useful, but Rachael doubted that was possible. She didn't have the natural affinity Cephy had.

Had whatever Aeron taught Cephy helped her after all? But why help her in the first place? Aeron couldn't have cared less about them. All she'd done was distract Rachael with books about magic; she'd never planned to do anything for Rachael. But Cephy was more controlled. Her magic no longer leaked out if she wasn't careful enough. Why do that if Aeron wanted them both dead? Maybe Cale was right. Maybe this really was just a game to her, and Aeron had nothing to gain from it except the thrill of the hunt. Rachael had seen it many times in Blackrock. Cats often played with mice and killed them when they got bored. Sometimes, the mouse died by accident when the cat had played a little too rough. That's what Aeron was—an excitable predator that didn't know when to stop.

"I'm sorry." She jumped to her feet at Cale's voice, her heart racing. "We didn't want to tell you like this." She scolded herself; he shouldn't have been able to sneak up on her. What if he'd come to finish her off since she disagreed with their plan? She knew too much, after all. As far as Cale knew, she could take the information to King Aeric and bargain for her freedom.

She frowned at him. "I didn't know you were there."

A small smile played on his lips. "Is it okay if I sit?" He nodded to a patch of frosted grass next to her.

She shrugged; he hadn't come just to walk away again.

He sat down as carefully as she had extended her hand to the rabbits. She was tempted to bolt like they'd done, but unlike the rabbits, she had nowhere to run to. No burrow where her family was waiting. No hideout only she knew about.

"I should have said something," Cale said. "I wasn't there for long, I promise."

His words meant nothing. He and Arlo could still kill her and Cephy. Lure them in first, then strike when they least expected it. She'd seen it happen plenty of times in Blackrock's more corrupt corners. Cephy had let her guard down and even liked the two men, and Rachael herself had been too lost in thought to hear Cale approach.

Rachael wouldn't make it easy. She refused to be another mouse caught in the cat's claw.

"How did you sneak up on me? No one has ever—" She hadn't meant to say the words and show her weakness, but they were out now. He'd already seen her jump, anyway. Only her future reactions mattered.

"Arlo taught me since I was a child. He knew my parents, but he's known this place even longer. For a big guy he can move as silently as a deer when he wants to."

An uncomfortable silence settled between them. Rachael wanted to say something but didn't know what. Cale already knew her opinion on their plan, and she wasn't about to tell him that yes, they did have a point. She wasn't ready to confess it to herself just yet.

"I grew up in a small village on the other end of Rifarne," Cale said. "My parents were farmers. My sister is two years younger than me. Only Ailis has inherited their gift, but our mother's grandfather was a great wizard. Four times every year, Arlo visited us. My parents grew crops but they loved to eat meat, too. Red meat was expensive back then, and they could never save enough to buy it for us. Arlo has been a hunter since he was ten and brought them game, pork, and other meats for a much smaller fee than the local merchants. That's how I met him. Barnaby was a present from him.

"One summer, some men came to our farm. They came on black horses, wore black armour. They waved a flag as red as blood behind them as they rode to our house, burning my parents' crops as they went. It was the most terrifying thing I'd ever seen. I thought death had come for us. Was right, too. Our mother told me to take Ailis and run. Dad held the back door open so we could slip out undetected. I'd never run so hard in my life, but I have done many times since then."

He stared at the snow, his eyes far away.

"Who were they?" She dreaded the answer.

"Tramurans. From the north? My mother was born there, past the Boneanvil Mountains. I've never been. Magic is outlawed there, always has been. They'd murdered her grandfather for it, but she escaped in a similar way to how I and Ailis got out when those same men came for her and father."

"But your parents were farmers," Rachael said. "Did anyone here know they had the gift?"

Rachael thought she saw a tear glistening in his eye, but maybe the sun was playing a trick on her.

"No. They stuck to farming and didn't tell anyone about their gift or her heritage to keep us safe. But my mother was related to her grandfather, and that was enough.

"In Tramura, everyone with magic has to die, even if there's only a slim it got passed down. My parents never hurt anyone and hadn't lived in Tramura for over a decade, but Tramura came for them anyway. They hate magic so much that my parents' existence was offensive to them. I hid in the forest and tried to keep Ailis from crying. I knew the general direction Arlo usually came from and thought it best to wait for him. By the time he visited again, our parents had been dead for weeks and we were weak. Ailis and I weren't sure which berries were safe to eat and only drank water from puddles when it rained. We were sick for a while, but Arlo took us in and helped us. We moved out as soon as I was old enough and built a small house outside the White City."

Rachael was speechless. Here she was, feeling sorry for her miserable life, when Cale had lived through all that. "That's awful. I'm sorry."

"What's done is done, but I appreciate it. The Tramuran king doesn't influence King Aeric, but his leadership is slowly taking us in the same direction. It won't be long before magic is officially outlawed here too, and then it'll be as bad here as it is there. I can't let that happen, Rachael. With or without you, the Sparrows will stand against him."

This was too heavy a weight for her to carry. How could she possibly stop Rifarne from plunging into such dark times? Its people already feared magic, and she wouldn't help that if she took the throne because of prophecy. King Aeric only had to officially declare war and she'd have a whole country against her.

Cale said he would fight. He'd rather die than live in the world his mother had escaped from and died of. Would Rachael? Cale's parents had run and fought but in the end, they were slaughtered in their own home anyway. Would the same thing happen to her? Would the White Guard find her no matter how far she ran, like those men had tracked Cale's parents across the border?

"Why are you telling me this?"

Cale couldn't have been much older than her. Her parents had abandoned her with nothing but a blanket to her name, but she didn't know what had become of them. Had they been hunted down, too? She had the gift. Maybe they had it, too. Maybe they had hoped she'd have a better life without them.

A deep-burning anger rose in her chest. How could they be anything than what they were born? How could anyone punish them for it?

"I'm not doing this on a whim," Cale said. "We've been preparing for years. I understand why you're suspicious—I would be too if our roles were reversed—but we're on your side. The Sparrows help the gifted. With you, we could help many more. You can trust us, but I understand not wanting to trust a stranger."

He got up, shook some wet grass off his trousers, and turned to leave.

Rachael looked up at him and squinted when the sun shone into her eyes. "Where are you going?"

"I said you don't need to decide right away and I meant it. It's true that we're running out of time, but you have a big decision to make. You shouldn't rush into something you might regret."

She watched him walk back to the hut and close the door behind him. There was a lump in her throat she wasn't sure how to swallow. Everything he'd said could have been a lie, but her gut told her there was at least some truth in his words.

She didn't need to have been to Tramura to know the mentality here. Rifarne's people feared the gifted. King Aeric was desperate enough to send his White Guard after two children. What would his next move be now they'd escaped his commander? Would he send more men after them or declare them dead, hoping they'd die a slow death in the forest? Either way, he wanted her dead. All that hate, because her dreams sometimes showed her the future.

Rachael stood and walked back to the hut with her heart racing and her eyes burning. She was done hiding.

Chapter Twenty-Two

Cephy was sitting on Arlo's legs when Rachael stepped into the cramped kitchen. He was putting new bandages around her hands. Her face didn't twist in pain this time but into a big smile. Rachael wished hers was as honest, but she felt too queasy for that.

Cephy bounced on Arlo's legs. "Rachael!"

"Hold still, lass, or these won't sit right." Arlo's low grunt made Cephy go rigid but didn't dim her smile.

"Arlo says my hands are looking much better," Cephy said. "He told me about a bunny that lives by the river that had injured its paw and he fixed it."

Rachael couldn't help but smile at seeing her so much happier. She still didn't like how quickly Cephy had come to trust these two strangers, but she was glad to see Cephy's frown gone.

"I'm sorry I ran out." It had been rude, and the apology soothed the burning in her chest a little.

"Don't mention it, lass. Can't say I blame you, given what we told you."

She took a seat opposite Cephy but got up again when the restless tugging in her chest was too much.

Her racing heart was making it worse.

"I've thought about what you said." She glanced at Cale, who was busying himself with something she couldn't see at the fire. The worry that everything he'd told her was a lie spun was still there, but her mind was made up. Lie or not, they'd suffered enough. She had lived his story to a smaller extent. Chances were someone else in Rifarne was still suffering the same life. So what if it was a lie for him? It was her truth.

Arlo looked up from the bandages without stopping his work. "And what did you decide, lass?"

She tried again to swallow past the lump in her throat, but the more she tried the worse it got.

"I want to help you," she said. "But I don't know what I can do or where to start."

Arlo's thunderous laugh boomed through the hut. "That's fantastic news, lass."

Even though his laugh made her jump a little, something about it put her at ease too. Cephy beamed at her. Cale gave her a reassuring smile over his shoulder. Their confidence in her was maddening.

"But I don't know what to do. Killing King Aeric, this prophecy... How do I fit in?"

Cale opened his mouth to speak but Arlo raised a hand to keep him quiet. "Don't worry about the details, lass. That's where Cale and his Sparrows come in."

Cale poured some tea into mugs by the fire. His hands were shaking. "You're not so unimportant yourself, old man."

"Aye, I don't do much. I just get the occasional Sparrow back on their feet."

"You're placing too much hope in me," Rachael said. "I can't control my visions and if I did, they wouldn't help." She was beginning to feel frustrated. Relying on luck was never the way to go. It took skill to survive, and she didn't have the needed skill to accomplish this.

"That's why my sister is willing to help you," Cale said. "She's used to teaching people who have the gift but don't how to control it. I know she's never taught a seer before, but she'll still be able to aid you a little."

"Can she teach me?" Cephy asked from Arlo's lap. With her feet dangling in the air, she looked like his granddaughter and he her proud grandfather.

Cale smiled at her. "If you ask her nicely?"

"Let's not get ahead of ourselves," Arlo said. "First, you'll have to get there. The White Guard will be looking for you. If you don't plan your steps carefully, all this celebrating will be for nothing."

"I know," Cale said. "I have a plan, but we shouldn't ride until Cephy's hands have healed completely. Just in case."

"Aye, that's fine with me. You can stay as long as you need, but you should let Ailis know you're coming. She'll want to prepare."

Cale laughed. "She's been prepared for months."

Arlo sighed and gave Cale a look a father might give a son who'd made the same mistake twice. "There are other people to inform too, lad. The Sparrows should know."

"No need to tell me," Cale said. "It'll be good for morale. But for now, we celebrate."

Arlo grunted but his smile betrayed him.

Chapter Twenty-Three

A week passed before Cale was happy that Cephy's hands had healed enough to ride. Rachael was still struggling with everything they'd told her, everything they believed she could do, but it was nice to be important for once. She was happy to go along until Cale and Arlo moved on to a better—a real—saviour. She knew she couldn't learn magic like other people learned to read or walk. They'd drop her once they realised it, and maybe then she and Cephy could live in peace while an actual hero saved Rifarne.

The ride to Cale's sister would be long and exhausting and take them close to the White City. Rachael had never sat on a horse for this long before. She was in no rush to do it again unless she had to. After just one day of riding in disguise, her entire body was stiff and aching. Her hands refused to hold on to the reins for another minute. She stayed on the horse by sheer willpower alone, but Kaori didn't seem to mind, so Rachael didn't complain, either.

The disguises Arlo had made were simple but effective. Rachael and Cephy were wrapped in long linen and cloths, and Cale treated them like they suffered from some contagious fever. Everyone gave them a wide berth. Cale only allowed them to take the heavy disguises off when they found shelter for the night. The rush of fresh air felt incredible every time even though the cold was still biting. Once they began to shiver, the disguises kept them warm.

After almost a week of gentle trotting to make their fever more believable, the capital appeared in the distance. Blackrock and the forest had been large to her, but they were nothing compared to the White City. Its white buildings stretched as far as she could see, King Aeric's palace higher than the rest. She couldn't imagine how its citizens dared sleep in its shadow. She wasn't sure how she'd be able to sleep herself once they reached Cale's home.

The palace aside, the home of all this slaughter and bloodshed was a beautiful place. The white buildings looked proud and exotic. Everything had been covered in years of soot and dust in Blackrock, but even from a distance she could tell the White City was clean and pristine. Several large ships were anchored in the port. The sea lapped at its beaches, which stretched away from the city in both directions.

If she set aside what she knew about King Aeric, even the palace looked beautiful. She'd never have guessed at the cruelty coming out of this place if it hadn't come after her.

She was grateful they wouldn't be staying inside the city walls. Cale and his sister lived in the nearby forest, so Rachael wouldn't have to set foot beyond the gates. A part of her wanted to see more of the city and explore its shadows, but a much larger part wanted to stay away from the king.

Thanks to their disguises, the guards that had passed them hadn't given them a second glance, but her stomach twisted every time their white armour came into view regardless. Cale said the White Guard wouldn't be looking for them this close to the capital, but she didn't miss that he wore his leather hood lower.

When the road got busier, Cale led them into the forest. Rachael was sad to see the ocean disappear behind them but didn't protest.

Cale jumped down from his horse. "We can walk from here."

Rachael had hated jumping off Kaori when they'd first set out, but she was used to it now. She wasn't as skilful as Cale but she no longer tripped and knew how to land without hurting her feet. She was also grateful to stretch her legs.

Cephy moved closer to Rachael as they led their horses through the trees. "Is it far?"

Cale shook his head. "It's a twenty-minute walk into the forest. We could have continued on horseback, but I figured you'd want to use your feet for a change."

Rachael gently petted Kaori's side as they walked through the trees. She didn't enjoy riding but she liked the animal itself. Kaori seemed to have warmed to her too and whinnied every time she spotted Rachael. This close to home, Kaori moved with more purpose and without relying on Rachael's leadership as much, like she knew the way back.

Every tree looked the same to Rachael. There was no path, no signs to follow, and no clues anywhere. It was beyond her how Cale found his way so easily.

A small cabin came into view. It was larger than

Arlo's with a small second floor. Smoke rose into the air from the chimney, and a small vegetable garden peeked out from behind the corner. She heard gently flowing water nearby. It wasn't at all like Rachael had expected. Cale acted nice enough, but he was rough around the edges. She'd assumed his house would reflect that, but it looked inviting. The smoke from the chimney promised warmth.

"You can tie Kaori and Shelbie up over there by the lake," Cale said. "They can drink and rest there."

Rachael took her time to allow Kaori to nuzzle her before she followed Cale to the house. A woman's faint voice sang through the air and the smell of fresh bread wafted outside from an open window.

"Ailis?" Cale opened the door and stepped inside. He waved for them to follow. "Ailis, we're here."

Footsteps rushed down the stairs and a young woman entered the room with wide eyes. There was no denying she was Cale's sister—save for the scar that marked his face, they were near identical. The same brown hair fell over her shoulders and the same youthful spark lit up her features. The only real difference were her bright blue eyes, a clear summer day to his storm.

"Cale! You're— Is this—?" Her eyes flashed between Cale and Rachael before settling on Rachael.

Cale hugged his sister. "Ailis, these are Rachael and Cephy. Rachael is the Sparrow. Cephy is her friend, a fire user."

Ailis swallowed whatever she'd wanted to say and threw her arms around Rachael. Then, she fell to her knees.

"We've waited so long to meet you, Sparrow. I'm

Ailis, and you're welcome in our home. I'm honoured to be your teacher. If there's anything you need, please don't hesitate to tell me."

No one had ever been so happy to meet her, let alone bowed to her. Rachael didn't know how to react.

Cale held out his hand and pulled his sister back up. "No need to be so formal. Rachael isn't used to people bowing to her."

Ailis's face was bright red and she offered an embarrassed smile. Rachael didn't understand her odd reverence, but she did understand feeling out of place. She offered an unsure smile back.

Ailis beamed at her. "Forgive me. We've been waiting for this day for a long time. I grew up hearing the prophecy. Actually meeting you, I... I didn't know what would be appropriate."

It was refreshing to meet someone as lost with the situation as she was.

"Be yourself," Cale said. "I don't think Rachael wants to be treated like royalty."

"I can do that." Ailis looked more at ease if still a little sheepish. "You must be hungry. Why don't you show them to their rooms while I make us something to eat?"

The mere mention of food made Rachael's stomach feel hollow. By the look on Cephy's face, Cephy felt the same way.

"Thank you," Rachael and Cephy said.

Cale ushered them towards the stairs. Ailis got started in the kitchen, already chopping vegetables when Rachael's feet stepped onto the narrow staircase.

Upstairs, sunlight flooded the corridor. Dust only visible in the warm light danced through the room.

Cale gestured to the two rooms opposite the stairs. "Pick whichever one you like. We have no other guests at the moment, so it doesn't matter. The only one off-limits is Ailis's room." He pointed to the room at the end of the short corridor. "She's a great cook. Feel free to rest until she calls you down."

Rachael raised her eyebrows. "Where do you sleep?" She hadn't seen another room besides the two he'd given them and Ailis's.

"I sleep in one of our hiding places where I can be near my Sparrows." He smiled. "Ailis will love having the company."

Rachael nodded and opened the door on the left. Cale looked like he wanted to say something but stopped himself and went back downstairs. Cephy was already inside the room on her right, so Rachael went into her small chamber, sat on the bed, and tried not to think about how close to the people that wanted her dead she was.

Chapter Twenty-Four

Living with Cale and Ailis was so different from living with Aeron. The Mist Woman had carried herself with a cold confidence, and while Cale was every bit as confident, he had welcomed them into his home and did his best to make sure they had everything they needed. Ailis was shy and nervous around Rachael. She had calmed down after their introduction, but still seemed more self-conscious around Rachael. Ailis sounded relaxed when she was alone with Cale but straightened when Rachael entered, the easy tone gone. Despite her awkwardness, Ailis was a wonderful host and let Cephy help her prepare their meals. Aeron had told them which spices to add and when, but Ailis was happy for Cephy to help in any way she could. They worked together, whereas Aeron had given orders.

Ailis loved feeding people. She wore a content smile every time she served food—and there was plenty of it. No matter how much Rachael ate, Ailis had more.

For the first time in her life, Rachael was too full to continue. Her stomach had never complained that it had too much food before. It was a nice feeling.

Cale and Ailis would have been the perfect parents if they weren't siblings. Cale took Cephy along when he went hunting, and Ailis had the warm glow Rachael thought only a caring mother could have.

But Ailis had done more than feed them and make them feel welcome. Ailis had healed them. She'd worried that Rachael's life on the streets had infected her with all sorts of diseases and had healed her on their first evening in the cabin. Ailis had tended to Cephy as well, to make sure neither of them carried any infections in them. Rachael had felt Ailis' magic work its way through her body—a warm, soothing wave that had slowly spread through her and settled in her chest. Afterwards, Ailis had sent her to her room and asked her to sleep as long as she liked.

They'd arrived a week ago, but the cosy cabin already felt like home. Rachael was more careful than ever, the familiar warning of things that seemed too good to be true at the forefront of her mind.

Although, the longer she was here the harder it was to believe they had any dark intentions. If Ailis wanted to, she could have easily killed Rachael and Cephy by poisoning their food or by using her gift. Cephy had gone into the forest with Cale a few times and trusted him. He could have run her through with his sword or shot her with a bow if he wanted to.

Ailis placed another slice of bread in front of Rachael. "How is your breakfast?"

Rachael pushed her plate away from herself with an apologetic smile. "I can't eat any more. Thank you."

Ailis smiled back and carried the plate over to the counter.

Their kitchen was small but as cosy and homely as

the rest of the house. The furniture had been carved from a light wood, which seemed to absorb the sunlight and radiated warmth back into the room. Fresh flowers sat in the middle of the table and in the windows. Ailis had spread a red tablecloth over the smooth table. She often left the window open to let in a fresh breeze. Ailis had offered to close it if Rachael or Cephy were too cold, but Rachael didn't mind the chill. The cold had always kept her senses sharp and alert. It was exhilarating compared to the warmth, which made her sleepy.

Ailis sat down with her. "I'd like to discuss your gift with you, if you're done eating."

Rachael nodded. She'd wondered when Ailis would bring it up.

Cephy ran down the stairs and sat down next to Rachael. She beamed up at Ailis. "Can I stay?"

Did Ailis twitch or had Rachael imagined it?

"I thought you promised Cale you'd help him hunt?" Ailis asked.

"I did, but I want to learn magic. Can I stay? Please?"

Cale walked in and leaned against the door frame, a bow in his hand and a quiver over his shoulder. His eyes met Rachael's. There was something strange in his gaze, something she had never seen before, but she couldn't identify it. She was grateful when he turned his attention back to Cephy, even though his eyes had only lingered on her for a few seconds.

"Are you ready?"

Cephy pouted. "But—"

"We'll do it another day," Ailis said. "Our dinner is important too, hm?" Ailis sounded encouraging, but Rachael didn't miss the glance she exchanged with

Cale.

"You promise?" Cephy got up and walked over to Cale, her eyes fixed on Ailis.

Ailis smiled. "Go on. Cale is showing you how to track animals today."

Cale nodded. "It's quite difficult. Are you sure you're ready?"

New fire flashed in Cephy's eyes. "Yes."

He closed the door behind them., leaving Rachael alone with Ailis again.

Ailis sighed. "I'd like to start your lessons today, if you're rested enough."

Rachael wanted to ask what had happened, but decided to wait. Ailis wasn't someone who talked behind her brother's back.

"I am. How does this work?"

"I've never taught a prophet before, but I'll do what I can. The most important step is that you learn to sense the source of your gift inside yourself. Once you can find that source at will, you'll be able to use it at will too, but it will take some practice."

Rachael didn't know how much time she had to learn what she needed to know, but she was willing to try.

Ailis was sitting opposite her on the floor in Rachael's room. "Try to focus."

"I *am.*"

Rachael didn't want to sound harsh, but the sun had stood high in the sky when they began their session. Only a few weak rays of dying sunlight fell through the window now, and she was tired. All they'd done was sit together like this while Rachael tried to focus on some energy within herself she'd never felt before and which she wasn't convinced existed.

"I don't know where my dreams come from," she said. "They just happen to me. I can't control it."

Ailis closed her eyes and breathed deep as if showing Rachael how to do it. "Finding the source of your magic is often difficult. Most people are like Cephy. Their gift leaks out of them, but they can sense it. It usually responds when the person starts trying, but it can take a few days or weeks. I admit, it doesn't normally take this long, but that shouldn't discourage you."

Cale's sister had been a patient teacher. Since they'd begun her lessons a month ago, they'd sat like this on most days, trying to tap into Rachael's gift until they were both too tired to continue. Rachael was struggling to concentrate because she knew she couldn't do it. She was trying, but there was simply nothing there. However, for reasons beyond Rachael's understanding, Ailis refused to give up.

Rachael shrugged. "It leaks out of me too, but always when I'm sleeping. I don't even know what magic is supposed to feel like. Usually, it scares me."

She blushed at the confession, but Ailis either didn't notice or didn't mind. Something about Ailis put Rachael's worries at ease. She was a kind person and they always did Rachael's teaching in private without Cale or Cephy interfering. Rachael could relax around her, and her gut told her it was fine. Ailis was the most gentle and generous person; Rachael couldn't imagine her jumping up and attacking her. Ailis's stature was too frail for her to even swing a sword, let alone take Rachael down. When Ailis got flustered or blushed, she looked even younger than Cephy despite being twenty-three years old.

"Have you had any visions recently?" Ailis asked. "Maybe if I observed you while it's happening I could learn how to teach you."

"No, not since..." Rachael hesitated. The last time she'd had a vision was before they met Aeron. She swallowed. "Aeron made me a tea to make the dreams go away."

In the low afternoon glow, Ailis's face paled. Every mention of the Mist Woman had the same effect on her; Ailis was a timid person, but Aeron drove a whole different fear into her.

Rachael had the uneasy feeling that Aeron had stopped her dreams for her own selfish reasons, but there was nothing she could do about it now. Whatever was coming, it would take her by surprise. Dread chilled her bones and made her shiver. She needed to learn to control her visions, but it wasn't looking good.

"Do you know what was in the tea?"

Rachael shook her head. "She didn't tell me."

"Do you think you'd be able to identify the herbs by smell?"

"Maybe. It smelled strong at the time, but I don't know if I'd still recognise it." She was no cook. Common flavours like deer or chicken were obvious even to her, but she hadn't known the herbs Aeron had used. She doubted she'd know them by smell alone.

"We'll try it. Without your visions..." Ailis bit her lip. "I'm sorry, I shouldn't."

"Shouldn't what?"

Rachael stared at her. She hadn't realised it before, but Ailis looked exhausted.

"I leave most Sparrow business to my brother," she

said. "He is their leader and founder, after all. They are the ones on the front lines, doing the fighting. I just help new recruits like you. I heal their injuries."

"So, you don't know anything about what's going on?" Rachael was disappointed. Cale hadn't said much about the Sparrows since they'd arrived, and his silence had made her curious.

"Oh no, I do. Cale keeps me informed. They are our family. Hasn't he told you?"

"He said he'll take me to them when the time is right, but I don't know when that'll be."

"He's so cautious lately." Ailis's smile spoke volumes of her love for her brother. "I'm sorry, Rachael. He told me you don't trust strangers easily, and from what little I know of your life I can't blame you. We're on your side and I want to be your friend. Cale does, too. In his head he's always planning five steps ahead. It's hard on him when Sparrows fall. He takes every loss personally. If he hasn't told you when he'll take you to them it's only because he wants to make sure it's safe."

Rachael was uncomfortable. She'd known people died in this war, but until now she hadn't thought about it. Hearing Ailis state the obvious with such pain in her voice made Rachael feel guilty for not having asked sooner.

"How many?"

"We started with two hundred Sparrows. Out of those—"

"*Two hundred.*" Rachael hated herself for interrupting but couldn't help herself. Two hundred was a tiny number compared to the king's army. They couldn't hope to win this war with so few.

Ailis nodded. "It's difficult to find people like you and Cephy. Most of the ones we tracked down are too terrified to stand in this war and openly admit they have magic or support those who do. Even if they're telling only us, they're not used to saying it out loud. They'd rather be on the first ship to Midoka or Krymistis than stay here." Ailis's eyes burnt, and Rachael felt her pain. She still felt like running most days. "They are good people, Rachael. They have never hurt anyone."

"Why are Midoka and Krymistis so different?" Rachael had never even heard of those places.

"Magic isn't hated everywhere," Ailis said. "The people we help, those who don't want to fight, know they'll find refuge and protection there. It's the safest place for them, and the White Guard would never chase them across the Far Sea. Over there, they don't have to worry about being hunted. They are accepted for what they are."

It sounded too good to be true, but Rachael had no reason to doubt her words. If places like that really existed, she couldn't blame people for going when given the chance.

Rachael reached across and took Ailis's shaking hands into hers. She understood the desire to be away from here and live in peace, but there was something more in Ailis's past. She had a personal reason for fighting. How much did Ailis remember about the day the Tramurans came for her parents?

"I'm sorry."

Ailis nodded and squeezed Rachael's hands, but there was a distant look in her eyes. "To answer your question, we started with two hundred Sparrows.

We're now down to one hundred and twelve. Five of our healers died in the last raid."

"Raid?"

Ailis's face paled and Rachael wished she hadn't asked. "There's a prison, high up in the White City. The White Guard would have taken you there to rot and be tortured until your execution. We watch the roads, so we know when more people are brought in. Cale always goes with the Sparrows and they always take at least ten into the walls, but last time only Cale and two others came back. He still can't sleep. He believes they died because he failed."

Rachael took a deep, rattling breath. If she and Cephy hadn't evaded the commander's forces, they would have ended up in the same prison. That others were in there right now—experiencing the hopelessness she'd felt in her dream, being tortured by those demons—hurt her deeper than anything else had ever cut. Would Cale have found her within the walls? Would it have made a difference or would she have died trying to run?

She balled her hands into fists in her lap. Better to run and die than to stay and wither away. Cale risked his life to save people like her. He was the only hope they had left. Only, according to him, she could do more than free them from prison. And all she did was sit here and complain she couldn't do what Ailis asked her to.

It wasn't good enough. She'd try until it either worked or killed her, but she wouldn't just sit here and feel defeated. She'd thought she failed at finding her gift, but that wasn't true. She only failed if she stopped trying.

The strong need to hug Cephy and never let her go again overcame Rachael. If it hadn't been for her, they'd both be rotting in that prison now.

"I've seen the place," Rachael said. "I dreamed about it, before we left Blackrock." Most of it had faded, but a few details were still all too vivid.

"Then you understand."

"What do those demons do to the prisoners, exactly?" She feared the answer, but she had to ask. Next time she felt like giving up, she'd remember it.

"Demons?"

"Yes. I saw them in my dream. They came to kill me I think, but I can't remember the details."

"You must mean the guards. Or that horrible man, Commander Videl." Ailis shuddered and Rachael's breath caught in her throat. "I often thought of him as a demon. He's cruel enough."

He'd seemed like a demon to her too, but he wasn't who she'd seen.

Ailis looked haunted just thinking about it, so Rachael decided to drop it for now.

"But why?" she asked. "Why do all this? Why raid the prison, build a resistance?" Why find one orphan girl on the streets of Blackrock to set it all right? So much effort for something that was doomed to fail.

"Because a terrible injustice is being done to innocent people. Cale knows he can't save all of them. Every Sparrow is prepared to die if it means saving two captives. The prison will be the first thing we tear down if we win this war. There are many gifted who would gladly offer a hand."

This had been about her and Cephy living in peace. About Cale's parents finding peace. Now it was about all those other people whose names she didn't know, who she'd likely never meet herself, who desperately needed her to go through with this insane plan because they would die if she didn't.

"Let's try again," Rachael said.

"What do you want to try?"

"My lesson." Rachael closed her eyes and tried to find the place within herself she knew didn't exist but that she needed to reach regardless.

Chapter Twenty-Five

Cephy shut her eyes and *listened.* Aeron had taught her how to focus on her gift, and when she did it well she could sense the slightest of movements around her without needing to see. She found the place within herself where her magic resided, and let that spark feel out around her. The faint sound of water rushing around rocks and muddy soil. The flapping of bird wings. A squirrel cracking a nut. They all sounded like they were happening right next to her.

They were close to the White City, but their little spot in the forest made it feel miles away. Cale's place sure was nice. His sister was nice too. Ailis let her help with the cooking and other household chores, and Cale allowed her to accompany him deeper into the forest when he went to hunt. He taught her how to use a bow and she even got to swing his sword a few times. Ailis taught her how to cook the most delicious things—delicious things Cephy was proud to have made herself. Maybe, if things had turned out differently, she could have been a great baker like her parents. Instead, she'd been born with the spark of magic and her father had cast her out like the rest of the rubbish. If it hadn't been for Rachael, she wouldn't have survived the winter.

But she'd gathered all her courage and approached Rachael. Cephy had known from gossip around town that Rachael was dangerous—her father had said mean things about Rachael many times—but the opposite was true. Rachael was real nice and had helped her escape.

But they wouldn't have needed to escape at all if the White Guard hadn't come after them. Who'd called them? A stranger, or could it have been her own father? He hated magic as much as anyone…

Apart from Cale and Ailis and Arlo. They'd been real nice to her too. Arlo had even fixed her hands. The tincture he'd used on her charred skin had been magic in itself, the way it had worked on her blisters and healed hurt flesh. Her hands were still a little rough in places but unmarked.

Cephy hated Aeron for what she'd done to her, for how easily she cast them aside. Cephy also loved her because Aeron had taught her without fear or prejudice. She'd been so indifferent when Cale had taken her and Rachael away, almost relieved, but she *had* taught Cephy control. If it hadn't been for Aeron, Cephy would never have found that place within herself where her magic slept until she called it. If it hadn't been for Aeron, the squirrel cracking the nut would be hidden from Cephy.

Cephy grimaced. Her hands also wouldn't have suffered like this. Aeron had said sacrifice was necessary if Cephy wanted to accomplish anything, but she'd taken it too far. Her hands had hurt worse than anything Cephy had felt before and would still be hurting if Arlo hadn't intervened and if Cale hadn't saved them from the evil Mist Woman.

Still, Cephy couldn't hate Aeron completely. It was beautiful here with Cale, but all they did was focus on Rachael. Ailis spent all her time teaching Rachael how to find that place within herself, which Rachael struggled with but which Cephy could tap into easily. Their priority was always Rachael, even when Cephy helped with dinner and even when Cale taught her how to hold and shoot the bow. She felt like an unwanted tag-along. No one cared what happened to her. In a way, life with Cale and Ailis wasn't that different from her old life with her parents and siblings. Aeron's lessons had been harsh but Cephy had felt useful.

Maybe Aeron would take her back. The Mist Woman had been more open with Cephy than with Rachael; maybe, if she went back now, Aeron would teach her once more. Cephy wouldn't be in Rachael's way then. Hadn't Aeron said she was welcome in her home at any time? All Cephy needed to do was find the way.

What King Aeric did to people like her was terrible. She hated him and his people's loathing for it. If they hadn't run—if, if, *if*. Cephy was tired of it. Cale said the Sparrows were trying but their numbers were non-existent compared to the White Guard. They'd all be wiped out before they even got a glimpse at King Aeric. And then what? People like her would be left to suffer forever.

Rachael was trying, too. At night, after they'd gone to bed, they talked about their days. Rachael still couldn't sense the magic inside her. Ailis was beginning to lose faith. She hadn't said so, but she looked more exhausted each time she left Rachael's room. The King had to die. Cephy was happy Rachael had agreed to help, but Rachael wasn't making any progress. And where did that leave her?

They needed to take more drastic measures if they wanted to win. It was risky, but she wanted to find Aeron. She wouldn't turn Cephy down if she went back now. She'd said herself that Cephy would always be welcome in her home.

All Cephy had to do was leave and find her way.

Rachael saw only hazy shapes. There was red and black and different shades of grey, but she couldn't tell what they belonged to. It was dark. There were sounds somewhere in the distance. They were muffled and unclear like she was wearing something thick over her ears and had just been hit over the head. Were they screams? They were too garbled for her to be sure.

All she knew was that they made her skin crawl. Whatever this was, it was wrong. Her heart nearly doubled over itself in fear of what was to come. There were distant bangs, like explosions or a door slamming shut.

There was a sense of recognition and the terrible emptiness only lack of hope could bring.

Finally, there was pain. It was searing through her and burned into every corner of her being.

Rachael sat up with a start. She was soaked in cold sweat from her damp shirt, but she was fine.

Confused, she looked around. She was safely tucked away in her bed in Cale's cabin. It was silent save for the soft cooing of owls. Everyone was likely asleep since it was the middle of the night.

She got up and looked for a cloth to dry her sweat and fresh clothes she could change into.

It didn't make sense. The dream had felt like a vision, but it had been too unclear to be one. Her visions had always been lucid—there'd never been a doubt about their meaning. But this had been nothing but a blurred, confused mess of colours and sounds. It had lacked the distinct sharpness of her visions, but it had felt like every other vision she'd ever had. It had left her disoriented, her head throbbing and her heart racing. Rachael couldn't even tell if this dream had been about her or someone else. Whether it would happen in this house, in the forests, or somewhere else. Something terrible was coming and she was defenceless. What good was a warning when it was too vague to be useful?

Rachael went downstairs for some fresh air. It'd be cold outside, but the breeze would be perfect for her racing mind.

She was surprised to find Cale sitting by himself in a corner.

Their eyes met, and he straightened. "Are you all right? Why are you up?"

A part of her had started to believe his worry for her was real, but she couldn't convince herself to let her guard down. For all she knew, her dream had tried to warn her about him. Despite Cale's kindness and everything they'd done for her and Cephy, Rachael still barely knew him or Ailis. She only really trusted Cephy, but Cephy had earned that. Cale was still a long way off; although, she wasn't sure what he could do to earn her trust, either.

She shrugged. “I can’t sleep. Why are you up?”

A small candle dipped his sad smile in a warm light. “It’s complicated.”

“Try me.” Her whole life had been complicated. She was good at it by now.

He sighed, but it sounded more exhausted than frustrated. “I’m thinking about the Sparrows and this war. About how many have died and will still die if we don’t figure out a way to stop King Aeric.”

Rachael remembered her conversation with Ailis and asked, “When can I meet them?”

He kept telling her how relieved they were she was alive, how much they supported her and believed in her, yet he stalled every time she brought it up. How could they place their trust in someone they didn’t know? How could she fight for them with all this secrecy? She had to meet them—people who put their faith in a stranger and risked their lives for other strangers.

“It’s difficult,” Cale said. “There are things to prepare. The White Guard is always watching; I can’t risk them finding us. The time isn’t right.”

“I can sneak without being seen,” Rachael said. “You always say they want to meet me, so take me to them.”

She had no idea what she’d say to them, but she was curious. The Sparrows were people who fought the king and his men to defend people like her, to create a better future for the gifted. They had sworn that no one else would have to go through what she and Cephy had gone through. Even if she couldn’t think of anything to say to them, she had to see for herself that people like that existed. She had to see if they were genuine, if their hearts were in this fight. She didn't know what difference it would make if they were, but she had to know.

"All right," Cale said and her heart jumped. "But you need to give me some time. I need to make sure that our route is clear. Would you mind going at night?"

"I've always searched for food at night without anyone spotting me."

"That was different, Rachael. You were in Blackrock then. There were no White Guards looking for you."

"There were the night we escaped, and the people there were always looking for me."

He sighed again. "You're right. It's time you met them—you're their hero, after all."

She blushed. How could *she* be someone's hero? "They don't even know me."

"They know enough. Trust me, they'll be happy to see you. We can't go tonight, I need to prepare things first. Get some sleep. I'll let you know when it's time. Maybe in two, three days. Just be prepared—they are... excitable."

Chapter Twenty-Six

"Are you ready?"

Rachael barely saw Cale in front of her in his hood made of dark leather and his cloak made of midnight, but she heard him just fine and she could make out his silhouette. He had stopped to make sure she was ready to go on, and she almost bumped into him.

They were drenched from the heavy downpour and struggling to see in the harsh light from the oil lamp. Darkness had always spelled safety for her, but tonight it was difficult to move forwards in the unfamiliar streets. The heavy rain nearly blinded her and, despite her protests, Cale had led her by her hand for most of the trip. They couldn't stop anywhere for long or a patrolling guard might spot their silhouettes in the shadows. Dreadful as this weather was, it provided perfect cover. Cale pulling her onwards had been the best solution, whether she liked it or not.

He'd told her it was time and to be ready two days after their late-night conversation. She thought she'd been prepared, but now they were here her mind was racing. Behind that door were the people that had invested all their hopes for a better future in her—all that blind faith, all that unjustified belief, and in return she had nothing but the truth. They'd drop her in an instant when they learned she couldn't control her visions. Cale had assured her they wouldn't, but she found that hard to believe. Blind faith didn't outlast bitter disappointment.

Rachael wasn't sure how long they'd been walking. She wasn't familiar with these roads, didn't know the scratches on the worn buildings. She'd been on edge ever since Cale had led her out of the forest and onto the main road through the gates into the city's walls. They'd been safe so far, but she couldn't trust this place. The Sparrows' safe house was just within the city walls and they hadn't seen another soul, but she still saw danger in every twitching shadow.

She shivered through the wet fabric and walked next to Cale. "I'm fine. Let's go."

"Remember, I'll be right here with you if it's too much. We can leave at any time," Cale said with a reassuring smile. His warning that the Sparrows were excitable came to mind. How bad could it be? They were all grown-ups who'd seen their friends die. They'd been hunted for their beliefs or for having magic. Little children who didn't quite understand the situation might have been excitable, but Rachael struggled to picture a group of adults acting like children receiving a new toy—because of her, no less.

Cale knocked on the door in a sequence Rachael knew she'd never remember. It opened barely wide enough for the smallest sliver of light to leak into the night.

There was a gasp from the other side and the door

flew open.

A young man jumped into the rain and grinned at them. "You made it! We were worried something happened when it was getting late." He turned his attention to Rachael. "You must be Rachael." He grinned wider and offer her his hand. "Pleased to meet you. I'm Lon. Cale hasn't stopped talking about you since he got back from Blackrock. Come on in. The others are waiting."

Rachael felt a little overwhelmed already but followed Cale inside and waited as he shut the door behind them. If the others were anything like Lon, then *excitable* was an understatement.

Rachael stayed close behind Cale as they walked through a faintly lit corridor, while Lon filled in Cale about everything that had happened since the last time Cale had stopped by. Lon didn't seem to need to breathe, and Rachael stopped paying attention to him.

The building had looked old and abandoned from the outside, with barred windows and moss on the walls. It didn't look much better on the inside. The staircase had large holes in several steps, and most of the doors were either hanging off their hinges or had been taken off completely. The floorboards creaked with every step, and the smell of mould and rot filled the narrow corridor.

Rachael could see why the White Guard hadn't searched this place. Apart from a lack of dust, it looked like it hadn't been lived in for years.

Lon opened a wide oak door—the only one still attacked—to a bright chamber. "Everyone, Cale is here. He brought the Sparrow." Lon's voice was shaking with excitement. Cheering from the other side of the door told her the room was filled with a lot of people who were just as excited.

Cale grinned at her and led her inside. "Remember, we can leave any time if this becomes too much."

His words barely registered with her. This was already a little overwhelming, but she'd only just got here. As tempting as leaving right away was, she nodded. It was never a good strategy to show fear, and despite her vows to herself, she trusted Cale to get her out if necessary. Besides, these people were on her side—in theory, she had nothing to worry about.

Rachael entered and blinked to adjust to the much brighter room—and all those people smiling at her. There wasn't a free floorboard or corner. Every Sparrow greeted her with a smile wider than the last like they were competing for who was more welcoming. And they were *cheering*. Some of them looked barely older than Cephy, but there were no young children in the room unless they were hiding from the noise. Some of the heads were greying, their faces marked with deep wrinkles and the spark of wisdom only a long life could teach. The biggest difference was in their clothes, some worn and patched by hand but others of finer materials and adorned with lace and jewellery. They all stood together, at least fifty people, and watched her just like she was watching them. She saw the most amazing mix of social classes. What did they see when they looked at her? Ailis had given her nice clothes, washed and brushed her hair, and fed her, but did they still see the street rat under the mask? Did it even matter to them?

She had never felt immediately accepted or loved. That she felt it now made her eyes burn and warmth spread through her. It also made her heart sink. She'd expected them to be upset, beaten, and mourning their fallen friends but instead, they were celebrating. Because she was here. How could she disappoint them now?

"Rachael, these are the Sparrows," Cale said. "My family."

They formed a loose circle around her and Cale, which was buzzing with whispers and offered names. Everyone was talking at the same time, and it filled the room with an impossible to understand chatter.

Cale held up his hands. "One at a time, please."

Just like that their voices died, but their smiles remained.

Cale gave her a soft nudge. Her turn to say something. But instead of getting the words out, her throat grew tight. She'd never addressed this many people before, let alone people who were paying attention. She couldn't shake the feeling that she should have prepared a speech, no matter how short. Anything would have been better than silence.

"It's all right." Cale took her hand as if to comfort her, but Rachael pulled away. She could do this—she *had* to do this—on her own. She wasn't a helpless child who couldn't stand on her own feet. She just needed to find her balance, and she couldn't do that if he steadied her. "They just want to know it's really you," he whispered. "Tell them you're okay."

Rachael took a deep breath. "I..." What did they want? Her name? How old she was maybe? She had never felt so out of place anywhere. Blackrock's streets had been cruel, but they'd been familiar. This, here, was overwhelming, but she wouldn't run. She owed them honesty for their dedication and losses. "I'm Rachael. Cale thinks I can help you somehow." The Sparrows shuffled a little closer. Rachael took another deep breath and braced herself. "But I can't. I'm not this Sparrow you think I am. I can't control my dreams. I've only had one since Cale found us and it was useless." For all she knew it'd been a normal dream, but she felt like she needed to give them something, even if it wasn't much. "I can't control any other magic, like Cale says some of you can. I can't move anything with my mind or set fire to things. Cephy is the one who—"

Cale gave her another nudge. Her hands were shaking, but at least they knew the truth now. They could find someone who could actually help, and she could stop pretending. She turned around to leave, but an impenetrable wall of people made that impossible. No one moved aside so she could pass. Their smiles were gone, but they still looked just as hopeful.

"Didn't you hear me? I can't help you."

Their silence was deafening. A young woman with hair like fire moved to the front of the crowd. Her leather armour was scratched, a fading bruise on her cheek, but her step was confident and unintimidated. She wore her hurts like earned trophies.

"Yeah, we know," she said. "Cale told us you're struggling."

Rachael didn't know what to say. She'd assumed they had no idea, that they'd cheered because they thought Rachael would change everything, but they knew. Why would they risk their lives if they knew? Had their losses driven them mad?

"Then what do you want from me?"

The fearless woman with red hair winked. "You'll find a way, somehow." She reached for Rachael through the crowd and gave her hand a brief squeeze.

A man stumbled to the front and almost fell over his own feet. "We believe in you."

Offers of support and encouragement came from everywhere at once as more Sparrows chirped up.

It was hopeless. Why couldn't they accept that prophecy had been wrong? Whoever had created this nonsense about her bringing in a new age of freedom for the gifted had clearly lost their mind and now, hundreds of years later, she suffered from their insanity.

Rachael sighed in frustration. "But I can't. Don't you understand? *I can't kill the king*. We can't even get close to him. You're out there every day, losing your lives for some future foretold by someone who lived in completely different times, and for what? Because prophecy says I'll kill King Aeric? I don't even know why you think we can get past his guards!"

Finally, the faces around her fell into stunned shock. Even Cale had gone limp.

"Find someone else who knows how to do this."

Their belief in her had been nice, but like everything else it had faded like she'd known it would. People were like that, pledging their undying love one minute and changing their mind the next. Unshakable faith could be shaken quite easily once someone was honest. She could finally find a dark alley and get back to her old life.

She began to walk, but Cale took her hand the moment her foot left the floor. "Don't worry about any of that. We're your diversion. If you can't control your magic by the time we make our move, then so be it."

"But you can't—"

He smiled. "Oh, but we can and we will. It's fine if you can't believe in the prophecy, but we do. We thought prophecy was wrong countless times too, but here we are. We're not giving up no matter what you say. With or without you, we'll retake the White City. Maker help us, we'll retake all of Rifarne. It's true that we want you to do this with us. We might not even stand a chance without you, but if we don't do anything we've already lost. It would be an insult to our fallen friends if we gave up now."

Rachael blinked away tears. How could he still believe in her after everything she'd said? Worse yet, the Sparrows looked more determined than ever.

The same woman as before stepped forwards, her red hair glowing like fire in the dim light of the oil lamps. "No one expects you to have all the answers. That's what we're here for. We have war specialists and strategists." She gently placed one hand on Rachael's shoulder. "We know of your background. We know how you grew up and how you were treated. Many of us have similar backgrounds. There isn't one person here who doesn't understand how hard it is to believe in yourself. We're here for that, too. We'll believe in you when you can't find a reason to."

An agreeing murmur spread through the room. Several people stepped up to give her a reassuring pat. All Rachael could do was nod, desperate not to let them see how much their words affected her.

"I'm sorry," Cale said. "I should have told you how much they knew, but I wanted them to see you for you."

They hadn't said a word on the way back, until now. Rachael needed time to process everything, and Cale had given her the space she needed. Really she wanted him to stay back a little but he'd never agree to that until they were back at the cabin, so she'd accepted his silence instead.

The rain had stopped and pale moonlight reflected off the wet cobblestones. They'd be easy to spot for any guard patrolling tonight. Rachael couldn't argue against caution, so she stayed close.

Rachael sighed. She was tired after their overwhelming friendliness. "That makes no sense."

They'd stayed for another hour after everyone had sworn their loyalty to her. Kiana, the fearless redhead, had talked to her the most, but everyone had tried to get a few words with her. They'd all introduced themselves, but she'd never remember all their names.

She did want to try, with or without magic; although, she didn't know what she could achieve if she didn't learn to control it in time.

"I could have told you how much they knew, but then you'd have prepared excuses. This way, they saw you react. They saw what their words meant to you, and you saw that they genuinely care."

"I don't understand how. Just because a prophecy makes me sound important? You could still have the wrong girl."

Cale stopped walking and turned around to face her. "Think of it this way—morale is a powerful thing. Even if it turns out that you're not the Sparrow, they believe that you are. They'll fight harder and with more determination because of it. Many of them might live another day because of it. Would you take that away from them?"

If there was one thing she knew for certain about Cale, it was that he was determined.

"No, I wouldn't." But something else had been bothering her and she couldn't keep quiet any more. "Why did you ask me to be quiet?"

Cale started to walk again. "When?"

"When I mentioned Cephy. I was telling them that Cephy knows more about magic than I do and is better suited to this Sparrow role, and you gave me a nudge to be quiet."

At first, she'd thought that he didn't want her to be so harsh on herself, but it wasn't just his nudge. He had promised Cephy that Ailis would teach her. Cephy had been thrilled to learn more, yet all she'd done since coming here was help with the household chores. Cephy didn't say so, but Rachael knew she was bored and disappointed. She was eager to learn and would have made a great student, but Cale seemed to have forgotten all about it.

"Well?"

She nearly walked into him when he stopped and turned to face her again.

"They can't know everything about Cephy."

"Why not?"

"Because they think prophecy names her as the one to betray you."

That was the most ridiculous thing she'd heard all night. "That's nonsense, Cephy would never—"

"Maybe not, but they don't know her as you do. I wouldn't have recognised her either if Aeron hadn't told me."

Rachael was getting irritated. Cephy was only a child, and Aeron had made it clear that she wanted them out of her life. More to the point, she hated Cale. Why would she tell him something that would help him?

"What did Aeron say?"

His eyes were grim as he looked into hers. "She called Cephy her Fox."

"So?"

"'The Fox will lead you to ruin.' According to Aeron, that's Cephy. You've boosted their morale, but if they found out who came here with you that morale would shatter. I'm sure you can see why I don't want that to happen."

Rachael nodded without taking her eyes off Cale. She didn't believe any of it, but he was determined. He knew more about morale than she did, and she'd seen for herself how her entering the room had affected the Sparrows. Cephy would never betray her, but Cale was right—they didn't know Cephy like she did, but they did place a great amount of faith in prophecy.

"We should get going," Cale said. "It's cold and it'll be morning before long."

It had been a long night. Rachael was desperate to lie down and let everything sink in. She wasn't done talking to him about Cephy, but she'd think clearer once she'd slept.

Cale held out his arm and signalled her with one hand to be quiet and get down. She froze but did as he asked. Something was wrong. Now they'd stopped talking, she heard it—hurried footsteps on wet ground. Her heart was hammering, and she clamped one hand over her lips to stop her fear from escaping. Cale knelt beside her, sword drawn. Had the White Guard followed them? Did they know where the Sparrows were hiding? The footsteps grew louder. Branches cracked too close to them.

Cale jumped up. "*Ailis*."

Rachael breathed a heavy sigh of relief and got up after him. Ailis was standing not far from them, but it was too dark to see what she was doing. The forest was thick in this part and the moonlight wasn't strong enough to get through the army of branches.

"Cale! Oh, thank the Maker. Have you seen Cephy? Did she come after you?"

Rachael went cold.

"What?" Cale ran to Ailis. "No. Why? Isn't she in her bed?"

"No. I went to check on her before going to bed, but she wasn't there."

Rachael caught up with them. "Why were you checking on her?"

Had this prophecy clouded their judgment so much they needed to make sure Cephy wasn't plotting Rachael's murder? Had they checked on her too, while she was asleep?

But Rachael saw the worry in Ailis's eyes now she'd caught up. Her eyes were bloodshot. She'd been crying.

Ailis folded her hands before her and looked at the ground. "Cephy likes a glass of milk overnight. It helps her sleep. She takes one when she goes to bed, but I always see if she needs more."

Ailis was shaking. Cale wrapped his arms around her and she sank into him.

"She wasn't in her room tonight or in Rachael's. I've

been out here for nearly an hour looking for her, but there's no sign of her. It's like she's disappeared."

Rachael paled. "She could be anywhere."

Had Cephy come after them? The White City's layout was confusing and the rain had been so heavy. Had she run into guards? Had they taken her to the prison?

Rachael turned on her heel to run back, but a strong hand around her wrist held her back.

"Stay here," Cale said.

Rachael tried to wriggle out of his grip, but it was no use. "I have to look for her, Cale. There are guards in the city, what if she—"

"I know, and that's exactly why you're not going. Ailis, take Rachael back to the house and stay with her. I will search the city. If I can't find any sign of her there, I will search the forest." He didn't sound like the Cale she'd got to know. This was a commander, a leader, taking charge of another rescue mission.

"But what if you—"

He placed his hands on her shoulders. "I appreciate that you want to help and maybe one day I'll teach you, but right now you don't know this city. If you come with me, you'll create a larger risk for me. Stay here. Ailis will be with you."

Cale moved to run off, not waiting for a reply or a promise, but she needed his. "Cale!"

He stopped and turned back around, the look in his eyes saying that whatever she had to say had better be important.

"Promise you'll find her."

He gulped, his eyes flitting to the ground and back to her in what might have been regret. Then he was gone.

Chapter Twenty-Seven

The sun had begun to rise and a soft yellow-blue illuminated the waking forest by the time Cale returned. He was alone. Despite the morning glow, the air was heavy, promising more heavy rain later to wash away the last of the snow.

It had been a long night of waiting and twitching at every sound. Rachael hadn't been able to sleep and sat in the kitchen instead. She'd been furious with Cale but once she sat down for a while with some calming, hot tea for her nerves, she had to admit that he was right. She was angry he hadn't promised her what she wanted to hear, but now, in the cold light of the morning, she understood. He didn't make promises if there was a chance he couldn't keep them.

Cale looked tired. The weather had stayed dry, but his clothes were muddy and his hair ruffled like he'd been crawling through the dirt to find Cephy.

Ailis got him a towel but he shook his head. "I'll need more than that." He leaned against the doorframe. "It took a while to track her footprints in the dark, but she went straight to the stables. I think she left the

White City."

"Did you follow her?" Rachael asked.

"There were too many hoofprints in the road. She could have been any of them. I could have followed any track for hours without finding her or getting any closer to her. I'm sorry, Rachael. She's gone."

"Do you know why she left?" Ailis asked. "Is there any family she might have missed?"

Rachael scoffed. "Not likely." She sighed. "I don't know. She didn't say that she wanted to leave. I thought she was happy here." The second the words were out, Rachael wanted to take them back. "It's your fault she's gone."

"Rachael, I—" Ailis started, but Cale shook his head like he was giving Rachael permission to talk. She wanted to punch him for it. Who was he to allow her to speak? When had she given him so much power over herself?

Rachael glared at Ailis. "If you'd taught her, Cephy would still be here. And *you*." She turned to Cale. "She asked you if Ailis could train her and you said she would if Cephy asked nicely. How often did she ask, Cale? Did either of you care? You didn't let her do anything once we got here. You only taught me and I still can't find the source of my gift." Her hands, balled into fists on the table, were shaking. "You should have taught her. You should have—" The words choked her, so she ran upstairs and locked the door behind her. She didn't want to see either of them. Cale had allowed this. Ailis hadn't argued. Their fears had ruled them, and now Cephy was gone because of it.

By the time Rachael stepped out of her room, the rain's

gentle drums had comforted her and numbed the screaming accusations in her head. Ailis must have left her a warm breakfast outside the door, but it had got cold and looked unappealing.

Rachael was ashamed of how she'd reacted. She still meant every word, but Cale and Ailis had been good to them. They shouldn't have neglected Cephy, but judging by Ailis's bloodshot eyes last night, she knew that too. Rachael felt terrible that she'd made Ailis feel worse.

Cale wasn't in the kitchen when Rachael went downstairs, but Ailis was cooking what smelled like stew over the fire. She looked up when Rachael entered and smiled.

"Just in time," she said. "Come here. Taste this for me, please? I can't decide if it needs more ground pepper."

Rachael was in no position to argue after her outburst, so she stepped up to the hot cauldron and took the ladle from Ailis. The stew smelled delicious, its meaty scents warming and comforting. The wonderful fragrances worked their way into her mind and soothed any remaining anger.

She took a sip. "I think it's fine."

Ailis smiled again and took back the ladle. "Thank you, I'm glad to hear it."

Rachael intertwined her fingers and hugged herself. She'd come to apologise, but now that she was here the words wouldn't come. After a few moments of awkward silence, she couldn't take it anymore.

"I'm sorry. I shouldn't have—"

"No, Rachael. You were right." Ailis's voice was shaking. "Cale asked me to teach Cephy shortly after you'd arrived. And I wanted to, I really did, but teaching you seemed more important. Cephy already had such a good grip on her gift, I could only have taught her so much. But you… We need *you*. The prophecy named *you*. It doesn't excuse the way I treated her, but it's the only reason I can give."

Rachael understood. Ailis regretted it, and that was all Rachael needed to know.

"It does. This is new to all of us." The kitchen suddenly seemed far too small. "Where is Cale? Is he outside?"

Ailis's smile didn't reach her eyes. "He is, but not near the house. He's taken Barnaby and Shelbie to look for Cephy. There are three main roads she could have taken. He rode out early to search all three."

Cale wouldn't find her. Rachael felt guilty; if she hadn't said those things the night before, Cale might have stayed. She still didn't trust him, but she was starting to—and now he'd left without saying a word because of how she had reacted. Even Cephy had left her. Trust, once broken, didn't mend easily. It was only a matter of time before Ailis left her, too.

Arlo inspected every corner of his house one last time. He hadn't packed much, but he hated being under-prepared.

The Sparrows had sent him disturbing news from the capital. King Aeric was up to something, and to make matters worse, they'd seen a woman with raven-back hair and an aura as evil as the Dark One himself close to the White City. If it was Aeron… Maker's soggy breeches help them all if it was Aeron.

Arlo closed the door to his home with a grunt,

satisfied that he'd packed everything he needed—a sword, his axe, medicinal herbs, bandages, and some spices for cooking. He was tempted to throw away the key; he had a feeling he wouldn't be back to see the leaves change colour again.

He saddled his horse and mounted the great beast with ease. A great horse for a great man, as Cale had said the day he gifted Arlo the animal. A thank you for Barnaby, he'd said. A thank you for everything else, Arlo suspected. He scratched the horse's right ear to comfort it. It was clever and seemed to know that something was wrong—a trait Arlo had counted on many times over the years. It was an old horse now, nearly as old in horse years as Arlo was himself, but he still trusted its instincts like he trusted his own.

If his gut was right, then things would be heating up in the city soon and he didn't want to be away from the lad or the Sparrows when it happened, but he also hoped they had just a little more. He'd be able to gather information along the way if he didn't have to ride hard until he reached the city, and information wasn't something to be dismissed. It could turn the tide of a losing battle, and the Sparrows wouldn't turn down the advantage. He'd lose a day or two. Was it worth the risk, or was his sword arm worth more?

He grunted—a command his horse understood well after many years together—and his horse turned around and began its long trot to the White City.

His chest ached as they left the clearing. Would the critters be all right without him or would the wolves have the rabbits for supper now he was gone?

"Look at me, growing soft at my old age." His horse huffed in understanding. "Are you up for one last battle, old friend?" The horse whinnied and briefly stood on its hind legs before it fell into a fast trot away from the peace Arlo had built for himself.

"What can I get you, sugar?"

Cephy shook her head. "Nothing, thank you."

The waitress scowled. "You sure? You look frozen right to the bone."

That she was, but it didn't change that she had nothing of value, no way to pay for food or a room. She wasn't going to steal from anyone. "I have no money."

Again, the girl scowled, apparently unhappy at losing a seat without gaining profit. "Suit yourself."

She was about to dance off to take a wealthier patron's order when Cephy remembered the reason she'd come.

"I'm looking for someone."

"Aren't we all, sugar." The waitress didn't even turn around. She was too busy flirting with a man twice her age.

"Please, I was told that she came this way. She's got dark hair, dark eyes, and—" How could she describe Aeron to someone who'd never met her? Cephy didn't dare mention the gift, but she'd realised over the last few days that she didn't know much else about Aeron.

The waitress huffed and turned around after all. "So? Lost your mother or something?"

Cephy nodded. "We got separated yesterday. I've been looking for her ever since."

"Well, sugar, if your mother isn't looking for you then maybe she doesn't want—"

The older customer gave her a pat on the back. "Come now, Lin, the girl's looking for her mum. Be nice to her, eh? And get her a pie on me. She looks like she hasn't eaten in weeks."

Lin rolled her eyes and sighed. "Fine. But I've not seen your mother, girl. Don't forget to thank Thomas here." With a sour scowl, Lin hurried off to the kitchen.

Thomas leaned over his table. "Don't take it personally, eh, girl? Lin's job's a hard one, it is."

Cephy nodded, grateful that he'd interfered. "Thank you, sir, for the pie." She hadn't seen her parents in a long time, but she hadn't forgotten the manners her mother had taught her. *Always be kind to the people who are kind to you.*

She looked towards the kitchen, pretending to see whether her pie was on its way yet. Rachael and Cale and Ailis had been real kind to her, and she'd repaid them by running away—to Aeron, no less. Rachael was likely worried sick about her, but it couldn't be helped. She hadn't got anywhere with them. Aeron wasn't kind like Rachael, but at least Cephy would learn a thing or two and she wasn't planning on staying forever. She'd learn everything Aeron could teach her, maybe stay a month—two at the most—and then she'd go back. Then she'd be able to help in the war. If she could do that, she'd be real happy that she'd repaid Rachael and Cale and Ailis. And Arlo, too—kind Arlo, who had fixed her hands for her.

Her throat tightened and Cephy wiped her eyes dry on her sleeve. She couldn't cry in a place like this. Her mother had warned her about these places—taverns and bars and worse. Cephy knew what the men in these places were like. Thomas had bought her a pie, but she didn't believe that he didn't want anything in return. Rachael had taught her that people *always* wanted something in return for kindness.

"Everything all right, girl?"

She turned around to see Thomas watching her.

She swallowed her fears. "Yes. I'm just missing my mother, is all." It was close enough to the truth and fit the story she'd told them.

"Say, what does your mother look like again?"

"She has long, dark hair. Dark eyes."

Thomas frowned. "And a personality to freeze you to your core?"

Cephy beamed. "That's her. Have you seen her? Is she here?"

He scoffed. "I've seen her, all right. I know where she's gone off to, but why you'd want to go back to someone like that… Well, I suppose she's your mother, after all."

"Where is she?"

"She rode north around five hours ago, left just as I arrived. Gave me a right cold stare, she did. Thought she'd kill me on the spot."

Cephy's heart sank. Any number of places lay north. She thought Aeron's house was that way, but so were two busy main roads and several towns.

"Did she say anything?"

Thomas laughed. "Say anything? Nuh, girl, that she didn't. Had no reason to, did she? She doesn't know me and I don't know her, even if her glare suggests we're old lovers. Sorry, girl, that's all I know. You mother went north about five hours ago, but listen. Lin over there's right—your mother isn't looking for you. You didn't get separated, she left. Might be better to stay here and start over rather than chase after her."

But Cephy had already got up and tied her coat

around her until it wouldn't go any tighter. It wasn't much, but it was better than nothing. She was grateful to have it in this cold, and if it rained more it'd protect her from that too.

"Your pie," Lin said. "On Thomas, as promised."

Cephy didn't turn back around to see the disapproving scowl on Lin's face. She turned on her heels and headed for the door.

Thomas spat. "Ungrateful little bitch. Your mother is trouble, girl, I'd think again if I were you." He sighed when she opened the door. "Well, Lin, if she won't have the pie I'll have it. Paid for it already, haven't I?"

Cephy stepped into the night and the door fell shut behind her, slowly taking the warm square of light by her feet with it until only muffled laughter filled the night and she was alone once more.

Chapter Twenty-Eight

Two weeks passed and Cephy hadn't returned. Cale had given up his search after the first. There was nothing more they could do. But knowing it and accepting it were two different things, and Rachael was struggling to understand why Cephy had run away. Where did Cephy think she could run to? Her parents were dead, but even if they weren't they'd cast Cephy out. Arlo likely had better things to do. Aeron wasn't an option, the way she'd treated Cephy. Where did someone, who had nowhere to run, go? It bugged Rachael more every day that Cephy was gone.

"Rachael?" Ailis's voice pulled her back into the room. They were sitting opposite each other on the floor in her room. Ailis was trying her best to help Rachael find the source of her gift, but Rachael still felt nothing.

"I'm sorry," she said. "Let's start again."

Ailis sighed. "No, you need a break. You've been pushing yourself too hard since you met the Sparrows."

"And it's done me no good, has it? It's not enough,

I'm still useless to you." Most of all to Cephy, but Rachael wasn't about to say it. Ailis was doing her best not to bring it up, so neither would Rachael. There was nothing else they could do except move on and focus on her lessons.

"That's not true," Ailis said. "You might not even need magic to defeat King Aeric. All these lessons might be unnecessary."

Hollow words. How else would she reach the best guarded man in Rifarne? His guards wouldn't let her walk up to him and stand by as she killed him. Even if they did, the king would know how to defend himself. Getting close enough to try was one issue—a big one, at that—but defeating him was another problem.

"You know that's not true." People kept telling her she wasn't useless, promising they wouldn't leave her, while she wasn't making any progress and Cephy was still missing. Just once she wanted them to be honest with her.

"I know the prophecy wasn't specific," Ailis said. "It only said you would kill the king. It didn't say how you have to do it. And if you think about it, it didn't even say that much. It says you'll lead us to victory, but that could mean you'll lead someone else to the king, who then kills him."

Rachael sighed. Ailis had a point, but she just couldn't picture his defeat without magic and she couldn't get herself to believe that it didn't have to be her. The Sparrows had infiltrated the prison several times. If they wanted, she was sure they could infiltrate the castle too. If morale was enough, she wouldn't need to be here for it. She wouldn't even be in the prophecy.

Rachael got up. "Is Cale outside?"

Ailis hesitated. "He went into the White City to buy supplies. Why?"

She was suddenly desperate for fresh air. "Because I want to be alone for a while."

With long steps, Rachael hurried away from the house. Staying here had been great at first, but now the house was nothing but a reminder of everything she wasn't.

She wasn't good enough for the Sparrows or their belief in her.

She wasn't good enough for Cephy to stay.

She definitely wasn't good enough to go through with this crazy plan.

Even Ailis had given up on teaching her. Why else would she say the lessons might be unnecessary? Rachael was no closer to finding her source of magic than she'd been as a newborn baby. She wasn't going to find it tomorrow either or any time soon, so maybe Ailis was right. Rachael wanted to help the Sparrows, let their sacrifices mean something, but she didn't know how and that was more frustrating every day.

The night Cephy had run away, Rachael had hoped she'd merely stepped out for a bit, maybe to the nearby lake. But after two weeks without a sign, Rachael couldn't pretend that was the case any more. Cephy had left her, and only Cephy knew why.

Cephy had promised she wouldn't leave—the one person Rachael had trusted—but she'd left after all. If Rachael couldn't trust Cephy, she couldn't trust Cale and Ailis either. It was better to expect the inevitable than to spend her life hoping for something that would never happen.

Rachael fell onto the grass by the lake. The impact

when she hit the ground knocked the air out of her, but she ignored the pain. Spring had come early. Its heavy downpours had washed away the last of the snow and the sun was slowly getting stronger, but it was still cold and the ground hadn't thawed completely.

Disheartened, Rachael looked around. Cephy could sense nearby animals, but all Rachael could do was see the birds perching on a nearby branch and watch the rabbit drink from the lake. Without her eyes, she wouldn't have known they were there. Cephy had known with her eyes shut.

Rachael picked up a rock and threw it as far as she could into the water. Small ripples spread over the lake where it sank. Cale should have picked Cephy. Prophecy got it wrong—Cephy was better suited to this role.

Although, part of the prophecy had come true. Cephy had betrayed her by leaving. Could Cale be right? Could Cephy be this Fox the Sparrows were so scared of?

Not that it mattered. Cephy was gone, so the Sparrows didn't have to worry about her any more.

Rachael relaxed into the cold grass and squeezed her eyes shut. The thick leaves were good cover from the sun, but a few stubborn rays found their way through the branches anyway and made the darkness behind her eyes dance with brightness.

"Rachael?"

She jumped to her feet, her heart racing. Cale's eyes clouded over with a deepening frown.

"*Cale*. Can't you—" She couldn't ask him to knock since she was outside, but she felt like he should have said *something*. Something gentle, so she wouldn't jump.

He smiled apologetically and walked closer. "Ailis said you went out for a bit to clear your head."

She frowned. "I was."

"If you need to talk to someone, I can—"

"If you wanted to talk, Cale, you should have talked to Cephy."

Her words were sharper than she'd intended, but they were out now and she wasn't going to take them back. So what if it was her fault Cephy was gone? Cale and Ailis hadn't helped.

His shoulders slumped and he slowly sank to the ground like a wounded man. "I'm sorry. I know we weren't fair on her."

"Being sorry won't bring her back."

"I know. I tried to find her, Rachael. Please believe me. It's hard to track someone once they leave the White City. There are so many different roads she could have taken, all of which split into more roads. I would have had to follow her as she was leaving to have a chance."

Rachael closed her eyes in defeat. Over the last two weeks, he'd explained this so often but it didn't help. She no longer believed the words. She never really had.

"Are you sure that's why you haven't found her?"

"Of course, I'm a good tracker. What other reason would there be?"

Her fingers dug into the dirt. "The prophecy. That stupid thing naming her as the Fox. You said yourself that the other Sparrows wouldn't trust her if they knew. Are you relieved she's gone, Cale? Are you glad she can't interfere with your ridiculous plot?"

"Rachael, I'd never—"

"Wouldn't you? I don't even know you. Or Ailis or Arlo. You're all strangers to me. Cephy was all I had, and now she's gone and you're grateful she left."

Rachael hated herself for it, but she couldn't help it—she started to cry. The tears she'd held back for so long finally blurred her vision. She barely made out Cale's silhouette until his arms wrapped around her and held her as she cried.

"*Let me go.*" She scratched his skin, punched his chest, bit his arm, but it was no use. Cale was much stronger than her and refused to let go no matter how deep her teeth went, no matter how much blood her nails drew.

He didn't speak. He simply held her until she stopped struggling and sank into his arms, where she cried and screamed until there were no tears left.

After years of trying, life had broken her.

"You're wrong," Cale said. "Cephy wasn't all you had. You have me, and you have Ailis. Arlo is far away right now, but you'll always find refuge in his home. We'll never turn you away. You only need to ask."

She wanted to hate him—how she wanted to punch him and make his lies stop—but she couldn't. All his words did was cut a little deeper.

"I know there's nothing I can say to change your mind, so let me show you."

"How?"

He made it sound so easy. Someone like her couldn't just ask a stranger for help and receive it. She'd tried years ago, when she'd still been naïve, but Blackrock had taught her differently every time. Kindness like that didn't exist. Not for people like her. People with magic. Homeless, orphaned people with magic, who'd grown up in the dirt and hoped for other people's unwanted leftovers just to live another day.

"I don't know," Cale said. "I would put down my life to save yours, but I'd prefer not to get you into such a situation. Just look at where you are. You're right outside the White City. You can see King Aeric's castle from your window, and his guards are all over the city. If I wanted to betray you, I could have turned you in when we arrived. King Aeric would pay a lot of gold for just a hint about your location. Imagine what he'd pay me if I handed you over. I could bargain for my Sparrows' freedom."

She was sick of his excuses. How had his lies ever fooled her? "You wouldn't. I know where the Sparrows are hiding."

"We have more than one hideout, Rachael. Not all are here, in the capital. If I wanted to turn you in, I'd move them out first and then your information would gain King Aeric nothing."

Her legs were shaking. She sank deeper into Cale's arms and hated herself for being too weak to break free. How was she supposed to assassinate the best protected man in the country when she couldn't even escape this one's arms?

"You're lying." But her voice had lost all energy like the rest of her.

"I'm not. If you want, I'll show you where our other hideouts are. I'll take you to each of them personally and you can stay for as long as it takes to convince yourself that they are ours."

"Why?" She'd pegged him for a better strategist than that.

"Because, Rachael, while you don't trust me, I trust

you. I don't know how to prove it to you short of dying for you but as I said, I'd rather not get us into that position; although, I don't think we'll have a choice much longer. When the time comes, I hope my actions will change your mind."

Her heart clenched. She didn't want Cale to die, least of all because of her. He could lead an army. He could make a difference. She was just another unwanted orphan.

"I'm truly sorry about Cephy. I tried everything, but the truth is that she could be anywhere by now." Rachael believed him. "You have every right to be upset, but I need you to move on. Cephy chose this. She's a smart girl—she'll get by. You know better than anyone that she can defend herself."

Rachael forced a smile; he was right about that.

"You've been a great friend to Cephy while you were together, but she's old enough to make her own decisions."

"She's a child."

"A mature one. She wouldn't have left if she didn't think it the best decision."

Rachael hated to admit it, but Cale was right again. Cephy was young, but she wasn't stupid and she'd grown up fast in the time they'd spent together. Because of everything Rachael had taught her, Cephy could look after herself.

She braced herself. "I can't do this, Cale."

"Okay."

Rachael let him hold her while his response sank in. She'd expected a lecture or a speech, not acceptance.

"I don't understand how prophecy works, Rachael. But I know that sometimes, it's not how hard you try that matters. Sometimes, you need to accept things as they are and work with what you've got. I don't care that you can't find the source of your magic. If you don't kill King Aeric with magic, maybe you'll stab him with a dagger instead. Maybe he'll be so terrified of you and the prophecy that he'll take one step back too many and fall out of a window when he sees you. Don't worry about the *how*, Rachael. I believe in you, even if you don't. I know you'll try, because you've been trying since I brought you here. That's all I ask. Prophecy will see itself fulfilled if it's meant to be."

Rachael couldn't remember the last time she'd been held like this. It was nice. Comforting. Knowing he didn't care was soothing—it meant she couldn't disappoint him. She wanted to believe him, even trust him and Ailis, and for the first time since they'd met, she thought that she could.

Cale needed to put space between him and Rachael. Holding her like this was too close, too personal. He couldn't allow his feelings to get in the way of what he needed to do. How could he fight a war if he let his emotions blind him? He'd tried it once and it had shown him that it wasn't possible.

He pulled Rachael closer for a moment. It hurt to see her so fragile and so defeated, but if holding her and believing in her made her feel safer then he'd do both every day until he died. Or he'd do the latter, anyway. Holding her every day would be difficult with all this necessary distance between them.

Maybe, once this war was over, he'd tell her how he felt, but it wouldn't accomplish anything. Rachael hadn't shown any interest and he couldn't fault her paranoia. Suspicion was healthy, especially in times like these. If it kept her alive, then so be it. Even if it meant that she didn't trust him.

Once Rachael had calmed down, she could go back inside and he could train behind the house. His sword in his hands always calmed him. It was just what he needed before he said something he'd regret.

King Aeric was growing impatient. There were rumours of him forging strange alliances. Cale couldn't be sure, but he was worried this mysterious alliance involved Aeron. There was only one way forward if it did. King Aeric had stalled until now, but Aeron was impatient. She'd convince him war was the only way.

Cale let go of Rachael and gently pushed her away. "Are you feeling better?"

Her tears had dried, but her eyes were still red and puffy.

"A little."

She didn't look like it. Her body had sacked in his arms as if the fight had gone out of her, but at least she wasn't crying anymore. Her sobs had hurt him deeper than any wound, because there was little he could do to stop her pain.

Cale would have loved to bring Cephy back, but the girl knew how to hide. He suspected it was a result of having been homeless and of having had Rachael as her teacher. Even if Cephy had run to Aeron, he wouldn't have known where to look. She had more than one lair and wouldn't give up Cephy a second time.

But that was the worst-case scenario. He wouldn't jump to conclusions.

“Why don’t you go back inside?” he said. “Ailis will make you a tea, it’ll help you feel better.”

Rachael nodded and moved away, but stopped after a few steps. “Where will you go?”

“I’ll be right here outside the house if you need anything.”

He reminded himself that she only asked to be polite, not because she cared.

Chapter Twenty-Nine

The Sparrows' hideout was nearly empty this time. Rachael was sitting at a table in the large room she'd been in before, but without all those excited people crowding around her it looked like a different space. There was a table on the other end with maps and markers. Chairs and smaller tables lined the room on each side. She observed Cale as he discussed the next raid with four other Sparrows over one of the maps.

She wanted to join them—not just in the discussions but on the raids—but Cale wouldn't let her. He'd been reluctant to let her come along at all, in case a guard saw them and realised who she was. Not that she would have been much use to them anyway. She couldn't fight and she had no useful magic, but she wanted, *needed*, to do something helpful. She knew she'd only get in the way if she insisted, and she hated it.

Kiana's bright red hair entered the room. It was like a beacon in the otherwise dimly lit room; not noticing her would have been impossible. She walked over and sat down on the table, one leg crossed over the other.

Her bright green eyes smiled at Rachael. "How's

Cale treating you?"

Rachael shrugged. How was he supposed to treat her? The Sparrows were excited to see her amongst them, some even treated her with a reverence she found extremely awkward, but Cale was reluctant to put her in danger whereas the others seemed to want to fight beside her.

"He's been kind to me."

She wasn't sure how else to put it. He and Ailis had fed her twice a day, sometimes three times, and they'd given her a room with a soft bed. She'd even put on a bit of weight thanks to Ailis. The oils Ailis had given her put a shine into her hair. She felt better since Ailis had healed her, too. Her body felt stronger and her mind was sharper. In fact, she'd never been so healthy. She liked Cale and Ailis, could maybe even trust them with a bit more time. But she was missing something she couldn't quite put her finger on, and that pulled a veil over their generosity.

"They've both been kind," Rachael said.

Ailis looked after her most of the time since Cale was often out during the day to hunt or buy supplies. When he wasn't doing either, he was with the Sparrows.

Kiana winked at her. She was like a cat that had claimed the highest position and relaxed until it was time to pounce. Dressed in brown leather and with twin daggers at her hips, she looked every bit the hunter. The bruise from before was gone, but the small cut on her cheek looked fresh. Neither seemed to bother her. Rachael was grateful Kiana was on their side.

Kiana smiled. "You're in good hands, Rachael. I know what you've been through and how hard this must be, but Cale won't let anyone as much as scratch you."

Rachael frowned. "How would you know what I've been through?"

Kiana looked like she might well have been a thief-turned-hunter. Rachael couldn't imagine her struggling to survive. If she were hungry, she'd kill a deer or take the still-warm pie from the window sill.

Kiana shrugged. "Cale told me." Rachael thought she saw a light dim in Kiana's eyes, but it must have been the weak light from the oil lamps. "Well, that, and I used to live on the streets too. Not here—in Tramura's capital, Grozma. I grew up there."

Rachael felt herself drawn to Kiana. She couldn't have been much older than Rachael, but unlike Rachael, she was strong and unapologetic. If someone had prophesied her killing the king, she'd have drawn her daggers and thrown herself into the challenge. At least, Rachael couldn't imagine any other reaction.

"How long have you been here?" Rachael asked.

"About five years. We have scouts all over the place, and one of them recruited me. Reeve. He also found you in Blackrock, but he had orders from Cale not to interfere directly. We had to know it was really you, that you wanted to survive."

Rachael's head was spinning. There'd been a Sparrow in Blackrock? A Sparrow that had watched her, maybe every day, and she hadn't realised it?

Kiana giggled, a joyous sound of mischief that matched the gleam in her eyes. "Don't feel bad, our scouts are good. Reeve especially takes his job very seriously. If they don't want to be found, you'll never know they were there. I've trained a few of them."

Rachael's heart was racing. If they had scouts all

over Rifarne, maybe she could use them. "Who do they look for? Does Cale tell them?"

Kiana's smile faded but didn't disappear completely. "You're wondering about your friend. Cale mentioned you've recently lost someone close to you." Rachael nodded. "Cale has told his scouts to look for her, but he also told me that she has some powerful magic. She's skilled for her age, from what I understand."

Rachael doubted Cale had told them everything—they'd never look for someone they suspected of being the Fox—but she was grateful he was trying.

"Gifted children often can't control their magic, especially if it's an element they haven't practised before," Kiana said. "If your friend doesn't want to be found, she might be using her gift to conceal herself without realising it. Our best scouts won't have much luck if that's what she's doing. They are successful as often as they are because their targets don't know we're looking for them. If your friend is as clever as I've heard, she'll suspect Cale might come looking for her."

Rachael sighed. It didn't soothe the pain in her chest.

She focussed on something else. "Do you think we can win this war?"

"War?" Kiana laughed. "Rachael, this is no real war. Now, the sorcerers of the old world, they knew how to fight each other. Don't let Cale's war speech intimidate you." If Rachael had thought Arlo and Cale odd, then Kiana beat them both. "I think we have a good chance of winning." Kiana winked. "We have you, don't we?"

Rachael scowled. "I told you before, I don't know how to control my gift."

"And *I* told *you* before, we've got your back. You

might not be able to get to King Aeric on your own, but we can clear the way for you." A playful spark lit up her eyes. "Or are you saying you don't trust me with these?" Kiana pulled one of her daggers out of its sheath, twirled it between her fingers, and threw it into the air. She caught it between two fingers. The blade came close to Kiana's skin several times, but Rachael doubted it was ever close to cutting her. She pitied whoever had to fight Kiana.

Rachael smiled and shook her head. "I think you can handle yourself."

Kiana lovingly ran the blade between her fingers as it slid back into the leather.

"See? You've got nothing to worry about while I'm alive, and I promise you I don't die easily. Ask any White Guard in this city." Her smile turned mischievous. "Oh, wait. I killed the ones that attacked me. Never mind."

Rachael laughed. Despite only just having met Kiana, Rachael knew beyond a doubt that she could trust her. She was so unlike anyone Rachael had ever met, so sure of herself. Kiana had fought for and earned every ounce of her confidence. If Kiana said she could trust Cale, maybe she really could. She couldn't just change her mind no matter what Kiana said, but she wanted to try harder.

Three men had approached Cephy two days ago. She'd only left the main road for a few minutes to get fresh water from a nearby stream, which she'd heard with her magic-sharpened senses, but they'd followed her and cornered her. They had threatened her with things she couldn't repeat.

She'd tried not to use her magic, but she'd seen that she couldn't slip past them and it had leaked out of her. They'd burned to ashes by the stream, away from prying eyes.

Cephy was grateful no one had seen it—she didn't need any more trouble—but she hadn't meant to kill them. She'd only wanted to escape.

Some of their money had survived in their ashes, so she'd taken it for later. She needed money if she wanted to eat, and they didn't need it any more.

There'd been no sign of Aeron anywhere. Cephy had travelled in the wrong direction. She didn't know for how long. Aeron was probably on the other end of Rifarne by now, warm and well-fed, while Cephy was fading away.

She sank into the comfort of a hard tavern chair, exhausted after another long day of walking. Her feet were aching terribly, and her stomach even more so. It was mild outside, but the chill from lack of food and sleep had seeped under her skin. Most tavern owners had let her sleep with the animals, and while they were friendly enough Cephy hadn't dared nod off completely. You never knew who was watching—Rachael had taught her that.

She'd followed a merchant, hoping he'd have coin to spare. When he'd left the main road, she followed him, just in case her magic leaked out again. She'd asked nicely for food or money, whatever he could spare, but he had ignored her, laughed at her when she was persistent and threatened her when she hadn't gone away. He had grabbed her arm and balled his free hand into a fist and she had panicked. Her magic had leaked out again. She didn't want to hurt him, but it had burned him to ashes. She was ashamed of it, but she'd saved what little money hadn't melted from his charred remains.

To scold herself, Cephy bit down on her lip, hard. If her magic hadn't leaked out, the merchant would have reported her to the authorities. It was better this way. Rachael had taught her to do what was necessary to stay alive. Cephy wished killing him hadn't been necessary, but he hadn't given her a choice.

She felt guilty for spending his money now, but if she didn't his death would have been pointless. She'd only ordered a pie, because she didn't want to be greedy. The money would have to last for a while, so, even though the sugary bakes sure were tempting, she rationed herself.

She couldn't wait to go back to Rachael and live with Cale and Ailis. Ailis could bake for them then. Until then, Cephy would wait and save what little money she had.

The promise of a real bed was too much. She asked the innkeeper for a room and was relieved when he didn't charge too much.

She'd pray for the poor merchant tonight as she'd prayed for those other men that had followed her to the river. Rachael didn't believe in the Maker and Cephy herself doubted his existence, but if they were wrong she wanted the merchant to have a good afterlife, at least. She owed him something. This was all she could do for him.

Cephy opened the door, and it creaked. The room was small but had a bed, a small table with a chair, and a chamber pot. There was even a small wardrobe. It wasn't fancy or comfortable, but after all these nights of sleeping between cows and horses it was better than good enough.

Exhausted, Cephy sat down on the bed and ignored the hard straw digging into her skin. She closed her eyes to let the feeling of having a bed under her tired bones sink in.

Her floorboards creaked.

Cephy jumped up, ready to defend herself if she needed to—

And her heart soared and fell at the same time.

"Aeron!"

The Mist Woman smiled. "Now, now, is that how you greet an old friend?"

"You're not—" But her old injuries no longer mattered. She had finally found Aeron; she wasn't about to ruin it. "How long have you been here?"

"In this room? Mere moments, my Fox. Around you, watching your every step?" A sly smile ruined her pretty features. "For about two weeks."

Cephy was so angry she wanted to hurl the next best object at Aeron's beautiful head. If only she had any objects to spare.

"Why didn't you say anything?"

"Because I needed to know that you are strong enough to be my student, of course. You remember the suffering your hands underwent before, I trust?"

Cephy swallowed. How couldn't she?

"There will be worse in your future if you come with me. I needed to know that you can take a bit of pain before making my decision."

Cephy felt the colour drain from her face. Aeron was going to do worse? Could Cephy let her?

She clenched her hands in defiance. Yes, she could.

If it meant learning to control her gift and helping in this war, helping Rachael, then she'd bear it.

"And what have you decided?" Cephy asked.

Her terrible smile extinguished what little light there'd been in Aeron's eyes. "My, haven't you grown. You have become feisty in my absence. I shall need to teach you respect, my Fox."

Her legs were shaking, but Cephy didn't move. She wouldn't be intimidated. Aeron couldn't see how terrified she was.

Aeron laughed. "You have grown quite a bit, it seems. I will take you with me. I will teach you to control your gift and use it as I see fit."

Cephy straightened and nodded. Maybe Arlo could fix her once more when her training was over.

"Thank you."

Aeron's smile would have been pretty on anyone else. On Aeron, it looked like the Dark One's bride had come to toy with Cephy's soul.

"It is late and we cannot waste time. Grab your things and we shall be off."

Cephy wanted to protest, but she picked up her small bag and went to Aeron.

Everything was on fire. The sizzling flames devoured everything in their path except the screams of the injured. Rachael had hurt her leg in the fall. Careful not to make it worse, she got up, putting as much weight on the bone as she could bear. It shot white-hot aches through her leg and up her body, but it wasn't broken. A small victory.

The flames had formed a vicious circle around her. If any part of her touched the fire, she'd burn to ashes, she was sure of it; she didn't want to find out the hard way.

There was nothing she could use around her. There was no sign of Cale or the other Sparrows, either. She was cut off from the rest of the city.

"How does it feel to be helpless?"

The shock of hearing that voice again was almost too much. It stung more than the pain in her leg, more than the burns on her skin. Rachael stared at the small figure on the other side of the flames. She hadn't changed a bit—apart from the light in her eyes. That had become a vicious gleam.

Still, Rachael had to try. "What do you—"

A deadly ball of fire whizzed past her ear. Her skin had to be singed, but Rachael didn't dare touch it. This wasn't the time to mourn small hurts. Not when her regret was glaring at her from across the flames.

The girl she'd once known threw another fireball at her. Rachael jumped out of its way, but felt the heat of her prison when she got too close. She needed to get out, or she'd burn.

"I asked you a question."

Rachael had no answer. If it weren't for the evidence in front of her, she wouldn't have believed it to be the same girl. She looked the same, but she sounded so much like Aeron. It stung to even think it, but she emanated a similar aura of evil, too.

"What happened to you?" Rachael asked.

Another fireball barely missed her. She couldn't win this; even if she could control her magic, it'd be useless against something like this. Her only hope was that she was still alive. Her old friend was toying with her.

The ring of hungry fire around her flared up. Her old friend stepped through like it was any normal door, more flames already sizzling in her hands. No magic in the world would save Rachael from this madness.

The girl's smile was darker than moonless midnight. "And how does it feel to know you're about to die?"

"Stop it. Please." But there was no point. Better to say the one thing she'd been dying to say ever since her old friend had left Cale's house than to die with it still unspoken on her lips. "I'm so sorry, Cephy."

Rachael woke with a gasp and bathed in sweat. She sat up, grabbed for something to hold on to but only found the soft fabric of her blanket. She needed something else, something that could steady her while she trembled and calmed down. Her heart was racing, her breathing too fast as sweat trickled from her temples onto her neck and left her shivering.

This wasn't the incomprehensible swirl of colourful fog and muted voices she'd been having lately. It had been a vision, and no amount of wishing otherwise would change it.

Rachael clutched her forehead with her free hand. She wouldn't accept this. Her visions had always been this clear, yes, but this had to be something else. It had felt *real*, not like a possible future she could avoid if she took all the right steps. The unforgiving heat of the fire had felt real. Cephy's merciless glare had been real.

A nightmare. Nothing more.

Rachael had worried about Cephy ever since Cephy had gone missing, and she'd felt inferior because Cephy could control her magic. Of course her dreams would feed off that. Nothing odd about that.

She didn't dare close her eyes so soon after the dream, so she sat still on her bed and focussed on the sliver of moonlight that fell in through the window. Once her heart was beating normally again, she got up and put on the jacket she'd been working on with Ailis's help. Ailis was far better at knitting and Rachael wasn't sure she even wanted to learn the craft, but Ailis had insisted on making her something to keep her warm. It wasn't quite finished and her lack of skill showed in the stitching, but it was cosy and felt like a hug. Rachael was grateful for the normality.

She sat back down on her bed, but she was too alert to sleep now. The dream was fading, but the feelings off terror and helplessness remained. She had promised herself she would get her act together after she'd broken down in front of Cale. His words had comforted her. Thanks to him, she no longer felt bad that she couldn't sense the source of her magic. If Cale said he believed in her even when she didn't, then she could believe at least that much. It wasn't quite trust yet, but it was a big step towards it.

Only, he'd been more reserved since their conversation. He went into the White City on most days to meet with the Sparrows, to get supplies, and sometimes for raids on the prison. The last raid had been a week ago, and he'd returned so bloodied Rachael and Ailis had feared for his life. Ailis had bandaged his cuts. Rachael had helped too, washing the dried blood off him where it didn't feel too intrusive. It was the least she could do. Ailis had put him on bed rest for the rest of the night, but he was up and training again come morning.

Rachael had asked him several times if she could

come with him into the city, but he insisted it was too dangerous. Security had increased. They weren't willing to risk Rachael's life just because she wanted a change of scenery. His words had hurt—she wasn't bored, she genuinely wanted to help—and she'd let him withdraw from her after that. Instead, she had joined Ailis more often. She helped with the cooking, the cleaning and tidying, and sometimes the knitting, but she wasn't any good at those and still felt like she wasn't doing anything. War was coming—a war Cale said only she could win—and here she was, knitting jackets and boiling potatoes.

A faint noise from downstairs startled her, and she shot back to her feet. It sounded like someone was panting. The *thud* of something heavy hitting wood was there, too. Rachael hugged herself; was something breaking in? Ailis was sleeping downstairs—Rachael wouldn't be able to sneak past someone breaking down the door to warn her. She didn't think Cale was home since he rarely slept here. There was a ledge under her window, but she'd have to jump. She could steal around the house and knock on Ailis's window.

Rachael pushed her window open and stuck her head out. The panting and thuds got louder. She pulled her head back into the room and clamped her hands over her mouth. Whoever it was, they were *right there* under her window.

Relief washed over her. If she hurried, she could get to Ailis through the house after all.

But first she needed to know what they were facing. Careful, she stuck her head out again. The trees blocked most of the moonlight, but she could see enough. She sank to the floor with a heavy sigh and a smile; Cale was training behind the house. No robber, no guards—just Cale who also couldn't sleep.

He'd been more determined after the last raid, but training at this hour seemed excessive even for him. Still, she felt better hearing him below. If beating up his training dummy helped him, she wouldn't interfere.

Although… Maybe there was something she could do. Rachael pulled the jacket tightly around her nightdress and silently hurried downstairs. She didn't want to give Ailis the fright Cale had given her only moments ago. Careful not to make a sound, she opened the front door and slipped outside. The cold grass between her toes told her she'd forgot to put on shoes, but she was too nervous to turn around now.

Cale didn't seem to notice her when she walked around the house, so she watched for a moment, unsure when the best moment would be to let him know she was here. This wasn't like the time he'd sneaked up on her. She hadn't wielded a heavy two-handed sword. It looked too big for him, but he swung it with ease. She could see why the White Guard was on their toes—Cale was a natural who made the heavy weapon look light. In the dim light of an oil lamp he'd placed on a barrel next to the training dummy, she could see the sword was intricately decorated down the middle. She was too far away and Cale too fast to see what it said, if it said anything.

Her heart was pounding when she stepped closer and cleared her throat. Cale lost his footing and missed his target. He stumbled over his own feet and looked like he was going to fall, but caught himself in the last second.

Her voice caught in her throat. He could have

impaled himself because of her.

Cale spun around and saw her. “Rachael!” He smiled, if a little awkwardly. “What are you doing out here at this hour?”

She blushed. This hadn’t gone at all like she’d hoped. “I couldn’t sleep and heard you out here, so I thought— I’m sorry I made you jump. I didn’t mean for you to—”

Cale laughed. “You think you made me jump? All the men of the White Guard couldn’t sneak up on me, Rachael. You’ve got nothing to apologise for.”

“But I saw you step over your own feet. You nearly fell.”

He looked at the ground. “You caught me unaware, is all.”

She smiled and walked up to him. His skin was glistening with sweat, but he didn’t look tired. He wasn’t even out of breath. He’d returned from the marketplace outside the city gates in the early afternoon with fresh fish and some spices Ailis had asked for. He’d come out here almost right away. Had he been training this whole time? His wounds were still healing, and he still wore bandages. Ailis could have healed them faster, but he wanted to feel the pain. He said it was a reminder to do better. Some of the bandages had loosened from the training. Blood seeped through here and there. If he was capable of this much effort while he was hurt, she could see why King Aeric worried.

He wiped the sweat from his forehead. “Bad dreams?”

Embarrassed, she nodded. He didn’t know the half of it.

"I'll ask Ailis in the morning to make you a tea so you can sleep. That should—"

She shook her head. Her visions were finally returning. They were the one thing she could do with her gift, even if she couldn't control them. She wouldn't risk losing them again because of some stupid nightmare.

"It's fine."

Cale nodded and leaned on his large sword. "Why did you come outside? Needed some fresh air?"

"I was hoping…" For a moment, she considered backing out, but then changed her mind again. Her magic would likely be useless in the war. She needed something she could do to help. "I want you to train me. I want to be able to defend myself when we attack."

Cale stared at her. "You want me to teach you how to use a sword?"

She nodded, determined to stay until he agreed.

"I'm all for you knowing how to defend yourself, but this isn't something you can learn in one night," Cale said. "We might have to move in one month or next week or maybe even tomorrow. You won't—"

"I know, but I'm sick of sitting inside doing nothing. I'm your Sparrow, aren't I? Let me do something, Cale. Let me help you win this war."

He looked her up and down, meeting her eyes last. She didn't dare blink even when her eyes began to hurt. If this was a test of her resolve, she would pass it.

"Okay," Cale said, and she grinned. It was a start. "I don't have any spare swords here right now, but you can try this dagger." He nodded to the almost-empty weapon rack against the wall. There was nothing on there besides the dagger and a bow. “If you still want to do this tomorrow, we’ll go into town together and find you a sword.”

Rachael couldn’t remember the last time her heart had raced because she was excited, not scared. Her smile was full of nerves. She picked up the small weapon from the too-large weapon rack and remembered Kiana twirling it through her fingers.

An amused smile lit up Cale’s eyes. “Not like that. Here, let me show you.” He took her hand into his and readjusted the dagger until her fingers were loosely but surely closed around the hilt.

“There, that’s better. Try hitting the hay stack now.”

She faced the stacked hay squares Cale had attacked and lunged herself at them, burying the tip of the dagger inside the hay. She tripped and fell forwards when the hay resisted more than she’d expected.

“Not bad. Stand like this.” He put one foot in front of the other, his knees slightly bent, and waited for Rachael to copy him. “Good. Don’t move your whole body when you attack, we can focus on that later. Now, attack.”

Adrenaline rushed through her. Rachael’s heart was racing when the dagger pierced the hay, and it raced even faster when it earned her an approving nod from Cale.

She was finally doing something useful. Even if she never learned to control her visions, she’d be able to defend herself to some small degree. She wouldn’t be helpless. She had a purpose again, a goal, and it gave her enough energy to keep her going until the sun rose above the trees.

Chapter Thirty

King Aeric had never regretted a decision as much as this one. He had been wrong to call a Mist Woman for help, unforgivable, and he knew he wouldn't live to tell his children about it. Not that he had any. This war had kept him busy for so long; he hadn't had the time for things such as raising a family or finding a suitable wife. Both would give his people hope and return normality to his country once the war was over, but until then he had more urgent things to worry about.

He paced around his throne room. The Mist Woman wasn't in the room with him yet, but that she was nearby was enough to put him on edge.

King Aeric stopped and clenched his fists in anger. He knew everything that was going on in his kingdom, yet Aeron… He knew nothing about her except what everyone seemed to know the moment they saw her—that she meant trouble. He'd lost sleep wondering whether her help would be worth it. She was driven, ambitious, and wanted to see this war end as much as he did, that much he was sure of. How she wished to achieve it… He wasn't at all certain about that, and not only because she hadn't shared her goals. Her methods, however, were bad enough.

He'd had an uneasy feeling in his gut since their first meeting. Aeron was full of ideas—a trait he usually admired—but he had to refuse most of them. He was against magic, yes, and he wanted this fight to come to an end, *yes*, but the things she wanted to do… They were unspeakable. The gifted were still people. Dangerous people without a doubt, but even criminals were his subjects. He had to subdue them, but betray them? He couldn't do that.

He and Aeron had finally agreed—after many hours of arguing back and forth—to simply find out where the Sparrows were hiding, round them up, and give them a choice. They could live in exile or be executed. The heathens of Midoka and Krymistis would take them in, he was sure, so the choice wasn't as cruel as it had first sounded to him. They were witches and sorcerers, but they left him and his kingdom alone. He knew when to be grateful.

But worse than any of Aeron's macabre ideas was that his commander had agreed with the vile woman. Commander Videl hated her as much as he respected his king, but they saw eye to eye when it came to eliminating the enemy. She had a talent for cruelty and he was still set on revenge for his men. King Aeric was sure the commander was going insane with grief, but his old friend denied it whenever King Aeric brought it up.

He sighed and sat on his throne. He couldn't remember the last time he'd felt this exhausted. By now, he was supposed to be married to a fine noble woman from Tramura or maybe Vistria with a son on the way. This war had halted everything. He hated to admit it, but those Sparrows were resourceful. Aeron needed to find them and bring them before him so he could finally do his job.

They were done talking, at least. Today, he'd set their plan in motion. Their imminent meeting would move the players into position and make the first move.

He sighed and sank into his throne. One more week. Then, everything would be over. Maker willing Aeron wouldn't have killed him out of boredom.

A heavy knock echoed through the room. His steward would be greeting his commander and Aeron and grant them entrance. A shiver ran down his spine and made the uneasy feeling grow. He cleared his throat, straightened, settled into his throne. He could act however he wanted while he was alone; it was time to be a king now, and kings had no room for doubt or uneasy feelings haunting their dreams.

The heavy-set doors opened smoothly—a marvel of old Rifarnee engineering—and his guests entered. Commander Videl wore polished white armour and a dark smile. King Aeric couldn't sense the gift, devout believer in the Maker that he was, but he saw it in the air around Aeron now. A dark fog that surrounded her and followed her, more shadow than substance. The Mists.

He gulped but wouldn't show his horror. As soon as this business was concluded, he would have her head. It would be saver for his people and better for his sanity to know she was dead.

Commander Videl bowed, but Aeron didn't look like she was about to do the same. Not once had she shown him the respect that befitted him. Weeks of negotiating and plotting, and not once had she addressed him by his title—at least, not without heavy sarcasm. His commander would be honoured to swing the axe. One more week.

"Your Highness," Commander Videl said.

Aeron remained silent. Was that impatience he saw? He'd take his time over this and watch as she squirmed. It was petty, but she'd give him no other satisfaction yet.

One more week.

He swallowed his pride and offered a courteous nod to them both. "You know why we are here today. I trust everything is in order?"

Commander Videl was about to speak up when Aeron stepped in front of him with that terrible smile. "Everything is as it should be."

She'd regret the tone she was taking with him, but there was something that bothered him even more. The darkness haunting her voice. The glimmer in her eyes. The evil in her twisted grin. Had she disobeyed him? The idea left him seething. Even his commander looked unusually smug, and King Aeric knew disloyalty when he saw it. Videl wasn't even trying to hide it.

He tried his best to stay calm. They'd been friends since childhood; Videl would never betray him. This was her doing, and she would no longer just die for it. She would suffer for turning them against each other.

"Why is it that you are here, in my throne room, when you should be out there rounding up Sparrows?" Many years of practice and being king allowed him to keep his voice controlled while his mind was furious.

Aeron's grin grew colder. "I gave your plan some

more thought after our last meeting, and decided it was insufficient. I have set another in motion."

The insolence! Worse, his people would suffer because of her. Every plan she'd suggested was more gruesome than the last. He didn't want to think which one she'd chosen, but he had to ask so he could prepare.

"What have you done?"

Which evil had she loosened in his city? The public burnings? The public gutting of children until their witch parents handed themselves in?

"You will find out soon enough. I expect the first… afflicted will be mourned very soon." Aeron turned around and walked back towards the doors. "I am done here. Enjoy your new kingdom."

His heart turned cold. She couldn't mean— Maker, had she begun *that* plan? Of all the demonic things she'd come up with… She couldn't leave. He had to deal with her now or he'd never see her again.

"*Do not move another inch.*" His voice was burning with his fury and he no longer cared to contain it. "Guards! Take that woman to the prison."

Five White Guards burst through the doors and crowded around the demon. How could he have been so blind? Had he truly been so cornered that he'd believed her to be the only way out?

Aeron looked at him over her shoulder and forced her hideous grin on him. One by one, his guards exploded. The cold stone floor and far walls ran red with his mistake. Aeron herself was covered in their blood and strings of skin but made no effort to wipe herself clean. His gut heaved. She finally looked like the foul horror she was—the horror he'd seen behind her eyes from the start but hadn't dared acknowledge.

"Do not come after me, *king*, or your fate will be worse than theirs." With that, she vanished into thin air.

His legs were too weak to stand, so he trembled in his throne. Commander Videl had gone ashen and refused to look behind him. Judging by the look on his face, he knew very well what had happened behind his back. Magic had killed even more of his men. He'd be glad to kill Aeron himself, but King Aeric was no longer sure she could be killed. Not with normal swords and bows.

"What is the meaning of this?" His voice had lost all power, but it didn't matter. It was silent enough to hear a mouse in the below kitchen sniff for cheese.

Grim determination settled on Commander Videl's face. "Don't worry, my king. Your country will be free soon, without the pest of magic infesting every corner."

Hearing his old friend's betrayal aloud was too much. King Aeric sank back into his throne. What would be left of his country, his people, when Aeron was done with it? He wasn't sure he still wanted to lead a country he had fought for like this. He wasn't sure he still deserved the crown.

Cale handed Rachael yet another lightweight sword. "Here, try this one."

They had spent all morning browsing the market. Her feet were aching, but she hadn't grown tired of feeling new weapons in her palm or seeing what the other stalls had to offer.

The White City's market was the most amazing

place she'd ever been to. People were everywhere and she often had to hold on to Cale's sleeve to stay together in the crowd, but even so she didn't feel backed into a corner. It was lively, not intimidating. The wonderful smells of spices and meats hung in the air. Accents she'd never heard before rang through the market like the excited chatter of birds first thing in the morning. And around all that she couldn't escape the lively banter as people tried new things and laughed at the beauties of foreign silks or local handiwork. No matter where Rachael looked, people were smiling. The tents were colourful, the merchants enthusiastic, and the crowd was swept up in the sales pitches and offers to try baked or cooked goods. The intensity of it was infectious, and Rachael wanted to see every stall.

Cale hadn't bothered to hide his face. Guards were stationed near the exits and by more expensive sellers, but the crowd was so thick that no one got a good look at any one face for long. Some people recognized him nonetheless, and her heart jumped each time someone greeted him or gave him a knowing nod. So many people knew him and supported the Sparrows. They were perfectly hidden and safe within the dense bustle of the market.

Those same people knew who she was, too. Cale introduced her to a few, yet no one called her *Sparrow*. No one even mentioned their movement. There was a silent understanding between Cale and the city Rachael found so fascinating. She was in the middle of the wolf's clearing—all it would take was a wrong move and the hungry predators would leap, but no one said a word. The bounty on their heads was impressive, yet the others stuck together to keep them concealed instead of going for the gold. She hadn't realised how many supporters outside the Sparrows they had. How many of them were gifted? How many afraid for their lives? For their children's?

Despite their relative safety, Cale had insisted she wear a veil. It was an exotic garment he'd bought the day before, and she enjoyed wearing it. Its colours were vibrant, its fabric so luxuriously soft and rich she never wanted to wear anything else ever again. Compared to her old life, this was bliss.

The sword Cale had handed her lay easily in her hands and her fingers closed around it naturally. Cale had assured her the price didn't matter, but she dreaded to hear it nonetheless. He was excited to teach her to fight and was happy to help, even if that help cost a small fortune.

"How's it feel, my lady?" the merchant asked. "Do you like it?"

Rachael gave it a few careful swings at the training dummy by the stall. It felt right in her hands, a perfect fit between her fingers.

She nodded. "What do these mean?" Beautiful, intricate designs ran along the middle of the blade. They looked similar to those on Cale's sword but seemed to have their own story. If the sun caught the steel at the right angle, they seemed to come alive, dancing across the blade to a music only they could hear.

"They're a charm, my lady. From the old kingdom. To protect and strengthen the bearer."

Cale crossed his arms. "A charm? And they let you sell it here?"

Merchants from Midoka and Krymistis, where the

gifted were accepted, had few stalls in the market, and the ones that were allowed inside the city walls were authorised to sell only spices and fabrics. Given King Aeric's hatred for the gifted, Rachael was surprised he let them into his city at all.

The merchant shrugged. "It's just scribbles, sir. Nothing dangerous."

Cale nodded, his eyes suspicious, and held out his hand to take the sword. Rachael was reluctant to let go, but placed it in his hand after giving it another once-over.

"How much for it?" Cale asked.

"A thousand gold pieces, sir."

Rachael choked. "*A thousand—*"

"Thank you, we'll take it."

"But—"

"Trust me, Rachael, it's fine. There are more expensive swords less worth their price. You like this one, don't you?"

He was right—they'd been looking at more costly swords all morning—but a thousand gold pieces was still a lot of money to her. She could barely imagine a thousand silvers, and that only amounted to one hundred gold. But then she had no real concept of currency. It had never mattered before because she hadn't owned any either way. Five bronze pieces would have been a small fortune to her. If Cale said this was fine, she'd have to trust his experience.

The sword was remarkably beautiful for something made to kill, more art than weapon. She couldn't—didn't want to—take her eyes off it. What did she know? Maybe it was worth ten thousand gold pieces, and maybe that would still have been a bargain for something so… so striking.

Cale opened a small coin pouch and handed over more money than Rachael had ever seen in one place. Just one of those coins would have been a life-changer once.

Cale accepted the sword and turned to her. "Allow me." He wrapped the sheathed sword in its scabbard around her waist and secured it on her new weapon's belt so it wouldn't come loose when she walked. It felt strange on her hip, like the unfamiliar weight had shifted her whole balance, but she liked it. Having a weapon right there by her hands was comforting, even if she had no experience in using it. Maybe it would at least make people think twice before they demanded her possessions—which, she had to admit, hadn't been a problem since she'd left Blackrock. Still, it calmed her old habits.

She couldn't help but keep one hand on the hilt as they walked away from the merchant, because she feared it would fall off if she didn't and because it soothed her.

"Thank you." No one had ever bought her anything, never mind something as beautiful as this. Besides the loaf of bread Cephy had thrown at her feet, this was her first present. Her heart raced, and she blushed. What would he expect in return? She gripped the hilt just a little tighter.

"You're welcome," Cale said. "A good sword is a good companion. You'll miss it when it's not with you, you'll see."

She already missed it, new as it was, and it was right there by her hand. It was like she'd found an old friend she thought she'd lost forever.

"You shouldn't have paid this much, even if it is cheaper than others."

Cale shrugged. "It's a fine weapon, Rachael. Believe me, that trader doesn't know what he lost." He pulled her away from the noisy crowd into a smaller tent of baked goods. "Swords like these are rare. It is said that, back in the old kingdom, swords had a mind of their own. They chose their owners, not the other way around. I think there is a charm on this sword, but not the kind he thinks."

Goosebumps crawled over her arms. She placed a tentative hand on the hilt, perfectly positioned so she could reach it instantly. She found it difficult to let go again.

"What do you mean, they had a mind of their own? How is that possible?"

"Magic isn't forbidden everywhere, Rachael. The southern countries don't just tolerate magic—it's sacred there. The Krymistian warriors use swords enchanted with magic, like yours."

"You mean it's a weapon like that?"

He nodded. "I saw how reluctant you were to hand it over. How did it feel in your hands?"

A smile curled her lips. "Just right. It's light, easy to swing. Warm." She hadn't thought anything of it when she'd first held it, but it *was* odd now Cale had mentioned enchantments. Was her sword made of magic?

"It was cold in my hand," Cale said. "It almost froze my fingers."

Rachael tightened her fingers around the hilt. It was definitely warm.

"How?" Had there always been this much magic in

the world and she just hadn't known where to look, or had it been buried beneath Blackrock's soot?

"It's proof of its magic," Cale said. "These swords are only a perfect fit in the hands of the right person. This is *your* sword, no one else's."

She drew the sword out of its scabbard to take another look. Knowing a bit about its history made it feel all the better by her side, even if Cale's story seemed a little unlikely; although, feeling the hilt's leather between her fingers, she wondered if there was an inkling of truth to it.

Rachael had never dreamed of possessing anything like this, but now she had it she felt like the sword was meant for her. Once again, Cale was right. This was her sword. She'd be worthy of it, whatever it took.

"Thank you."

Cale smiled. "Come on, let's find Ailis."

He took her hand into his and carefully navigated the busy crowd. Ailis had joined them to buy fresh ingredients for their dinners. A Krymistian spice merchant had set up his tent, and Ailis had looked forward to stocking up.

A woman with blue earrings so large they pulled at her ear lopes waved them over. "Fair lady, good sir, over here. Won't you take a look at my wares?"

Rachael had seen jewellery many times around the necks and fingers of Blackrock's wealthier people, but those pieces hadn't been like these. The brightest shades of every colour glistened in the sunshine like they were all diamonds. Rachael had never been interested in finery of any kind—jewellery especially had always seemed unnecessary and pompous to her—but some of these were almost delicate. She didn't want anything, but it wouldn't hurt to look if only to admire the shimmering colours.

She ignored Cale's dismissive wave and entered the tent. Cale sighed and followed her.

The merchant winked at Cale. "A ruby for your love? A sapphire, perhaps?"

Rachael flushed as red as the ruby. "Oh no, we're not—" How could she put into words what they were and weren't when she wasn't sure herself? She only knew they weren't *that*, but it was weird to even think about it.

"We're not a couple," Cale said.

An honest smile spread on the woman's face. "I'm sorry. I assumed, seeing you two hold hands. I meant no disrespect."

"No offence taken. Rachael…"

She cast a last glance over the gemstones. This wasn't why they were here; no matter how safe Cale felt, she knew he'd rather return to the cabin. They had what they'd come for. As much as she wanted to stay and see every last merchant, it'd be better to go home.

"Maybe another time." Cale smiled and ushered Rachael out of the tent, but the merchant wasn't done.

"Just the one, maybe? Allow me." She placed a pretty purple gem around Rachael's neck before Cale could protest. "A gift for the Sparrow, my lady."

The merchant's voice had been quiet enough that no one else could have heard her, but Rachael felt alarmed nonetheless. No one had named her as the Sparrow all day. Cale didn't seem concerned, however, and simply nodded at her kindness.

"I can't accept this," Rachael said. Even though the necklace was delicate, it somehow looked more expensive than her sword with its fine bands lacing around the gem and its flawless shine.

"Please," the merchant said. "As a thank you. If you truly don't like it, you can return it to me any time I'm here."

Rachael ran her finger over the smooth stone. It wasn't excessive or pretentious. She liked the way the sun made it sparkle, its smoothness beneath her finger.

"Thank you."

The merchant smiled. "It's called the Eye of Seers, my lady. For good luck." She took Rachael's hand in hers and gently squeezed it before letting go.

"Thank you," Cale said. "Rachael, we really should go. We've stayed too long already." He turned to the merchant. "Not a word about what you know to anyone."

She inclined her head. "Never."

He took Rachael's hand into his again and pulled her with him. They set one foot outside the tent…

And an uneasy silence fell over the crowd.

"My lady." The breathless fear in the merchant's voice sent cold shivers over Rachael's body. At first Rachael thought the White Guard had found them, but the merchant wasn't looking at Rachael or past her. She was looking up. Rachael followed her horrified gaze and Cale's fearful eyes.

Across the square, on top of a building, stood a woman with an infant in her arms. Her feet were too close to the edge.

Rachael felt sick.

The woman inched closer to the drop. The entire market square had fallen silent and watched as the woman prepared to jump with her baby still cradled in her embrace.

"My lady. Don't look."

Rachael didn't want to, but she couldn't look away. The harder she tried, the more her eyes fixated on the woman on the roof. She couldn't even blink.

The woman's voice shattered the market's silence. "*My child and I are tainted. We are sinners. We free the world of our evil with our death.*"

And she leaned forwards. A scream tore through the crowd when her body hit the ground. Rachael was grateful all these people were blocking her view, but they didn't hide the dull *thud*, the noise of bones breaking and soft insides splashing.

Rachael thought she was going to be sick, but nothing happened. Others weren't so lucky. The sour stench of stomach acid on the air made her gag more.

She could finally look away. Cale was still staring at the spot on the roof, where only moments ago the woman and her child had been alive. His face was white.

"Cale…"

He tore his eyes away from the roof. "We need to leave. Now." He faced the merchant. "You too. Get to safety."

The woman was already packing up her wares. All around them, the market had erupted into chaos. People were screaming. Children were crying for their parents, who they'd lost sight of in the madness.

"We'll run," Cale said, the hard tone of authority heavy in his voice. "Don't look back. Don't worry about what happened. Just get home, as fast as you can."

"But Ailis—"

"Ailis knows what to do in an emergency. She'll be fine. Right now, we need to leave."

The market was mayhem. Rachael grasped Cale's hand so she wouldn't lose him in the chaos. People farther away from the market had started to ask what had caused the uproar, and many were heading back the way she came to see the mess for themselves.

Together, Rachael and Cale dashed through the forest strengthened by adrenaline. Her free hand had clasped the hilt of her sword the entire time, and her knuckles had turned white.

"Get inside."

Rachael knew better than to argue when he sounded like this, like the Sparrow's commander. She saw him walk around the house through the windows, and guessed he was checking the perimeter. She didn't realise she'd been holding her breath until he closed the door behind him, his face dark and creased with worry.

Ailis hadn't returned.

Chapter Thirty-One

Ever since they'd returned from the market, Rachael had felt invisible eyes on her, waiting to strike the moment she let her guard down. Cale was sitting opposite her at the kitchen table with his head between his hands. She had expected him to pace, to think of something, but he seemed as shell-shocked as Rachael and it was unsettling to see him like this. Exhausted. Defeated. Speechless.

She didn't know how long ago they'd returned, only that the shadows hadn't been as long yet and that the sword by her waist wasn't as comforting as she'd hoped. They had sat in stunned silence for a while, but Ailis was still missing. For the first time since Cale had found her and Cephy, Rachael's gut feeling told her to run. But she wouldn't. She was stronger than she'd been, even if most of her strength went into sitting still and waiting for Cale to have an answer. She wanted to rush in and fix this, whatever had happened, but she didn't know where to start. Too many unknowns taunted her.

Rachael had seen many people die. Sick orphans.

Mauled hunters. Starved or mugged families. Nothing like this.

She had witnessed two suicides, too, but she'd never cared. This was a harsh world. If people decided to move on to the next one, she wouldn't judge them. But those people had killed themselves in secret, sneaked out at night from the overbearing eyes of their parents or abusive lovers and husbands. One had stabbed his heart, the other thrown herself off the wall. It wasn't easy to get up there—Blackrock's small town guard did everything it could to make climbing it impossible—but true despair always found a way. Those two people from Blackrock had.

But this today hadn't been secret. The woman had made a public showing out of her last moments, made sure everyone knew she'd been tainted. Rachael's insides twisted at the memory. 'Tainted' could only mean one thing—she'd had the gift, as had her baby. But to go so far... They were all right—Cale, Ailis, Cephy, the Sparrows. Rifarne was sick. It needed help.

"Cale..." She desperately wanted the haunted look in his eyes to go away, but she didn't know what to say. Words wouldn't make this better.

He must have seen people die many times, but his reaction now seemed almost personal. Maybe death was something people couldn't get used to, no matter how often they saw it.

"Her name was Anna." His whisper shook the heavy silence. "She was a Sparrow."

Rachael froze. Had they met? Her stomach twisted harder. Had she talked to the woman? Had Anna been one of those who'd offered her reassurances the first night she'd visited their hideout? There'd been so many Sparrows, and Rachael hadn't known where to look. The room had been dark. It was possible.

"Six months ago, Anna left to look after herself and give birth to her second child. The baby wasn't two months old." He closed his eyes and swallowed. When he opened them again to stare at the table, they were brimmed red. "She was one of the best, Rachael. So brave, so ruthless, but so kind. I don't understand why she'd do this. She loved her gift, hoped her baby would inherit it. Her daughter didn't, so she hoped…" He looked at Rachael with a desperate glint in his eyes. "I didn't know she felt this way. If I'd known how much she hated herself… I could have helped her."

Her throat was tight, but she had to say something, anything. "You couldn't have known. You said it yourself, she's been at home looking after herself and her family for the past six months. A lot can change in that time."

Slowly, Cale nodded. "I guess. And there's nothing I can do about it now. Tomorrow, I'll visit her husband and daughter. Maybe they know what happened."

They jumped when the door flew open and Ailis fell into the room.

"*Ailis*." Cale leaped to his feet and rushed to her.

Ailis looked as haunted as Cale. Her eyes were wide with fear and a nasty gash marred her cheek. Blood had stained her neck and clothes, but she seemed uninjured otherwise. "Thank the Maker. I'm so relieved you're both safe."

Cale cupped the uninjured half of her face in his hand and inspected the cut. "What happened?"

"The market place fell into mayhem after— Oh Maker, Cale. Did you see who it was?" Tears mixed with the blood and Ailis flinched.

"I did," he said. "Take a seat. Let me look at this."

Cale walked Ailis over to a chair, which she slumped into.

"Oh, Cale. Her baby, too." Ailis's voice was choked, her eyes red.

"I know. Have you spoken to her recently?"

Cale dipped a cloth into a clear liquid and held it against the wound. Ailis flinched and squeezed her eyes shut.

"No. I visited her once after the boy was born, but that was the same week he was born. She was so happy that she sensed magic in him. Her husband and daughter were ecstatic, too."

Cale gritted his teeth and swore under his breath. "I bet this is King Aeric's doing. He must have known she was a Sparrow."

Ailis held the cloth to her cheek. "But Anna has moved several times since they saw her face. Most of us didn't even know where she lived."

"Then they tracked her down. They must have found her and forced her to jump."

"But publicly, and even her baby? King Aeric would never—"

"We're at war, Ailis. He declared war today."

Rachael was shaking. Her eyes stung, and she shivered. Cale had only just bought her sword. She hadn't even started to train with it. If King Aeric was no longer holding back and had officially made the first move… What hope did she have?

Ailis shuddered and glared through the pain. "Don't treat me like a child, Cale, I know very well that we're at war. King Aeric has proven that he's ruthless and resourceful, but this is beneath him. He's never agreed to public executions before."

Cale scowled. "And yet Sparrows have hung in the square."

"That wasn't his doing. Do you remember the speech he gave afterwards? Saying his trusted commander had acted without his approval? King Aeric despises the gifted, but he'd never agree to something like this."

Cale scoffed. "No, that's what his prison is for. King Aeric doesn't gut people in the streets, he does it in secret so his loyal subjects never hear the screams and final words."

Ailis looked away. "That's not what I meant."

"It doesn't matter what you meant. We're at war now. Officially. We'll either rise or we'll fall." His icy stare met Rachael, and she shrank in her seat. "Are you ready for that?"

All she could do was stare at him. Was she ready? No. Did it matter? Either way, the end had come.

Cephy lost her footing and fell into the grass. She was exhausted. Her hands ached worse than ever. They were bleeding and worked raw, but it wasn't enough. Aeron would never be satisfied no matter how much she bled. Aeron demanded more no matter how much she suffered.

"Get up."

Even now, after all their failed exercises, Aeron's voice was molten gold. She'd lost her temper only once, and the memory still brought Cephy nightmares. Cephy hadn't been able to do as Aeron asked that time. The spell had proven too difficult for her charred hands, so Aeron had taught her a lesson. She'd taken Cephy into the next town and lured a small child away from his parents. In a clearing away from the town, Aeron had shown Cephy how to use the spell properly. The terror on the poor boy's face haunted her sleepless nights. His screams still made her ears ring.

Aeron had kept relatively calm since then. Cephy wanted to succeed so she could help Rachael, but she was stretched to her limit. She didn't want to learn most of the spells Aeron taught her, but there was no other way. Cephy feared what Aeron would do if she refused again.

"Cephy. Get up." A threat hidden under the sweet trill of Aeron's voice. Cephy had learned to listen for it.

She got up.

"Do it again."

Cephy focussed on that place within herself where her magic slumbered, thought of what she needed to do, pulled her gift forth and released. The hay bale in front of her caught fire. Cephy braced herself; when Aeron asked for an explosion, a small fire wasn't good enough.

To her surprise, no angry outbursts came. No scolding. Instead, Aeron sighed.

"Perhaps you should take a break, my Fox."

It had to be a trick. A test of her resolve.

Cephy shook her head. "No, I'm fine. I'll try again, it'll work this time."

Aeron shook her head, and Cephy stiffened. She feared Aeron's disappointment more than her anger. When Aeron was angry, she got it all out in one terrifying burst, but when she was disappointed, she had time to think of a fitting punishment. Cephy's back still hurt from the fiery lashes she'd received last time.

"Oh, my little Fox. I only want what is best for you."

Cephy nodded. Sometimes, she wished Aeron's best would hurt less.

"You came to me, remember? You asked for my help. I was kind enough to give you my full attention."

Eager to please Aeron and make her forget her disappointment, Cephy nodded. "Thank you, Aeron. I remember."

"Then believe me that this is not easy for me. You are my student, so, as you have been honest with me, I wish to be honest with you. The truth will hurt you, but you must know."

Cephy held her breath. She didn't like the look on Aeron's face one bit.

"What is it?"

"Come here, my Fox." Aeron held out her hands and a bowl appeared amidst swirls of black mist. "Take a look at this."

The bowl was filled to the brim with water. Aeron poured a night-dark liquid into it. The water rippled, but none spilled over.

"It is a mirror, of sorts," Aeron said. "It has allowed me to watch your friends in the White City."

Cephy's heart raced. She could watch Rachael with this? Make sure Rachael was okay? She came closer, excited and anxious to see a friendly face.

But as much as she stared, the liquid remained clear. "Why isn't it showing me anything?"

"Focus on who you want to see. The mirror will show you where they are right now and what they are doing." Aeron leaned in and whispered, "Some people can even hear them talk."

She needed to know that Rachael was all right. According to Aeron, the king had declared war after the suicide of a young gifted mother with her infant. Neither side had made the first move yet, but Rachael had to be in danger. It's why Cephy had driven herself so hard under Aeron, why her hands were blistered and bloody. Time was running out. She had to be ready when Rachael needed her.

The black liquid began to swirl into shapes and colours. Cephy dared not blink in case she missed anything and ignored the sting when her eyes stayed open.

Rachael appeared, and Cephy grinned. Rachael was swinging a sword at a hay bale, just like how she was flinging fire at her target. Cale was with Rachael, motivating her, showing her how to better hold the blade.

Cephy focussed more on Rachael and Cale to get a better view. She was surprised when she heard Cale speak.

"*...possibility*." Cale had that determined look in his eyes she remembered so well. She leaned in as if she'd hear better that way. "If you end up fighting each other, you won't have a choice. If you don't kill her, she'll kill you."

Cephy's heart grew cold. She hadn't heard her name, but... Aeron had told her Rachael would likely betray her, that Cale would convince Rachael and the other Sparrows to kill her if they got the chance. Cephy hadn't believed it. Until now.

Rachael didn't look happy, but that didn't change anything. They were plotting to kill her.

Maybe Rachael hadn't agreed to it. Maybe she wouldn't trust Cale and realise he was trying to set her up.

"*Promise me you'll kill her if you have to.*" Cale's voice had once been so warm and understanding. Now it made her nauseous and her stomach churn.

Cephy didn't want to look at him. Seeing him alone made her angry, but knowing that he was trying to set Rachael against her was too much.

Cephy focussed on Rachael.

"*I promise.*"

She didn't want to hear any more. Her heart ached worse than her blisters and lashes. How could Rachael do this to her? Her magic was boiling inside her, begging for release. Cephy pulled one more time and threw it towards the hay bale.

A deafening explosion tore through the forest. Hungry flames lit up her surroundings and devoured everything in their way.

Aeron extinguished the fire and renewed the hay with a flick of her hand.

"Now you know," she said. "You still love Rachael, but she would kill you in an instant given the chance."

Cephy balled her hands into shaking fists. "I don't. If Rachael tries to hurt me, I'll—" She couldn't say it, but she knew what she had to do. If Rachael tried to kill her, Cephy would kill her first.

Aeron gently cupped her face in her too-soft hands. "I'm sorry, my Fox. I wanted to spare you the burden of knowledge, but you deserve to know the truth. Never forget how her promise made you feel today. Let it fuel your magic, and the Sparrow won't get a chance to lift that sword at you."

Cephy smiled. Her own family had discarded her like rubbish, her neighbours and friends had alerted the White Guard, and now even Rachael wanted her dead. All because Cephy had the gift.

The war had to end, but it wouldn't end well for those who'd hurt her.

Chapter Thirty-Two

King Aeric was grateful that no one could see him weep as he sank onto his bed with his head in his hands. He'd sworn an oath to protect his people when he accepted the crown. Perhaps that was why the crown was such a heavy weight these days. It had become a burden—a reminder of failed vows.

Aeron had unleashed unspeakable atrocities on his people one month ago today. At least fifty people were dead, most of which had killed themselves publicly, but the count wasn't accurate any more. More people died every day and news travelled too slowly to know for sure how many were dead. His people were frightened. They demanded answers he didn't dare give. His country was in chaos, and he didn't know how to help.

Unless the leader of those damned Sparrows, Cale Spurling, gave himself up, he'd be forced to act, but that didn't seem likely. Spurling's indifference and lack of action proved how little the Sparrow cared for Rifarne's people. He'd given Spurling the chance, but many more would die if he kept waiting for the

Sparrow to hand himself in. Spurling didn't care, but King Aeric still cared a great deal.

His people had suffered enough. More than anything, he wanted things to return to normal.

Remembering the deaths he had witnessed himself made him nauseous, but he would remember them anyway, because he felt responsible. A young girl with her infant son had thrown herself off a roof in the busy market square. A five-year-old had thrown himself in front of galloping horses. An elderly woman, revered for her aid and healing skills, had gutted herself during her daughter's wedding by the altar. All fifty people had been cursed with magic.

King Aeric had wanted the war to stop. He had wanted magic to be harmless to his worried subjects. But he hadn't wanted this.

The suicides were no longer restricted to the capital but had spread across the country. He received reports of merchants, inn keepers, parents of large families that killed themselves in the most monstrous ways. What made this situation all the more desperate was that even children were affected.

Why had he ever believed they needed the help of that which they tried to stop? If he hadn't involved Aeron, his people wouldn't have suffered like this.

Magic had to end—it was hard to consider any other option after what Aeron's spell had done this month—but this wasn't humane. Even the worst criminal deserved a trial, yet these people hadn't received it.

And despite all that, Spurling still refused to come forwards. King Aeric rubbed an itch on his head. Maybe it didn't matter. He couldn't convince himself that Aeron would end the curse she had unleashed even if Spurling did present himself and his Sparrows. Aeron seemed to revel in cruelty. Sadly, so did Commander Videl.

So much had changed.

King Aeric wept for the souls of those who'd once believed in him. The Maker celebrated life and its joys above all else; He didn't forgive suicide. They were forced to wander the Mists forever, and King Aeric hated himself for having brought this fate upon them. What would the Maker say about him? Would his regret matter?

He wept for himself, too. He didn't deserve the crown. Maybe, should this nightmare ever end, he'd resign and give it to someone more deserving. It was a shame he had no heir—then again, his people had every right to demand a different bloodline on the throne after this last month.

But then their deaths would have been pointless. They shouldn't have happened but they had, and to render them pointless… No, he'd remain king assuming he survived. He'd live a life in pursuit of redemption in the eyes of his people and the Maker. He owed his people the kingdom so many had given their lives for.

"My, if your people could see their great king now."

Her voice chilled his blood and his bones, but fury burned through the frost. He jumped to his feet and rushed at her. She deserved a beating for intruding on his privacy, for her continued lack of respect, for all she'd done to his people.

"Stay your hand or you won't get the chance at the redemption you're so pathetically desperate for."

King Aeric hated himself for it, but he did as she

said. This was his palace, his people, *he was the damned king*, yet she commanded him so easily. Yes, if only his people could see him now. But he'd seen what she could do with a wave of her hand. One wrong move, one wrong look, and she would incinerate him if the fancy struck her.

So, instead of punching her hard, he bit his tongue and balled his hand into a trembling fist. "I ordered my guards not to let anyone disturb me."

That self-satisfied smile he loathed so much twisted her face into an obscure obscenity. How had he ever thought her beautiful past her flaws? She was as unattractive as a dead dog smeared across the gravel and just as disgusting to the eye.

"Why, my king, if you have skills like mine doors are no obstacles."

"What do you want?"

Aeron had never come to him on a whim. She always wanted or needed something from him; although, he no longer believed that lie. She'd neither wanted nor needed his help. The curse she'd spread proved that his permission meant nothing to her.

"Why so suspicious? I merely came to give you a gift."

"I don't want anything from you. Begone from my chambers." Why was he still making the effort? It seemed he couldn't stop trying. If he had any power over her, his guards would have stopped her, but since she was here and they weren't trying to drag her back outside, he could only assume they were dead, so he prayed for their souls.

He did an awful lot of praying these days. Did that still matter or was it something else that had changed?

He'd believed his entire life, like any good child of the Maker, but his faith had begun to crumble in recent days. Why would the Maker allow these crimes? Weren't the cursed still his children? King Aeric frowned; these thoughts didn't sit well with him.

"I believe you will change your mind, my king. Or have Cale and his Sparrows turned themselves in while I wasn't looking?"

He squinted at her. "What do you mean?"

She stepped up to him, placed one hand on his shoulder, and whispered in his ear, "I know where he's hiding. I know where his Sparrows are hiding. And I know where *the* Sparrow is."

Maker curse her. He couldn't turn down this information—he'd waited all month for it. Curse her for dangling it before him like a juicy cut of meat. Curse her for enjoying his desperation.

"Out with it, woman. Where are they?"

"Hm?" She chuckled. "Don't you want to know what I desire in return?"

The look she gave him froze him right down to the marrow in his exhausted bones. It would have stirred him on any other woman, but on her it was out of place, like a mask that didn't quite fit.

He'd have given her anything if it meant an end to this madness. If it meant closure and the chance to recover for his people. If he had to bed her to please her, then so be it. He'd wanted a wife, hadn't he? His people deserved an end no matter the consequences to himself. It's what a good king would do. It was about time he became one.

"Blast it, woman, out with it."

She sighed. "As you wish. The Sparrows are holed

up in a small building near the western city gate. Follow the main road and take a sharp left at the barber. Follow the road until you reach the end. The building appears abandoned to deter intruders, but they are in there."

He grunted in acknowledgment. "And Spurling and that Sparrow?"

"Just outside of town. You know the small stream that flows through the forest, I trust?"

He nodded. As children, he'd often played there with the commander, when they had been Prince Aeric and Videl, a poor farmer's son. No heavy responsibilities attached. It hurt to think about.

"He lives in a cabin there with his sister and the Sparrow. Kill all three and I will lift this curse."

"There's no other way?" So much blood had been shed already. He wouldn't shed any more if he could avoid it.

"Well, you could kill me." She chuckled again. "I'll return when their blood stains the cold forest ground. I will claim what I want in return then, too."

The promise made him want to retch, but he wouldn't show weakness while she was still here. The end was near. He just needed to see it through.

"How did you find out?"

Spurling and his Sparrows had been hiding right under his nose this whole time. It was inexcusable that his best men hadn't found them.

"Find out?" She laughed "My dearest king, I've always known."

She disappeared, leaving him seething and dreaming about twisting her neck so far not even Aeron could recover from it.

But there was no time for day dreams. He opened the door—was surprised to see his guards alive if a little dazed—and gave the command that would end the war.

Chapter Thirty-Three

Cale had promised Rachael he'd observe her training, but there was too much on his mind for him to focus. Too many bad omens for comfort. Something terrible had happened, he felt it in his scars. He couldn't shake the feeling that it was too late.

He only wished he knew for what. Had they lost one small battle or the entire war?

If he only knew where Cephy was hiding, it would have put his mind at ease. If he could only be sure that she wasn't with Aeron, but the witch had several lairs and he couldn't spare the men to scout them all. No one had seen Cephy in months. She could have crossed the Boneanvil Mountains, but why go to Tramura? It would have been suicide. She had to be somewhere in Rifarne, and his gut told him she was with Aeron, but it was pointless to lose sleep over assumptions. Prophecy always found a way. If Cephy really had betrayed Rachael… If Aeron was teaching her… He needed to make sure Rachael watched her back when he wasn't around.

Then there were the suicides. Too many Sparrows

had died because of them, and he refused to believe they'd all suddenly changed their minds. A few had had doubts, true, but most had been determined. Not one would have done this willingly.

But it worried him even more that this disease now also affected those without the gift. Everyone was a potential victim. He hated to admit it, but King Aeric wouldn't move against his people like this. Whatever was causing the infliction, he had nothing to do with it; however, this wasn't a simple disease either. People got the cold, the flu or nasty rashes when they were sick. They didn't throw themselves off buildings or gut themselves at family gatherings.

He hadn't slept in three nights. Something was coming, and he prayed they'd be ready when it hit.

Cale sighed. He couldn't put this conversation off any longer.

"Take a break," he said to Rachael.

She had got good with the sword. Rachael was a natural, and the weapon seemed to have taken an instant liking to her too. That an enchanted Krymistian blade had chosen Rachael for a fight where her magic would be useless was the first good thing to happen in a while. So, there were good omens too.

Sweating and panting, Rachael sat next to him on the grass. "Did I do something wrong?"

He smiled. A few months ago, she hadn't cared for his opinion. He couldn't blame her for being slow to trust, but maybe he'd finally got through to her.

"No, not at all," he said. "I wanted to talk to you about something."

The shadows which fell over her eyes reflected his own. This wouldn't be easy, but it had to be done.

"What is it?"

"It's about Cephy." Her eyes lit up. He hated that he had to crush her hopes. "I'm sorry, we haven't found her. There's something you need to be aware of. There's a chance she is with Aeron, and—"

Rachael leapt to her feet like she was ready to go after her.

"But Aeron is dangerous, you said so yourself. We have to get her out of there."

His heart hurt. If holding her could make all her pains go away, he'd do it without hesitation, but she was the Sparrow. It wasn't his place to be that close to her or to think about her in this way, but he couldn't help it. She was more than her prophecy, he saw that now. So much more.

"We can't. I'm sorry."

Rachael paced in front of him. "Why not?"

"Because we don't know where Aeron is. The hut you found isn't her only one, but even if we knew where she was hiding we wouldn't be able to leave the city. The fighting could start at any moment. I have to be here when it does, and so do you."

"But—"

"If Cephy even is with Aeron. No matter where she is, Cephy has chosen this path herself. Like it or not, she is where she wants to be."

He felt harsh saying it, but Rachael had to realise the potential threat Cephy signified. He didn't want to consider Rachael's chances if they were to face each other after the brainwashing Aeron had no doubt done. Cephy's magic was destructive, and Maker knew what Aeron had taught her. Rachael had a sword. She'd be no match for Cephy, no matter how much he wished it were different.

Rachael sagged into the mossy ground and closed her eyes. He wanted to spare her the next bit, but he couldn't. Not if it might save her life.

"Prophecy has named her as the one to betray you. Don't expect her to go easy on you should you meet again."

Rachael took a ragged breath in. He knew she wanted to object, but they'd been over this so often she likely knew there was no point.

"What do you want me to do then?" Her voice was strained with pain. She gulped. "Kill her?"

"Yes. You might not have a choice if you see each other again. If you don't kill her, she'll kill you."

"Cale, I can't—"

"I'm sorry, Rachael. There is no other way. Promise me you'll kill her if you have to."

Rachael closed her eyes. A small smile caught her tear. "I promise. If I have to and can't see any other options, I will."

His heart hurt more at seeing her smile. She thought she'd found a loophole. There was no harm in allowing her a sliver of hope, so he didn't take it away.

She'd find out how wrong she was sooner or later.

Rachael's eyes watered from the bright sunlight and from Cale's expectations. He'd left her alone after their talk to give her time to think, but there was nothing to think about. Was there? Cale expected too much. Rachael still missed Cephy and hoped she was safe. She couldn't go from wanting to see her again to killing her.

Rachael remembered the dream she'd been trying to

forget and tasted bile. Had it been a vision, after all? Rachael and Cephy trying to kill each other amidst the burning ruins of the White City. Had Cephy's fire caused that? *Would* Cephy's fire cause that?

Rachael remembered the evil, vile glare in Aeron's eyes. The Mist Woman could easily turn Cephy against her if she wanted. Aeron cared only about herself and something so dark Rachael didn't want to consider it; she wasn't sure that she could if she tried. If Cephy had really run to Aeron…

She'd be no match for Cephy. Maybe it was irrelevant whether she could bring herself to kill Cephy—it was more likely that Cephy would burn her to ashes before Rachael's sword got anywhere near her. Cephy had killed seasoned soldiers to death while they'd been panicked and on the run. Rachael was nothing compared to that.

She sighed, and stood to continue her training. They'd both been alive in her vision, so Cephy wouldn't kill her immediately. Maybe Rachael could talk her down, convince her to stop the destruction she'd witnessed in her vision. But if there was no hope for that, if she couldn't change Cephy's mind…

Yes. Rachael could kill her.

She'd always done what was necessary to survive. It couldn't matter that Cephy had been a friend—a threat was a threat. She had more to live for now. Even if she ended up alone again once this was over, she wouldn't live in fear any more. That was worth fighting for. It wouldn't matter if she died, but she wanted to fight to give other gifted a chance.

Rifarne's gifted had lived in fear long enough. If Rachael could end it, she would.

She didn't like it, but Cale was right—Cephy had made her decision. She was still young but almost old enough to marry, and she was clever. She was a survivor too, if a bit too trusting.

Rachael paused mid-swing and lowered her sword when Cale and Ailis ran towards her. She didn't like the grim look on his face.

She steeled herself. "What happened?"

His hands were tight fists, his knuckles white. The fire raging behind his eyes put Cephy's best efforts to shame. "The Sparrows are dead."

"What do you mean?" Cold dread settled in her gut. They'd lost some to this terrible disease which had driven people to suicide, but more were still alive. He couldn't mean they were all gone.

"King Aeric found the hideout I took you to. He sent twenty men to raid them. Another twenty surrounded the building in case anyone got out. One of the Sparrows managed to send a warning and a report with one of our pigeons. A spell hides the ink, only I, Ailis, and a few other Sparrows can read it."

Rachael felt dazed. Forty seasoned soldiers for a few resistance fighters? King Aeric had left nothing to chance.

They'd been so careful. Had they been followed one night? Cale had remained hidden for so long and the city was in nervous uproar. People were leaving to live with relatives either elsewhere in Rifarne or in another country. Doomsayers occupied the streets. It had been easier than ever to slip past a guard since they were watching everyone carefully, in case anyone tried to kill themselves. Had Cale felt too save in the chaos?

"Someone has to have made it out," Rachael said.

She didn't know most of them well, but Kiana could look after herself. But with the building surrounded…

"Not everyone was at the hideout when the White Guard attacked, but many were there. We can't be sure, but the letter was written in a hurry. It doesn't look good."

Cale sounded defeated and angry. Ailis's eyes were bloodshot and watery. Rachael felt somewhere in between. If the Sparrows were gone, they had no chance. It was just her, Cale, and Ailis, but Ailis was no fighter and Rachael wasn't confident with her sword. The hay bales Cale had given her had been great for practice, but they weren't strong, angry soldiers that wanted her dead. Their chances had always looked slim, but at least they'd had some.

Ailis sobbed. "I can't believe everyone's dead. All our friends. We were family."

Rachael wanted to hug Ailis, but a hug wouldn't end her pain. Her friends would still be gone. Everyone they'd known would still lie slaughtered in their safehouse. No hug or words would make this right or better.

Cale punched the hay bale. "We'll avenge them. I swear by the Maker, we'll avenge them."

But Ailis didn't seem to hear him. Her eyes had clouded over with an indifferent stare.

"Let's get inside," Rachael said. "I'll make you tea for a change, and Cale and I can plan our—"

Ailis didn't move. Her blank eyes found Rachael's.

"I'm a sinner and a disgrace. I will save Rifarne from the vile taint of my kind."

Chapter Thirty-Four

Faster than Rachael could think, Ailis grabbed for her sword. Rachael barely held on to it and stumbled out of Ailis's reach, but the illness made Ailis strong and fast. She tugged at the bare blade while Rachael tried to keep the tip away from her. Cale tackled Ailis to the ground. Her hands were bloody where Rachael's sword had cut into her flesh, but she looked unharmed otherwise.

Now that Cale was pinning her down, all Rachael could do was stare. She'd acted on instinct before, but she didn't know what to do now. Ailis kicked and flailed against Cale, but he was stronger.

"*Kill me.*"

Rachael had never heard so much force behind Ailis's voice. The difference in personality was too much; it was like staring at a stranger. If Cale hadn't been here, Ailis would be dead. Because Rachael hadn't reacted fast enough. Even with Cale here, Ailis had cut her hands deeply and more blood than Rachael had ever seen soaked the ground. Ailis didn't seem to care about the pain. Did she feel it?

Cale gripped Ailis's face and forced her to look at him. "Snap out of it!"

Husbands and children of the afflicted had tried their best, too. Their spouses and parents had committed suicide nonetheless. If the love for one's child wasn't enough to break out of this insanity, then Cale wouldn't get through to Ailis. But Rachael let him try, because he needed to.

With incredible strength, Ailis shoved Cale away from her and jumped to her feet. He stumbled and fell, and Ailis launched herself at Rachael's exposed blade. Rachael hurried to sheathe the weapon, but Ailis was faster—she only had time to turn the tip away again. Ailis threw herself at full speed into the hilt's blunt end. It knocked the air out of her and she staggered backwards. With a mad look in her eyes, Ailis launched herself at the blade once more. This time, Rachael managed to sheathe it and stepped aside. Ailis glared at her. The disease's insanity was written all over her once beautiful features.

Then, she ran towards the lake.

"*Cale.*" Rachael doubted she'd have the strength to tackle Ailis down like Cale had done, but she had to try. She sped after Ailis…

But wasn't fast enough. Ailis threw herself into the clear water. She didn't struggle as water began to fill her lungs.

Rachael tried to pull her out, but Ailis's soaked clothes dragged her down. Cale jumped in beside her. His head was bleeding—he must have hit it when Ailis had shoved him off—but he pulled Ailis out of the water without effort. She coughed up water when her body fought where her mind had surrendered.

Cale grabbed a large rock and hit his sister over the head with it.

Rachael's eyes went wide. "*What are you doing*."

He slumped down next to her. "She's fine, or I hope she will be. Don't worry, this only knocks her out for a few hours. Help me get her to the house."

Rachael was grateful to do something useful. She put one of Ailis's arms around her shoulder while Cale took the other. Together, they brought her into the house and sat her down on a chair.

"Clear out her room," Cale said. "Don't leave any sharp objects or anything else she could hurt herself with. Lock the window. If you're not sure if something could be a weapon, get rid of it."

Rachael swallowed the lump in her throat and entered Ailis's room. She'd never been inside. Ailis had only ever entered Rachael's room when they'd tried to tap into her gift together, and likewise Rachael had never entered Ailis's room. Their sessions seemed like another life now. The bedchamber was a perfect fit for kind, caring Ailis. Soft lavender tones adorned the walls. White bed sheets brightened the room. Only one small window let in a little sun, which cast rays of gentle light through the chamber. There weren't many sharp objects—everything was as soft and tender as Ailis.

Rachael threw what little she did find out of the window. She didn't know what Cale had planned, but she wouldn't take any risks. They couldn't keep knocking her out until this illness was lifted, if that ever happened.

Cale staggered into the room with Ailis still unconscious on his back. He set her down on the bed and carefully slid her onto the floor, then crossed her wrists behind the bed's legs and tied a thick rope around them.

"Will this be enough?" Rachael asked. She wasn't convinced that a bit of string would do.

"I hope so." Cale tied the rope into a knot. "It's not easy to escape one of these. I've never seen anyone just pull their hands out. She might hurt her wrists a little, but it won't be enough to kill her. If we're lucky, she'll knock herself out next time." His head jerked up. "Hide."

"What?"

"There are men outside. Hide. Now."

Her heart sped up. "Where?"

"Anywhere they can't find you."

The look in his eyes scared her too much to argue, so she slid into the small space under the bed and held her breath.

"Wait here." Cale left her alone with Ailis tied to the bed.

It was silent for a few moments. Then—

"Are you the owner of this house?"

She didn't need to see the man to hear the danger in his voices.

"I am," Cale said. "Who's asking?"

"Show some respect, kid," another man said. That made two. "You're talking to—"

"Enough." The first. "There'll be time for that later."

"How can I help you?" Cale asked.

"Are you Cale Spurling?"

Her stomach twisted.

"I am."

"We have orders to bring you before his Royal

Majesty King Aeric for execution. Come quietly or put up a fight, it's all the same to us."

Rachael clamped a hand over her mouth. This wasn't happening. They couldn't take him, she didn't know what to do.

"On what accusations?" Cale sounded calm, but she heard fear under his resolve.

One of the men laughed. "For leading those Sparrows, you idiot. Now, what will it be?"

Cale hesitated. "I'll come quietly."

By the *thud* that followed, Rachael guessed they didn't care for that.

"Search the house," the first man said. "Find those girls we were asked to bring in so we can take them to the commander."

Rachael whimpered into her hand. They'd definitely find Ailis, but the knot around her wrists was too tight for Rachael to move her.

The door to the room flew open. White steel boots stomped into the chamber. He stopped before Ailis and bent at the knees. Rachael didn't dare move one toe, but she hated that she didn't know what he was doing.

He straightened. "Dead."

Rachael held her breath against every wish to scream. Finally, the White Guard grunted, smashed the mirror, and left. She listened as he searched the house and shattered objects. The floor boards creaked under his heavy boots. She was worried he'd crash through the ceiling, but seconds later she heard him walk down the stairs.

"There's a dead one in there, but the other isn't in here."

"Which one's dead?" the first man asked. Rachael

guessed he was in charge.

"She looks like him, so I'd say his sister."

"That other girl must be around here somewhere. I'll take Spurling to the king, you search the area around the house. Follow me when you've found her."

"Want me to burn the house?"

"No. She won't know we were here. We'll station some men outside if you don't find her, they can wait for her to come back."

The shuffling of feet followed. Then everything went silent.

Rachael hoped she wasn't leaving her hiding place too soon and slid out from underneath the bed. It had been quiet for a while. The guard must have gone back to his commander by now, which meant they'd position more guards soon. It was either take the risk now or wait too long and get surrounded.

She placed two fingers on Ailis's neck. Years ago, she'd seen some men do the same with a friend who'd been robbed in the streets. They had said if they could still feel his pulse, then he was alive. If they felt nothing, then…

Rachael held her breath as she searched for that vital life sign and sighed when she found it. The guard had been wrong—Ailis was alive. Her pulse was weak, but it was there. Ailis likely wouldn't feel it, but Rachael squeezed her hand. Maybe she'd somehow know it was Rachael and that she was safe for now. Maybe, despite what Rachael had seen outside, Ailis was still in there somewhere.

Her sword felt heavy when she got up. She hadn't been this conscious of it before, but her life hadn't been in danger then. Immediate threats had a way of focussing the mind; she'd learned that years ago. She placed a hand on the hilt, felt its weight in her palm as she lifted it out of its scabbard. With Cale gone and a White Guard looking for her, she could count only on herself again. She was grateful to have the sword.

Rachael didn't want to leave Ailis behind, but she had no choice. Ailis was still unconscious—dead as far as the White Guard knew. She'd be fine, whereas Cale was on his way to the gallows right now.

She roughly remembered where the palace was from their trip to the market. If she hurried, she could catch up with them and free Cale. He was strong, and the guard was alone if his friend hadn't reached him yet. If she took them by surprise, it would give Cale an opening. They'd have the advantage. Determined, Rachael dashed out the front door—

And froze. Something was moving in the shrubs.

Something big.

The guard was still around, after all.

She swallowed and gripped her sword. If she didn't turn around, he wouldn't know that she knew. She could take him by surprise. She only needed to time it right.

Heavy footsteps broke out of the shrubs and walked towards her. She hoped she'd look intimidating enough for the guard to at least pause and give her an opening, drew her sword, and spun around.

"Maker's Breeches, lass, it's me."

Her heart missed a beat. "*Arlo*." She lowered her sword but didn't drop her guard.

"Aye, lass. I'm relieved you're safe. Who was that man searching the forest?"

She raised her eyebrows. "Was?"

A broad grin spread on Arlo's hairy face. "Aye. Was."

One less thing to worry about. It was a small consolation, but she'd take it.

"What are you doing here?" She sheathed her weapon and walked to Arlo, who looked more intimidating than any White Guard with the heavy sword on his back and his gruff appearance.

"I heard things were turning sour here. 'course, that was weeks ago. The rumours I heard on the way made me hurry. What's this I heard about people killing themselves?"

Rachael's heart sank; Ailis was still tied to the bed. Would she keep trying until she succeeded? Rachael doubted conventional medicine could fix this. A cure had to exist somewhere, but she didn't know where to look or how they'd ensure Ailis's safety while they were gone.

"It's true," she said. "People have been committing suicide in public and no one knows why."

Arlo's face darkened. "It's foul sorcery, is what it is. I be damned if this isn't the work of that Mist Woman."

"Aeron?" Aeron had seemed spiteful when Cale had taken her and Cephy away, but how would she get this many people to kill themselves? Why would she do something like this? What would she gain?

Arlo's grim stare turned deadly. "Aye, lass. I heard rumours that Aeron was seen in a tavern not far from Blackrock. Yesterday, I heard some women gossiping that King Aeric and Aeron were sticking their heads together, out of sight from everyone else."

"Then how did they know about it?"

“Gossip travels quickly, lass. It only takes one ear to overhear something it shouldn’t, and there’s always someone who snoops around. Of course, it could just be a washerwoman’s tale. You’d better pray it is.”

Rachael hoped he was right and it was just a made-up story, but she had a feeling it was more sinister than that. At least these rumours didn’t mention a girl with Aeron. Wherever Cephy was, she wasn’t with Aeron.

“Arlo, they have Cale.”

His expression darkened. “I feared as much when I saw you dash out of his house like a demon was chasing you. Do you know where they’re taking him?”

“To King Aeric. It’s just one guard. You killed the other one.”

Arlo frowned. “What’s the foolish boy doing, letting one guard take him?”

“When the guards arrived, we were tying up Ailis. He told me to hide and went out to greet them.”

“He’s got a soft spot for you, that boy. Clever lad.” Arlo looked every bit like a proud father—or so Rachael assumed. She’d never seen one. “But, say, what were you doing tying up Ailis?”

Rachael took a deep breath to steady herself. “She tried to kill herself, like all these other people. We had to tie her up to stop her from hurting herself. Just until we found a solution.”

“Maker’s Breeches, it’s been an eventful day, hasn’t it?”

Rachael nodded. That was one way to describe the madness unravelling around her.

A starving fire raged behind Arlo’s eyes. “You’ll find the solution with King Aeric, if the prophecy holds true. Stay close. We need to hurry.”

He took two large steps, and she already had to half-run to keep up.

"Where are we going?"

"We're going to gut a Mist Woman."

Aeron watched the people of the White City busy themselves from her spot high up in the bell tower. They scuttled about their daily lives like panicking ants, buying meats and vegetables and dragging their bawling brats behind them. And there, in their midst, a White Guard escorted Cale to his death.

Her lips twitched. How she had waited for this day. Finally, the Sparrows' wings had been clipped, and their leader would soon join them. Now she just had to find Rachael and kill her.

Cephy was also eager for that moment. The girl was so receptive to her lies, it had almost been too easy. She'd barely changed the vision she'd shown Ceph—or rather, she hadn't changed anything, merely omitted a thing or two. Her Fox was brave for her age, even determined, but when it came down to it Cephy was a naïve child who believed anything Aeron fed her. Her little Fox wielded such power. And now it was hers, to use as she pleased.

Oh, what a beautiful day this promised to be.

She'd give those ants a reason to panic. The king didn't know, but he didn't need to. He only needed to do as he was told and open his legs to her once this silly *war* was over. Then her child would sit on the throne and lead the world into the promised age of darkness and suffering alongside the Dark One. It was almost too beautiful to behold, but Aeron could appreciate art when she saw it in her mind's eye.

She had waited her entire life for this day. Today, she would stop prophecy.

The moment was perfect. Cale couldn't escape death now, the Sparrows were slaughtered, and Rachael would no doubt come to Cale's rescue. It'd be easy to pick her out from the rest once she scampered through the city.

"Is it time?" Cephy asked. She watched the people of the White City with a fire in her eyes that matched her talent.

Aeron smiled. Maybe she shouldn't interfere, let her Fox have some fun. It was the nature of things, for foxes to kill little defenceless birds, and it would be more amusing to observe.

"It is indeed, my Fox. Do you remember what I told you?"

Her pet nodded. "Set fire to the market stalls and explode a building or two."

Aeron was so proud. "And do it exactly like that. I have a reward for you, for being so obedient."

Cephy's face lit up, always so eager to please. "A reward?"

"I shall let you kill Rachael. Soak the streets with her blood. Let it run to the harbour, my Fox. The old ways fall today."

A bright grin twisted with excitement spread on her pet's face. "I will, Aeron. I swear it, I will!"

"Then let us get to work. Keep an eye out for Rachael while you're down there. She mustn't reach the king." Aeron doubted Rachael was capable of killing him, but she didn't want to tempt fate. Better to keep Rachael far away from him.

Together, they descended the tower and split up at

the base. Cephy had work to do, and so did Aeron.

Chapter Thirty-Five

The market was as busy as ever. The recent suicides had put a new fear of magic into the people, but it wouldn't stop them from going about their daily business. Their families still had to be fed and their children still needed to grow, and their husbands still had to be satisfied. Local tragedy aside, their lives continued.

Traders from other countries hadn't returned when the deaths had continued. The affliction had spread beyond the city walls, but the White City would always be where it had started and no one wanted to chance carrying it home. Local merchants seemed busier than ever as a result. Rachael didn't remember it being this packed at any one stall when she'd visited. The thick crowd made it harder to keep up with Arlo. They made room for him, but they barely noticed her trailing behind.

"Do you know where we're going?" Rachael asked as she tried to keep up.

"Sure I do, lass. It's not the first time I've been to the palace. Besides, it's easy to spot from here. See that up there, lass?"

She didn't need to look to know where he was pointing—the palace towered over most of the city. Even from a distance, she could tell it was extravagant. It signified Rifarne's wealth and was the first thing besides the prison ships saw. It was beautiful and imposing, a promise and a warning to all who visited. Only one structure stood higher right behind it—the prison cast an intimidating shadow over everything, including the palace.

"That's where they'll be taking Cale, so that's where we're going."

Rachael was glad she had Arlo to guide her through this maze. They left the market and turned into a smaller side road, where it was easier to follow his large steps.

She felt it before she heard it. A strange pressure in the air. Birds fell silent. Other people stopped and looked around like they instinctively knew that something was wrong.

A deafening explosion tore through the city. Liquid flames, bricks, and broken wood rained down on the buyers and set fire to everything they hit. Some hit people in the head. They died quickly. Rachael's ears were ringing, but she saw people scream.

The ringing only lasted a second before everyone's panic hit her and she could hear their screams, their terror, their crying children.

Arlo pulled her into a narrow alley. "Quickly, lass. In here."

The buildings to either side stood so close that nothing was likely to crash through.

A second explosion shook the city, farther away but

no less deafening.

"What's happening?" She gripped the hilt of her sword but felt like cornered prey. She couldn't fight *this* with steel.

Arlo cursed under his breath. "That'll be Aeron, I bet. The king has many faults, but he wouldn't destroy his own city."

"Then what do we do?" Aeron hadn't shown her true self to them, Rachael knew that now, but she remembered the way Cale had talked about her. If she was here, they had lost.

"Listen to me, lass. I need to get Cale out of there, but I need to keep you safe, too. You need to reach the king, but it's too dangerous with Aeron running rampant. Stay here. I will bring Cale. We can think of something together."

"I can't just—"

"I mean it, lass. Do not leave this spot. It's dark here and the buildings are sturdy. A few stray flames won't get through these brick homes. Aeron will die of old age before she finds you here."

She knew Arlo well enough to know there was no arguing with him. He was a hunter by trade, maybe even a warrior, and he spoke with the same authority as Cale. What did she know of situations like this? If he told her to stay put, she had no choice.

Not while he was still watching.

She nodded.

"There's a good lass." Arlo gripped his heavy axe, which had seen better days but looked as sharp as the day he'd purchased it. "I'll hurry, lass. Don't move unless the buildings come down around you."

Arlo sped back into the chaos, and Rachael waited

ten heart beats. Then she drew her own sword and went the other way.

A distant rumble tugged at Ailis's mind. Something wasn't right. The taint was still in her.

She frowned when she remembered. Cale had hit her over the head with a rock. It was his fault she hadn't succeeded. Rachael's, too. They didn't understand. She was evil, corrupted. There was no other way to get the darkness out of her.

She tugged at the ropes around her wrists but they wouldn't budge. If she could get to the kitchen, she could use a knife and open her wrists, but the rope was too tight.

"Cale!"

No answer. Ailis thought she remembered Rachael leaning over her, telling her it'd be all right. Rachael had left after that. Had they both gone? She had to act while she was alone, but she couldn't do anything while she was tied up. Cale's knots were too good, damn him.

She rubbed her wrists against the rough ropes, over and over again. If she could burn through her skin and through her veins, she'd be able to drain the vileness out of her.

But she couldn't. The ropes were too tight and there wasn't enough room to move. She wouldn't die this way, but she had to do something. Unless Cale came back and cut her free… But he'd never do that. He wouldn't understand.

Ailis looked around for something she could use, something sharp, but there was nothing. Someone had cleared out her room.

She sighed and sagged into herself against the bed. Maybe she could convince Cale and Rachael that she was fine when they returned. They'd release her and she could finally—

Shouting. Someone was giving orders. It wasn't Cale, but the voice was familiar.

She cried with relief when she realised who it was. Now all she needed to do was play her part well, and she'd join the Maker at his side at last.

Kiana ran through the forest as fast as she could. Trust the city guard to just walk in and blow up their hideout—she had only escaped because she blended into the shadows better than most, but it wasn't easy to focus on running away when you really needed to teach someone manners. With a dagger. In their faces.

Their building had gone up in flames shortly after she'd made it out. Maybe she'd be lucky and the guards had trapped themselves inside. It'd serve them right for barging in and killing her family. Rude bastards.

Aeric had sent an impressive number of White Guards to their hideout. She'd never had this many soldiers come after her at once; under different circumstances, she'd have been flattered. She'd still have killed them—they *had* come after her to kill her first—but it was nice to not be underestimated for a change.

Most Sparrows were dead, but some had escaped. Some lucky ones like Reeve hadn't been in town, so they'd be fine. Unless Aeric knew where they were, too—but she could worry about that later. Right now, Riane, Lon, and Oren were with her. Lon had a nasty gash around his leg and was losing blood, but he had insisted on coming along. Silly, persistent man, but that's why she trusted him. It's why Cale trusted him. Lon wouldn't have come along if he wasn't up to it. Besides, with the White Guard searching for them and the city on fire, running was safer than staying inside the walls.

Cale's cabin wouldn't be safe for much longer, though. Explosions shook the ground inside the walls but there was no telling if they'd stay confined to the city, and she'd overheard several guards talking about Cale's capture. Rachael wouldn't be far behind, wherever he was. Now things were really kicking off, they couldn't afford to lose either.

She only hoped she wasn't too late.

"Riane, stay here with Lon. Oren and I will go in alone."

Riane saluted. "Yes, ma'am."

Kiana rolled her eyes. Riane was still new to the Sparrows and hadn't got the message that Kiana wasn't big on formality. What did it matter that she was Cale's Second? They were all bleeding together today.

"We'll get Cale, Ailis, and Rachael and then we'll get to the next shelter, but I need you both well enough to run. Bandage Lon's wounds as much as you can. We won't be long."

Cale had named her his second in command months ago, before they'd located Rachael. The other Sparrows agreed with his decision, but it'd taken them a while to take orders from her. Something about her being less imposing? They weren't seasoned soldiers like the White Guard. They were farmers, tailors, and blacksmiths. A family. Some of them had been homeless like Rachael. None of them should have had to take orders from anyone, especially not to fight for their lives because of how they'd been born.

Riane began to look after Lon's wound right away. Oren was right behind Kiana. They were both ready for anything, but he was more likely to fall over his own feet. She'd have preferred to take Lon but, well... She'd look after the clumsy idiot. That's what family was for. And Oren did know his way around a man's vital organs. Useful, that. She almost hoped they'd run into a guard or two.

The forest was too quiet. Kiana had only been to the cabin a few times and had grown up in a city, but a forest wasn't supposed to be this... empty. No critters, no birds. Just an eerie silence that itched her bones to turn around.

"Cale? Ailis?"

The front door stood wide open and a vase had been smashed on the floor. Her heart sank. They were too late.

Maker be screwed.

She stopped abruptly inside the door, and Oren bumped into her.

"Search the upstairs," she said. "Maybe Rachael managed to hide."

The ground floor looked like a small battle field. Someone had emptied drawers onto the floor, the table cloth Ailis had handmade with such care had been torn in two, and the water from the smashed vase left a sad puddle.

"Maker, let them be alive or I swear you'll regret the day you let them die."

Could they win this war without Cale or Rachael? Ailis had saved their lives more often than Kiana cared to remember. Her healing magic would be vital.

Low groaning came from Ailis's room. Kiana ripped the door open—

And froze. Ailis was alive, but there was a huge bruise on her forehead and she was tied to the bed. Her wrists looked sore, like she'd been dragged through the forest by the rope. Small slivers of blood trickled down her hands. But she was alive, and Kiana knew when to be grateful.

Kiana cut Ailis free. "Bloody Mists, Ailis, what happened here?"

"A White Guard tied me up." She sounded weak, but that was easier to fix than death, so Kiana wouldn't complain. "He took Cale into the forest. I think he wants to—" Ailis sniffed. Kiana could guess the rest.

"Wait here, I'll look for him. Where is Rachael?"

"Another guard has her. He's taking her to the king."

"Maker be damned. I'm glad we saved you, at least. Rest here. We'll find them."

A weak smile graced Ailis's lips. "Please hurry."

"We will. Oren!"

His footsteps thundered down the stairs and into the room. "Ailis! By the Maker, what happened?"

"I'll explain later," Kiana said. "A White Guard has taken Cale into the forest for execution and another has Rachael. They are headed to the palace. I'm going after Cale, and I need you to go after Rachael. We can't lose her, understand?"

Oren nodded. "They won't get far."

Kiana turned back to Ailis. "Stay here, I'll be back with Cale as soon as I can."

Ailis smiled her thanks, and Kiana bolted into the forest.

Chapter Thirty-Six

Arlo was aware of every movement and shadow around him as he sped through the masses. Several guards had tried to stop him, so he'd cut them down; explaining what he needed to do would have wasted time and complicated matters, but he still hated himself for it. Battle wasn't supposed to be like this. It was supposed to be fair, a sport where both sides had equal chances, but war always brought out the worst in people.

He cursed Aeron for plunging the world into this mess. He couldn't be sure it was her, but he also couldn't think of anyone else who would set fire to an entire city. As far as he knew, she was the most powerful and most dangerous Mist Woman in Rifarne. If this was about Rachael and the prophecy, Aeron could have killed her without dragging all these other people into it. Rachael wouldn't have been a match for her. But then their plan would have failed a long time ago. He had to remember that they still had a chance because of Aeron's monstrosity, grim as that truth was.

This affliction he'd heard about had to be Aeron's

doing too, and now Ailis suffered from it. It didn't put his mind at ease that Cale had tied her to the bed. The sick developed incredible strength and were capable of overpowering anyone who stood in their way. A bit of rope—no matter how thick—wouldn't hold her for long.

But he couldn't worry about that now, when Cale's and Rachael's lives were in more immediate danger. The lad was too stricken with her to think clearly, but to let himself be captured to protect her? Lovesick fool.

Arlo scoffed. Cale's recklessness wasn't entirely about love. Rachael was their Sparrow. Cale would protect her until the world crumbled at its core—which it seemed to be doing now.

Arlo could smell foul magic miles away, and this reeked of Mist Woman. He'd bury his axe in her skull if he ran into her. He'd have searched for her too, had he believed he might stand a chance, but as it was he was happy to leave it to fate. No matter how much blood his axe had seen, it wouldn't be enough to slay that abomination. He wouldn't throw his life away.

Arlo turned from one street into the next, jumped over crates abandoned in the madness, and felled guards when they tried to get in his way. The palace wasn't far and therefore, neither was Cale. The mere thought of the boy in chains and screaming under torture made Arlo's heart and insides clench. He'd known the lad since he was a wee boy. He hadn't let him down when his parents had been slaughtered, had supported him all these years as he'd resurrected the Sparrows, and he wouldn't let him down now.

Someone was running after him. Arlo could give the White Guard credit for their persistence, if nothing else. It was a shame they fought against people like Rachael and Ailis. They'd have made formidable allies.

His follower was slowly falling back. Not many matched Arlo's years of experience of tracking in the woods; he had enough stamina to put any horse to shame. He wouldn't stop until he saw Cale safe and far away from the king.

"*Arlo*. Will you stop already!"

Arlo stopped at the sound of Cale's voice, axe raised and ready to kill any guards on the lad's heels. But Cale was struggling after him alone, no guards in sight.

Arlo laughed. "It's mighty good to see you, my boy. Why didn't you say something sooner?" No one kept up with him for long. Cale must have been nearby.

Cale frowned. "I've been calling after you for a good five minutes. You didn't hear me."

They hugged, and Arlo patted Cale's back. "What happened, lad? Rachael said some guard was escorting you."

"Some guard was. You mentioned her. Is she—"

"Aye, lad, she's safe." Arlo could no longer tell if the boy was worried about the Sparrow or if there were deeper feelings at play. "Safe and defiant as ever. She's waiting in an alley for me to bring you back." Cale smiled, so Arlo gave him that moment before he continued. "Happy as I am to see you're safe, it doesn't explain what happened. Did they not search you before they left your house?"

Cale grinned. "They did, but they found only my sword. They didn't think I'd have a dagger at my hip, too."

Arlo grinned in return. He'd raised the boy well.

"There's a good lad. The one that stayed behind is dead too. I ran into him on the way."

"Why are you here, Arlo? I'm glad to see you, but I don't understand why you came."

Arlo shrugged. "There's a war going on, isn't there? I thought you could use my help."

Cale sighed. "There is now. You timed your arrival well, old friend."

"So it seems. We need to get back to Rachael. I'm worried the lass might do something stupid." Rachael wasn't naïve or fairy-brained by any means, but she was fiery and wouldn't suffer inaction for long.

"Wait, Arlo, before we go—I heard explosions lower in the city. Did you see what happened?"

Arlo grunted. "Aeron happened. I'm sure she's behind this."

Cale's face went as pale as the coldest winter's snow. "And you left Rachael alone?"

Cale often got angry. It was a trait born of his time leading the Sparrows. He'd seen much and grown resentful over time. Usually, he didn't show his irritation, but Arlo wasn't surprised to see that he felt stronger about the lass.

"She's safe where she is, lad. Aeron won't find her where I left her."

"And if Rachael didn't want to wait? If she followed us?"

"That's why we should hurry back."

They started to run, Cale following his lead.

"One thing still doesn't make sense."

"What's that, lad?"

"I believe that Aeron is behind these attacks, I suspected as much, but why strike now? Why not a week ago or a week later?"

Arlo had wondered that himself. Only two options came to mind, and both were equally worrying.

"Might just be she's hateful like that, lad. If Aeron wants to destroy a city, she destroys a city. You know what Mist Women are like. They always act on passing fancies, no matter how many people get hurt."

"But that would be too much of a coincidence."

Their trip back down into the city was faster than his trip up had been. Downhill was always easier, especially when you were running and the few guards in their way were no match for their combined strength.

"Aye, lad. I believe Aeron's had her claws around the king's neck for longer."

He didn't need to see Cale's face to know he'd gone a dangerous shade of white. Arlo didn't like the grim implications either.

"You mean the suicides..." Arlo nodded. "Then everything we feared was true. Aeron is behind all this."

Cale cursed under his breath. He didn't swear often, so it was all Arlo needed to know.

"We have to find her, Arlo. She did this to Ailis."

Arlo grunted his approval and led Cale back onto the narrow side road.

Cale didn't need to speak for Arlo to feel the accusing glare in his back. He was just as shocked to see it empty.

Rachael didn't know where she was going. She only knew that she needed to head up. Once she was closer to the palace, she hoped it'd be more obvious. For now, she followed King's Road, hoping it was a reference to the other end of the cobblestones.

Two more explosions had shaken the city. Pillars of smoke turned the sky a dark grey. She was no longer near the market, but the breeze carried the screams of the scared and the injured to her. The fire was spreading. Only one person could make it burn with such ferocity, but Rachael didn't want to jump to conclusions. Aeron's magic was destructive too, and she was hateful enough to destroy a city.

Rachael's eyes stung from the ash in the air. She moved into a small square to blink the pain away and to plan her next steps. Reaching the palace would be easy. It was what had to happen next that worried her. Cale could be anywhere, King Aeric was one of many possibilities. Maybe Cale was in the prison. Maybe they'd already—

She had to believe that Cale was fine, alive, and hopefully uninjured.

Her blade had tasted first blood, and she would cut down more guards if she needed to. Thanks to Cale's patience, she wielded her sword well. One guard had injured her—a small cut on her thigh was throbbing every time she put her foot down and every time she took the pressure of—but she didn't have time to bandage the wound. She needed to find Cale.

She stepped out of the square, set out towards the palace…

And dodged the blazing ball of fire by luck.

Rachael readied her weapon, but her hands were shaking and her mind kept denying what her gut already knew.

"That won't help you." Another fire ball, larger than

the first, sizzled towards her. Rachael dodged it; her heart ached for that voice. “Nothing will.”

Another fire ball sped past her and flew into the house behind her, where it hit lamp oil. The explosion threw Rachael into the air. She hit the ground hard and the cut on her leg burst open. The piercing pain made her scream.

“Stop it, Cephy!”

The next fiery sphere came close enough to heat her cheek and singe her hair.

“No.” Cephy’s hands were already burning again, but the fire in her eyes burned even brighter. “I’m not here to talk.”

Rachael gripped her sword, but the firm hilt in her hand wasn’t reassuring. If she couldn’t talk Cephy down, then she wouldn’t win this battle either. Cephy would never let her come close enough.

But Rachael had to try. Even if Cephy didn’t want to listen. Somehow, Rachael had to make her care enough to stop her assault.

“Why are you doing this?”

Above her, a small explosion ripped through stone. The arch that connected the two houses on her left and right collapsed into a large pile of red-hot embers.

Cephy grinned. “You’re trapped. You’re not going anywhere until I’m done.”

It didn’t make sense—this wasn’t the Cephy she knew.

“I’m not your enemy, Cephy. Please stop.”

Cephy looked like a determined spirit of vengeance with her fists on fire and that glare. Deep down, Rachael had a feeling there were no words that could bring back the girl she’d known, but it was for that girl that she had to try. She couldn't just run Cephy through. Her old friend still had to be in there somewhere—Rachael refused to believe otherwise.

The fire around Cephy's hands flared into larger flames. "You're lying. Aeron showed me how you and Cale planned to get rid of me. You agreed to kill me. Aeron said you would betray me, and she was right!"

So, Cale had been right. Cephy had run to Aeron. Or maybe Aeron had found her, while Cephy had been on her way somewhere else? All that mattered now was Cephy's anger. Rachael would have to get close to hurt her or at least knock her out, but Cephy could kill her where she stood.

What a mess. Rachael couldn't imagine how Cephy had overheard their conversation, but she hadn't heard all of it.

"Then Aeron hasn't shown you the whole conversation," Rachael said. "I only agreed if you tried to kill me first. I'd never attack you without reason."

For a moment, the fire behind Cephy's eyes dimmed as she paused to think, but the lies Aeron had fed her burned hotter.

"*Liar.*"

Rachael saw the flame too late. She dodged fast enough that it didn't burn her skin, but it caught her sword which heated through and singed her hand. Rachael hissed and dropped the blade.

The flames of her prison licked ever higher as if to remind her that there was no way out. She had to get to Cephy, but if she touched the flames she'd likely burn to ashes—Rachael didn't want to find out the hard way. She had no way of reaching Cale or Arlo even if she had known where they were. It was just her, the hungry flames, and a sword that couldn't help her here.

In the dancing shadow-light of the fire, Cephy's grin turned into an ugly grimace. "How does it feel to be helpless?"

"This is madness, Cephy. Aeron is lying to you."

"Aeron is the only one willing to do something! She wants to fix everything, so people like us can rule and the people who hated us suffer."

"Aeron will get all of us killed." Rachael tied to keep her voice calm. Cephy's hands were still burning fists, but she thought some of the tension had gone out of them. They were talking. Rachael preferred that to the alternative. "I don't know what Aeron wants, but it's not a bright future for people like us."

"You don't know what she wants! You don't know her!" There was less madness in Cephy's voice now and more pain of a child that had been hurt one too many times. Rachael hoped it was progress and not her last chance to run before Cephy plunged into insanity.

Rachael inched forwards as much as the flames allowed. "And you do? Aeron has lied to you. She's behind all these suicides."

Rachael saw Cephy's resolve crumble. Aeron had got to her, but beneath all the lies was still the Cephy Rachael knew. Rachael just had to reach her.

"No. You're lying." Cephy stood still while the fire cast long shadows over her small body.

"I'm not." Or, at least, Rachael hoped Arlo's assumption had been right. "Let me out. We can talk."

The doubt disappeared from Cephy's face. "No. I still heard you. You're willing to kill me."

"No more than you're ready to kill me. I saw you pause. You don't want to do this any more than I do."

Cephy glared at her. "Nothing will change unless we *make* them change." Rachael's heart sank at the realisation that Cephy meant herself and Aeron. "I'm done being hated for what I am. I don't want to—"

The cage of starving flames around Rachael dropped to her waist. At first, Rachael didn't know why Cephy had stopped—it was hard to see anything past Cephy in the glare of her fire—but then Rachael saw it.

Wet and crimson.

Arlo's sword in Cephy's chest.

Cephy didn't gasp. Didn't protest when her eyes clouded over and their bright spark darkened.

Rachael's fiery prison died down to a weak flicker around her ankles. She jumped over what was left. "What did you—"

With a sickening sound, Arlo pulled the blade out of Cephy's body. Rachael caught her so she wouldn't fall onto the cooling cobblestones.

"I'm sorry, lass," Arlo said. "She would have killed you. I can't let that happen."

Rachael's surroundings blurred into a colourful mess of greys and too many reds. She didn't want to see the one thing she could, but she wouldn't leave Cephy alone. Cephy already believed that Rachael had betrayed her. If she couldn't say all those things she should have said, then she could at least stay with her until the last of Cephy's light was gone.

She could have talked Cephy down. Things could have been like before—just the two of them, living away from civilisation and hateful stares.

"Don't die, Cephy." A weak plea, but it was all she had.

Rachael had always known that, sooner or later,

Cephy would leave her. But she'd also assumed she'd be able to follow Cephy and watch over her. Better to have each other in some strange removed way than to be completely alone, but perhaps some people were destined to be lonely.

Cephy's lips twitched, but no sound escaped.

"I'm here." For what little it was worth now. "Take your time, Cephy. I won't leave you." Another pointless plea—Cephy didn't have time—but Racheal felt better for the lie. Maybe it made Cephy feel better too. It was worth it if it did.

"I—" Cephy coughed, and red spattered her lips. "I'm sorry I failed you, Aer—"

Cephy took one last strained breath. Then her eyes lost the last of their light and she went limp in Rachael's arms.

Rachael hated herself, but she hated Aeron even more. That Cephy's last words had been an apology to Aeron made her nauseous. The Mist Woman wouldn't care that Cephy was gone, wouldn't care that Cephy's last words had been meant for her.

Rachael ached for the way things had been before Aeron. Before Cale and Arlo and Ailis.

"Rachael."

Her head spun around to hurl insults and accusations at Arlo, but the fast movement drained the fight out of her.

"What do you want."

"I know you're angry, lass, but we need to keep moving. We need to reach King Aeric."

"Kill him yourself, you're clearly good at that. I'm staying with Cephy."

"And risk Aeron finding you? No, lass, you're

coming with me. Cale will be relieved to see you alive."

Rachael scoffed. This was Cale's fault, too. Also Ailis's, but she wasn't near enough for Rachael to accuse her. If they'd taught Cephy, she wouldn't have run to Aeron and she wouldn't be dead now.

Rachael kissed Cephy's forehead goodbye and gently laid her down on the ground. She'd come back and bury her when this was over. Right now, Rachael wanted answers. Someone would pay for what had happened here.

"Where is Cale?"

Arlo sighed. "Follow me, lass."

Chapter Thirty-Seven

Kiana knew a few tricks for tracking someone inside a forest. Cale had taught her most of them and she'd thought herself a good student, but there was nothing here. She'd found a dead guard and footsteps leading back to the house, but there was no sign of Cale or a struggle. Cale wouldn't have gone down without a fight—he was too good and too proud for that—and the footprints were too large to be his. Whoever had killed the guard was long gone, but it hadn't been Cale.

She had a bad feeling about this. Her gut said Ailis had lied, but why would she? Ailis loved her brother more than anything in this world. Kiana believed that the Whit Guard had taken Cale and Rachael, but why would Ailis lie about where they'd gone? She'd want her brother saved, but she's also sent Kiana on a cold trail.

It was possible Ailis had guessed. She'd been tied to the bed, after all, but Kiana had the feeling that something more was going on. Oren hadn't found anyone inside the cabin, and they had no basement. Could a guard have hidden behind the house, waiting for her and Oren to leave? It didn't make sense that they'd take Cale and Rachael but tie up Ailis. Even if there had only been two guards, they'd easily have overpowered three Sparrows. Ailis didn't fight and Rachael wasn't used to her sword. None of them wore heavy armour, unlike the White Guard.

Kiana frowned. She should have stayed with Ailis, rather than chased ghosts. Cale trusted her and had made her his second in command because he knew she was smart enough to lead them in his absence. It wasn't acceptable that she hadn't questioned Ailis more, that she hadn't realised sooner that the guards would have taken all three.

But there hadn't been time. Cale had taught her that rescuing someone took priority, that saving the innocent always came first. Ailis was alive, Cale and Rachael were in danger. Going after them hadn't been unreasonable, and yet…

Kiana sprinted back to the cabin. Ailis knew something, and Kiana needed to know what.

"Ailis?" Kiana threw the door open and dashed into the house. "I'm back. I— *Oh Maker*." Her blood ran cold and her stomach churned.

Kiana had seen many people die since she'd joined the Sparrows. Some had been tortured for days, others had died faster of horrific injuries.

But no death had ever made her feel like this.

Ailis lay in the middle of her kitchen, her throat cut. A warm puddle of blood spread across the floor and slowly soaked into the floorboards.

And Kiana had allowed it to happen, because she'd walked away.

Aeron stopped mid-spell amidst the ruins of someone's house. She'd placed wards around and inside of Cephy, so she would know if her little pet died.

Her Fox was dead. It was unfortunate, but of no real importance. Rachael would be weakened, saddened by the loss. Aeron just needed to find her—if only the stupid brat weren't so good at hiding.

Aeron had turned half of the White City upside down and inside out to find that damned Sparrow. She'd hoped her Fox had succeeded, but it seemed it no longer mattered. There was a chance her pet had killed Rachael before she'd died, but Aeron's gut feeling told her the Sparrow was alive while her Fox lay slain without having done as she'd asked.

Oh, how they'd pay for this. Rachael would suffer before Aeron let her die. Her screams would slice through the night and greet the Dark One.

There had been several explosions higher up not long ago—near King's Road, if Aeron wasn't mistaken. The Sparrow and the Fox must have met there.

Shaking with anticipation, Aeron stepped off the pile of useless rubble she'd used as a platform and began to walk towards King's Road.

"I will not let you harm her."

Aeron froze. That voice... Oh, how she hated that voice. She turned around to face the one witch she'd hoped never to see again.

"What are you doing here?" Aeron spat her words like venom and glared all her hatred at the woman.

She smiled, as striking and as treacherous as ever. "Is that how you greet an old friend?"

Aeron regained some of her composure. "Why, here

I was seeing you as an enemy instead. How foolish of me."

"Foolish indeed. If you had not abandoned your sisters, you would not be taking your last breaths now."

The nerve! The insolence! How dare she look sad behind her smile? How dare she believe she could kill Aeron? *Nothing* could kill Aeron.

She didn't have time for this. She'd teach her old *friend* a lesson and leave before the witch's soul could plague Aeron even in death.

"I do apologise, Kaida, I can't stay. I have a bird to kill."

Aeron threw enough of her gift at the smug witch—she abhorred the offensive slur, but Kaida deserved no better—to burn another three cities.

With a sad smile, Kaida dismissed her concentrated hatred with a thought. Aeron was seething, her rage as hot as her Fox's fire. The nerve, to dismiss her so easily!

"That is why I am here," Kaida said. "The Sparrow will come to no harm through you."

"And how do you propose to prevent it?" Aeron felt His power inside her, and tugged. "I have become the most powerful Mist Woman alive. Has this news not reached Midoka?" The others, her so-called sisters—didn't deserve to label themselves as Mist Women when none of them were brave enough to explore the Mists and delve as deep as she had done. None of them had the guts. None of them had the courage to command the magic Aeron now possessed.

Her last spell must have missed. She hadn't expected to see Kaida; the surprise had affected her focus or Kaida would be no more. But her surprise had grown old and she had as much of His power at her fingertips as she needed. Once, she could admit, Kaida had been stronger, but no more.

"We have heard of your delusion," Kaida said. Damn her knowing smile. "We do not argue that you are not the most powerful Mist Woman in Rifarne, but elsewhere there are those who would see you dead. It saddens me, but I have come to see that desire fulfilled."

Aeron grinned. The insolent pest had another thing coming! "I want to see you try."

The Midokan witch raised her hands. "I am sorry, Aeron. I wish we had been sisters."

White-hot flames unlike any Aeron had ever seen engulfed her. These were hungrier, burnt hotter, didn't seem human. They were alive. Her skin prickled under the heat. How had one Midokan witch done so much harm with one simple spell?

The flames flicked up around her body. The pain became unbearable, but she wouldn't scream. If she was to die here, then so be it. She had accounted for this unlikely event.

Aeron grinned. If Kaida had known what killing her would unleash—of the pact she'd made—the witch wouldn't have dared.

Her death meant nothing. She'd won.

Kaida watched Aeron's last moments, sad that it had come to this. It would be disrespectful to her prey if she turned away as they took their last breaths. Kaida would not allow herself to fall as low as Aeron had fallen.

She watched the flames go out and the ashes settle,

until she was certain there was no way to bring Aeron back.

Kaida wanted to meet the Sparrow, but this was not the time. She needed to return to Maishi Hou and tell Kei what had happened, but there was something more urgent she needed to do first. Aeron's arms and legs had been covered in scars. Kaida had recognised the short but deep incisions, but she hoped she was wrong. She would have to report those too, just in case Aeron had set the end of the world in motion.

Chapter Thirty-Eight

Rachael was panting when she reached a junction in King's Road moments behind Arlo. He still wasn't out of breath after all this running and fighting, while Rachael was struggling to keep up. She'd thought herself in good shape after Cale's merciless training sessions, but running after Arlo had shown her otherwise.

"Hurry, lass. Cale is waiting just ahead."

She wanted to protest, tell him she wasn't as fast as him, but more than anything she was still seething mad at him for killing Cephy. Seething mad at Cephy for attacking her. Seething mad at Aeron for having manipulated Cephy. So, instead of complaining, she followed as well as she could without saying a word.

Rachael knew she could have convinced Cephy, but Arlo hadn't given her the chance. That Cephy would attack her at all… That Arlo, who had healed her hands and comforted her, would kill her without the shadow of regret… Rachael didn't know how, but she'd make Aeron pay for destroying everything good in her life.

Since arriving at Cale's house, she'd slowly begun

to trust people as Cephy had urged her to do. And where had that faith got her? None of that would change for her once King Aeric was dead, but maybe it'd make a difference for someone else somewhere else in Rifarne. Growing up hated had been a long nightmare. If she could spare someone else that fate, then King Aeric needed to die. She needed to stop worrying about the details and stick her sword in his gut. This prophecy seemed certain about his death and her hand in it, and she was ready to believe the rest of it, too. She'd been reluctant to believe Cephy would betray her, but it had happened. If the prophecy could promise her an end to the madness, then she would do what it said and end the madness.

"Lass, did you hear me? We need to hurry."

Rachael didn't want to talk to him, so she nodded and picked up her pace. King's Road was long, spanning the length of the upper city and a small part of the lower city. They'd made good progress, but it would take a while to reach the palace on the other end.

The heavy clang of steel on cobblestone rang through the air. Her heart missed a beat; five White Guards headed down the road towards them.

"Shite. Rachael, run that way. I will catch up with you once—"

"Don't bother running from me, Sparrow."

Rachael would have recognised that voice anywhere—it still haunted her nightmares and always would. Commander Videl.

"I know this city better than most, know all of its hidden alleys and small side roads. There's nowhere you can hide where I won't find you."

Rachael had no one who could burn the guards with

their will alone this time. Arlo knew how to handle his sword—she'd seen proof of that several times following him through the city—but even Arlo was outnumbered against four trained soldiers and one commander.

There was no point in running. The city's layout was as confusing to her as her gift—she could have been born here and still wouldn't know all of its hidden nooks.

"Run, lass, or do you want to die here?"

But she wouldn't die here—she'd seen her fate in her vision. A dark cell with no hope of escape. Her punishment would be worse if she ran now, and she preferred a quick death to a slow, torturous one.

The commander and his soldiers surrounded her and Arlo.

"No need to worry about your Sparrow," Commander Videl said. "King Aeric wants to have a word with her. We've come to take her to him."

Arlo growled, more dangerous than a rabid wolf and just as easily provoked. "And I take it he'll shower her with gifts once he's done talking?"

The commander laughed. All Rachael heard was madness. Had he always been insane or had Aeron ruined him, too?

"Of course not. I'd cut her down right here, but my king insists. Once he's done saying whatever he wants to say, I'm sure he'll let me do my job."

Arlo stepped up to Commander Videl, who didn't look the least bit intimidated. "If you think I'll just let you take her, you're more stupid than you look."

"Arlo." Enough people had died. It needed to end. "I'll go with them. You don't need to—"

"And you, lass, are wrong if you think I'll let you walk to your death." His eyes didn't leave the commander. "Be a man and fight me, you shite."

"Hear that, men?" The commander laughed and drew his blade. "The old man thinks he can defeat me in a duel."

"A duel?" Arlo spat at the commander's feet, axe raised and ready to strike. "If you all charged me it wouldn't be a fair fight."

The commander scoffed. "Now, now, old man, you wound me already and our steels have yet to meet. Spread out, men, and don't lose the girl."

His soldiers moved aside. One grabbed her arm and dragged her with him.

Arlo attacked. His axe came down swiftly and nearly knocked the commander's sword out of his hands, but Commander Videl tightened his grip on his hilt and merely staggered a few steps. Arlo charged. The commander dodged in the last second, and Arlo's axe got stuck between the cobblestones.

It gave the commander an opening. Arlo jumped aside, but the commander's blade caught his arm. Blood stained the stones a slippery red. Arlo roared and pulled his axe free—seconds before the commander's blade would have split him in half.

Rachael watched frozen to the spot and held in place by the guard, who still had a tighter-than-necessary grip on her arm.

Commander Videl slipped on the blood. Rachael held her breath when Arlo aimed for the commander's middle, brought down his axe…

And the commander rolled onto his side, just out of the way, and launched his blade forwards through

Arlo's stomach.

Rachael screamed in shock. The guard's fingers on her arm squeezed harder. The commander laughed and pulled his blade out of Arlo's middle. Arlo toppled onto his knees. He held the gaping wound with one shaking hand while the other held him up on his axe.

"Ah, justice." The commander stepped away from Arlo with a smug grin. He turned to his men, his bloody sword raised high. "And he wanted to fight all of us at once. See what his arrogance has brought him."

Rachael was so angry she was shaking. How dare he call Arlo arrogant? Arlo was the most selfless and caring person she'd ever met. Her heart hurt at how she'd hated him after he killed Cephy. The decision couldn't have been easy on him either, but she'd been too busy hating him for it to understand it.

And where was Cale? Hadn't Arlo said he was waiting a little farther ahead? Surely he'd seen the White Guard approach, heard the screaming of steel against steel.

Rachael couldn't remember the last time she'd cried because someone had died, but tears ran down her cheeks now. Cale would be devastated that his friend was gone. She could have intervened. She had no idea how, but she should have done something.

"Hand her to me," Commander Videl said. "We can take her to King Aeric now this silly game is over."

"Don't touch me!" Rachael kicked and hit his kneecap. He hissed, and she glared all her pain at him.

His armoured fingers closed around her chin and forced her to look at him. "Do you know what we do to rebellious brats like you in the prison?" Her blood ran cold, but she wouldn't show him her fear. "You'll beg me to kill you long before I indulge you. You'll swear you'll do anything as long as I end your pain."

She spat in his face. He could torture her all he wanted; she'd never beg for that.

He punched her, hard metal against soft flesh. Sharp pain shot through her nose. Rachael tasted blood. She wouldn't show him how much it hurt. He'd have to do a lot better before she screamed.

She owed Arlo that much. Owed all of them a bit of defiance, most of all herself.

"Let this be a promise of what's to come, you little bitch."

She glowered at him and hoped he didn't see how much her legs were shaking.

The inside of the palace was as beautiful as the outside. Its halls, generously adorned with intricate designs and details, seemed to stretch for miles. It was even more of a maze than the city, but Commander Videl navigated the halls and corridors with ease.

They stopped before two heavy doors, which were almost as high as the ceiling. Two guards held their fists to their hearts and stood firm.

"Open the doors," Commander Videl said. "I have a present for King Aeric."

The guards did as they were told, and her eyes went wide. The throne room was huge, easily as large as the market square but empty and quiet. There were no buzzing crowds here, only a king upon his throne who watched them enter. Five guards on each side of the throne watched over him.

The commander shoved Rachael ahead of him halfway to the throne, where he gave her a final push and she hit the floor.

"Here she is, my king. The Sparrow."

Rachael didn't look up at the king's face. She'd heard enough to feel like she knew him, and she didn't want to see the cold, hateful glare in his eyes to confirm what she already knew. He hated her. He'd sent soldiers to kill her.

"Leave us."

His voice was a surprise. She'd expected it to be as cruel and calculating as his methods, but King Aeric sounded tired—even exhausted. Underneath his fatigue, she heard warmth. He wasn't a man who burnt down his city or wanted people dead for having the gift. Men with those ambitions didn't have the soft compassionate his voice had once held. It was thin, barely noticeable, but she heard it. King Aeric had once been a good man. Now, he was like every other criminal driven by hunger and necessity. Like every other peasant. She didn't like it, but she understood him. He was scared. He'd done what he thought he had to do to survive. But that didn't excuse that he'd sent the White Guard after her. It didn't excuse all those deaths. King Aeric had taken the easy way out, ordered someone else to do the things he didn't want to, and in that regard they weren't the same at all.

The commander cleared his throat. "My king, I can't—"

"*Leave*, Videl. Take your men with you."

Rachael smiled. He was tired, but he could still be firm when he needed to be. He was her enemy, but unlike the commander or Aeron, she could respect him.

Behind her, the heavy doors opened and closed as the commander and his men left the room. The guards by the throne hadn't moved.

"Come closer."

Rachael didn't want to be anywhere near him, but she supposed it was necessary if she was to kill him. Maybe she could run him through before he or his guards could react.

Rachael got up and dragged herself over to him, determined to defy the man who'd ordered her death. Her face stung from the commander's punch, which had left a dry crust of blood around her nose and more running down her chin.

She stopped just before the steps leading up to his throne.

He regarded her with… what? Curiosity? A hint of fear? No, just fatigue. "I know why you're here."

"Then why send your commander away and leave me my sword?"

She was surprised he hadn't ordered them to take her weapon away. Was he so confident in himself he didn't believe her to be a threat? Cale had trained her well in the short time they'd had, and the king didn't look fit for a fight. He looked as tired as he sounded, was thin and worn out from the conflict he'd started. His face showed deep lines shaped by worry.

King Aeric didn't look like a king. His clothes and crown were the only things that betrayed him. Without them, he'd have passed for a beggar.

With a heavy sigh, King Aeric stood and moved towards her with the grace of a dying lion.

He stopped an arm's length away from her.

"Because this is my throne. If you want my crown, you'll need to fight me for it, not him."

Her aching face twisted into a smirk. The man she

had worried about killing because she'd believed him to be impossible to reach had challenged her to a duel.

"You *want* to fight me?"

His forehead creased. With another sigh as heavy as the first, he shook his head. "I haven't been a good king, Sparrow. A good king would have prevented this war. A good king wouldn't have asked a Mist Woman for help."

There it was, the confession to everything Arlo had warned her of. Had King Aeric known what Aeron would do? From the remorse in his eyes, Rachael doubted it.

She could hardly believe it, but— "You regret your life."

She'd come prepared for an impossible fight, yet here he was, willing to cross blades. He looked too worn out to take another step, let alone defend himself.

"No. Only the last year of it."

He sat down on the cold steps leading up to his throne with a heavy grunt, like even that little movement cost him more energy than he had to spare. His guards glanced at each other, but didn't leave their positions.

"During my coronation, I swore to serve my people. I swore to protect them and lead them. They came to me, said that magic ruined their crops, forced their wives into stillbirth, and sold ill omens rather than charms for good luck on my markets. So, I put up laws that forbade the gifted to interfere with the lives of people that don't have magic. It worked for a while, but then the gifted took offence, called their accusers liars. Then the protests started. People were arrested. I sent them to prison like any other criminal, whether they had the gift or not. My commander assured me they were treated with respect, but it appears we have different definitions of the term."

Rachael wanted to say something, question him further, but all she could do was listen. It felt like King Aeric was giving his final confession. She wouldn't deny him that.

"The prison breaks started around that time. I was told a group called the Sparrows were behind it, sympathisers who rescued the gifted regardless of their own blood." He sighed. "Any resistance has to be stopped before it grows too strong. Through all that, my people kept complaining. They claimed the gifted had unfair advantages, an easier life, were too dangerous to be allowed free. I received reports from all over Rifarne of dangerous individuals that killed innocents with magic. I am their king, Sparrow. It was my duty to do something. But it was never enough, and then the rumour that a war was coming started. The Sparrows wanted revenge for the injustice while everyone else wanted the gifted locked up. I wanted to find another solution, a different way than Tramura's cruelty or Vistria's worship, but I could not. Things moved too fast. You know yourself how powerful one witch can be when several guards twice her size and in full armour confront her."

Rachael nodded. She'd never forget her escape from Blackrock.

"So, you called in Aeron? You decided to depend on someone you'd promised your people you would kill?"

King Aeric hesitated. He stared past her, his thoughts far away. "War is a terrible thing, Sparrow. If you wish to win, you have to use any weapon at your disposal, especially when so many people trust you to keep them safe. I pray you will never learn this truth the hard way.

"Now, I believe you are here for a reason. I'm not proud of the man I have become, but I owe my people a better tomorrow. I have no desire to fight you. Contrary to what you must believe of me, I don't relish in unnecessary bloodshed, neither do I want the gifted to suffer. Try to take my crown if you wish, but I can't simply hand it over. It would be an injustice to my people."

Rachael swallowed and nodded. She drew her sword and gripped the hilt tight for strength, but King Aeric's blade was twice its size and twice its weight.

Then, he charged.

Cale watched from the shadows as Commander Videl took his position outside the throne room's doors. Rachael was on the other side, alone with the king and his personal guard.

His teeth clenched, and his fingers clutched his sword's hilt. He'd already lost too much. The Sparrows were gone, and he couldn't be sure that Ailis was all right.

But worst of all, this sorry excuse for a commander had killed his best friend.

Cale had followed them up King's Road and into the palace. He wanted to help Rachael, but she had to win this fight by herself and for herself. While she fulfilled the prophecy, Cale had urgent business with the commander.

Arlo had been his only friend for years until Cale founded the Sparrows. He had saved him and Ailis from starvation, and he'd been a save refuge to them as well as many gifted and new Sparrows. That the commander of the White Guard had defeated him in a duel was an insult to everything Arlo had been.

Cale stepped out of the shadows and allowed his rage to fuel him this once. He'd have killed the commander before the duel, but he'd been too far away. He hadn't wanted to rush in and distract Arlo. He hadn't wanted it to be his fault if his friend died.

And it wasn't his fault. Commander Videl had laughed over Arlo's dying body. Commander Videl had killed him.

Commander Videl would die.

He had destroyed Cale's Sparrows—his family—he had a hand in all those people dying of that disease, and he had killed the only father Cale remembered clearly.

"Commander Videl!" His voice was shaking with anger. Usually, he'd try to control himself but today, he'd let his wrath guide him.

The commander turned around and an amused smile spread on his face. Smug bastard; he was probably boasting. With Rachael delivered to King Aeric and Cale coming to him willingly, this must have felt like his lucky day. Cale couldn't wait to ruin it.

He took three long steps and swung his sword. It caught the commander by surprise—he dodged, but too late. Cale's sword caught his leg and left a deep cut. Commander Videl hissed.

"You—" His men drew their weapons, but Commander Videl held up the hand that wasn't holding his leg. "Stand down. I have given you one lesson today and I will give you another." He grinned. "Never go into battle in blind rage."

Commander Videl stood and raised his sword—Arlo's blood was still drying on it—and brought it down towards Cale's head. Cale dodged. Unlike the commander, who had to be feeling the pain in his leg now the initial shock was likely wearing off, Cale was light on his feet. He stood behind the commander before he knew Cale was there.

After his parents had died, Arlo had raised him and taught him to fight. His real father had also taught him a little and instilled in Cale the morals of battle. He'd been brought up to fight fair. Both Arlo and his father had raised him to never attacked if his opponent couldn't defend himself.

Cale shoved that lesson aside when he thrust his blade through Commander Videl's heart. Hot blood poured down the hilt and over Cale's hands. His grip on his sword was getting slippery, but Cale held it tighter.

What would his father and Arlo think if they saw him now? Cale never killed in cold blood. He always gave his enemy the chance to fight back.

But Commander Videl hadn't deserved that chance.

Two White Guards raised their swords and surrounded him. Cale removed his blade from the commander's back—he fell to the floor with a satisfying, lifeless *thud*—and spun on his toes, bringing his sword down in an arc. He cut both men's middles in one move, and they fell onto a bed of their blood and insides.

The other guards hadn't moved. Their eyes were wide, and they seemed unsure of what to do. They'd hunted him and his family for years. Cale had a chance to end it here.

"Stand down and the Sparrows will show you mercy."

They were just soldiers, like him and his Sparrows. Their king had decided to work with Aeron. Their commander had given the orders. Cale knew enough about Commander Videl to know that no one disobeyed him without consequence.

Their eyes twitched between Cale and their dead commander.

"Attack me. I dare you."

They dropped their weapons and held up their hands in surrender. He would have to question them. With the Sparrows gone, he'd have to rebuild, but he needed to know where they stood first. His Sparrows were irreplaceable, but Rachael would need an army. She would need guards.

These were a start.

Rachael heard the ring of steel against steel outside the throne room. Something was going on, but she had no time to worry about it. She spun around just in time to dodge King Aeric's attack. His heavy sword crashed into the stone right beside her feet. Her heart missed a beat. She stumbled to the side. For a man as tired as him, King Aeric moved well.

From the corner of her eyes, she saw the doors open. Thick blood poured into the room, and her heart dropped. Then Cale entered the throne room soaked in blood, and her heart plunged all the way to her feet. If she died, Cale would go to prison. Cephy and Arlo would have died for nothing. Things would stay the same. All over Rifarne, children would continue to grow up without food, without safety, without friends.

King Aeric raised his sword for another attack, and their eyes met. He was *smiling*. A sad, beaten imitation of the real thing. He had allowed all this pain, all this suffering, and he was *smiling*.

Rachael spun on her toes, just like Cale had taught her. She brought her sword down in a fast arc, and buried the cold steel so deep in his gut it came out the other side.

The king froze. His eyes glazed over. A thin sliver of blood trickled down his chin as his lungs filled with blood. Someone gasped, and ten pairs of feet ran towards their dying king.

Rachael didn't know whether to celebrate or to mourn him. Had there been a better way? He had seemed ready to step down. He had regretted what he'd done. Would he have resigned if it meant that he could live? Or would he then have changed his mind later and claimed the throne as his after all?

Her heart was thudding hard as his life drained out of him. Whether he'd been ready to step down or not, he'd been their king and he'd wanted to do right by his people. After everything that had gone wrong, his life had been the last thing he could give his people. He'd needed her to earn it—she was sure now that's what his smile had meant. Permission.

Cale rushed to her side. "Rachael..."

What could she say? A king was dead along with so many others. His blood slowly soaked her shoes—blood she had spilled. There were no words to describe the emptiness she felt. She'd imagined this moment to feel more like a victory, but instead she felt hollow. Aeron was still a danger and Ailis was still cursed. Cale needed to hear about Arlo, too.

And where did any of this leave her? Rachael didn't want to be queen. She only knew what King Aeric had told her mere moments ago about ruling a country, and none of it sounded appealing.

Cephy had been desperate for a better future for the gifted. Aeron had manipulated her, but Cephy's goal hadn't changed. Whoever took King Aeric's place wouldn't change anything, for all she knew. Maybe he'd even see everything that had happened to the city as a reason to make things worse. If she were queen, maybe she could make all this death mean something.

Rachael had always done what she needed to survive. If becoming queen was next… But it was a big step. She wasn't sure if she could take it.

"What now?" she asked.

She was grateful that Cale was with her. Given what had happened here, she didn't want to be alone with the late king's guards.

"Now you become Queen of Rifarne." His words punched a hole in her gut.

"What makes you think anyone will accept that? They hunted me half an hour ago."

"That's exactly why they will accept you, Rachael. They fear you. There's an entire prophecy around you that predicts the end for their way of life. They'll accept you because they are scared of what you'll do if they don't." She frowned; she didn't want to rule with fear. Rifarne had seen enough of that. Cale took her hand in his. "They will come to love you, Rachael. I know I—" He bit his lips and pulled his hand back. "Don't worry about it. We'll take it one step at a time. Right now, I have preparations to make."

She nodded in defeat. Cale was right—becoming

queen didn't happen overnight, and she wouldn't be alone. Cale would advise her and guide her.

"There's one thing you need to know," Cale said.

She swallowed. "What is it?"

"Aeron is dead. I found her charred remains."

Rachael didn't understand the look of dread on his face. "That's good, isn't it?"

"In itself, yes, but what killed her? I don't know anyone who could have done this."

Shivers ran down her arms. The thought that someone more dangerous than Aeron was out there, in the White City, didn't sit well with her either.

But there was another way of looking at it, too. "Whoever killed her probably saved us."

A small smile struggled on Cale's lips. "You're right. I'm probably worried about nothing. Still, I can't help but think that this isn't over. It almost seems too easy."

Rachael frowned. Aeron couldn't have been easy to kill, and they'd lost Cephy and Arlo. Ailis was cursed. The Sparrows were dead, and the city lay in still smouldering ruins. Rachael didn't dare ask which part of this struck him as easy.

Arlo. Rachael took a deep breath in and readied herself. There was no point in talking around it; no matter how she embellished it, the outcome was the same, and Cale didn't appreciate being coddled. As Arlo's best friend, he deserved to know now rather than later.

"Arlo is dead."

A dark shadow chased away his smile and settled over his eyes. "I know. I found the—him. I found him."

Tears stung her eyes. "Cephy, too."

He gave her hand a brief squeeze. “I’m so sorry, Rachael. We’ll find her body and we’ll bury her. I promise.”

Her eyes watered, because Cale meant every word and she realised she could trust him—really trust him with her life.

“What do we do now?”

Someone cleared his throat behind her. “If I may speak.”

Rachael blushed. She’d forgotten all about the guards. Had they stood behind her and Cale this whole time, allowing them to have a conversation when she’d just killed their king?

The man who’d spoken sounded and looked less intimidating than Commander Videl, but no less authoritative. Rachael was glad Commander Videl lay dead outside the throne room—now the fighting was over, she could see his body through the open doors.

Cale straightened with just as much authority in his posture and stare. “She has fought late King Aeric and defeated him. She is the Sparrow prophecy has promised and your new queen.”

Rachael wanted to laugh but thought better. It sounded so ridiculous.

The soldiers looked unsure and cast glances between them and their leader, the man who had spoken.

He stepped forwards, his eyes on hers. “We know. King Aeric has left us clear instructions.” He clasped his hand over his heart. “May he find peace by the Maker’s side.”

“What kind of instructions?” Cale asked.

“He knew the prophecy and that he would likely die if he challenged you to a duel. Had you not agreed or lost too easily, he would have killed you, but he must have decided you've earned his throne. *Your* throne." His men drew their fists to their chests and bowed their heads. "These are strange times. Under normal circumstances, the throne would go to his first-born son, but his Highness had no children." He eyed the late king with a sad smile, and again clasped his hand over his heart and bowed his head in respect. "Protocol dictates we vote to determine his successor, but the people are in no shape to make such a decision. Too much tragedy. King Aeric has asked that you take his place should you defeat him. He has signed the papers. The throne is yours." He sighed. "I admit, I'd prefer a vote to decide our new ruler, but this isn't the first time a throne has been taken by conquest. If it means that this war is over and we can begin to heal, I won't challenge his final wish. We will serve you faithfully as we have served late King Aeric."

Rachael watched in disbelief as the commander as all ten White Guards fell to their knees with their fists over their hearts in respect. To her.

Next to her, Cale was grinning. She sighed. A gifted, homeless orphan on the Rifarnee throne? Times were strange indeed.

Epilogue

Arnost Lis threw his wine glass against the wall, where it shattered like his faith in humanity. What was Rifarne thinking, putting *her* on the throne? They were just as bad as the cursed people of the south that placed their beliefs in fake gods and goddesses—*goddesses*— and that practiced their unholy crafts like someone might bake bread or knit a jumper. And now, Rifarne had followed suit by making *her* their queen. His king would never bow to such monstrosities. There was no weakness in Tramura.

He tore up the letter and threw it into the fire, where it burned to ashes—just as she would once he got his hands on her.

This proved that he couldn't trust anyone to do his work for him. If you wanted someone killed, you had to do it yourself, and there was no way around it. He'd been foolish to think that he might be able to rely on other people this time.

That Mist Woman, Aeron, had been supposed to murder the girl, but the girl was alive and *queen* and Aeron was dead. If he'd actually contacted that cursed witch… He tore the envelope the letter had come in to shreds and threw it into the fire, too. It was no good now; what was done was done. Maybe a new plan would do the job better.

His thin lips broke into a smile. This wasn't a complete disaster. Aeron had been out of his control and had acted on her own volition, but Shyla had performed well. Of course, she hadn't known what she'd given the new queen, but her knowledge hadn't been required. The necklace had been a gamble, but it was worth it. Since she had accepted Shyla's gift—his gift—he'd been able to observe her. That fool late Rifarnee king had been right in one respect—in war, you had to do what was necessary to win. Arnost Lis wasn't someone who shirked away from his duty, so he'd called in a witch and asked her to enchant the necklace. Shyla's loyalties had surfaced when he'd given it to her disguised as a gift. To think that someone here, in his country, supported those children playing at war…

He shook himself. Simply unacceptable. Shyla had returned to tell him the good news, that Rachael had accepted the necklace, and Arnost Lis had ordered her execution. He couldn't allow any disobedience from his people. Shyla's death had served as a warning. Magic was an evil thing created by the Dark One, and Arnost Lis wouldn't allow it in Tramura. Bad enough that it had spread in Rifarne. He needed to deal with Rachael before she could spread her taint further and poison their king's mind.

"Erimentha!"

It was time he acted—time *they* acted.

His wife entered the room. "My lord?"

Her exotic Krymistian eyes and skin were as warm and promising as the flames that devoured the letter his spy had sent them. He supposed their daughter might have inherited his wife's beautiful features, but time would tell.

"It is almost time. Our king will be summoned to the White Palace soon, and I have no doubt he will send us in his stead." Their king was a busy man after all, and Arnost Lis his loyal ambassador. He'd go wherever his king sent him, even if his destination was poisoned. "We will need to make preparations."

Something played behind her eyes, something odd, but women were like that. Given the circumstances, he could almost understand it.

"My lord." She folded her hands before her and inclined her head. "We have begun to mix poisons and plan traps. Our best assassins are awaiting your word, my lord."

Ah, Erimentha. Such a wonderful, faithful, obedient creature. He'd had to have her the first time he'd laid eyes on her. It was a pity she was tainted and unlikely to breed him many heirs. His son Kleon was the only exception. He was still young but hadn't shown any signs of the taint. Arnost Lis was hopeful he'd make a strong heir, perhaps marry the king's daughter.

Kleon wasn't the only child Erimentha had birthed, but the others had all been born with that vile evil staining their souls. Arnost Lis had ordered their deaths to be quick and painless—unlike them, he wasn't a monster.

"Send one assassin now and have him meet with my spy. If he succeeds, we won't need to set foot in Rifarne."

She nodded and bowed. "He will, my lord."

He smiled. Kleon was getting older and no doubt wanted a brother. All children wanted siblings, and it would do him good to be the oldest child rather than the only one. Something for later.

"Don't be so sure, Erimentha. She is their queen now. Guards will protect the ground she steps on. Her Highness will be well protected."

Their best chance of success was the first attempt, before her guards suspected anything. Should that try fail… Rulers were always more careful once they knew assassins were after them, but Rifarne was still being rebuilt. Slipping in and out would be easy.

"What do you wish of me in the meantime, my lord?"

He smiled at her unspoken offer. "Get yourself undressed and wait in our chambers. I will be with you in a moment."

She bowed once more and left him to it.

What a day this was. Perhaps there were things to look forward to. Erimentha was always a good distraction for his troubled mind and would give him another son. The sooner the better.

And while his wife was heavy with child, Arnost Lis would travel to Rifarne and kill his daughter who now sat on the throne.

CONNECT

Thank you for reading *Rise of the Sparrows*. I hope you enjoyed it! If you have a moment, I'd really appreciate a review. Reviews are everything to indie authors because they get our books in front of new readers, so it would be a big help.

If you'd like to receive ARCs and hear about upcoming releases, early cover reveals, exclusive giveaways, excerpts, and all other announcements, join my mailing list on sarinalanger.com/stay-in-touch/

CONNECT ON SOCIAL MEDIA

My Website https://sarinalanger.com/
Facebook @sarinalangerwriter
Twitter @sarina_langer
Instagram @sarinalangerwriter
Pinterest @sarinalanger
Goodreads: Sarina Langer

Printed in Great Britain
by Amazon